I0778463

The PANGEA
LEGACIES

by *Ellis McBride*

Copyright © 2023 by Ellis McBride

Publishing all rights reserved worldwide.

All rights reserved as sole property of the author.

The author guarantees all content is original and does not infringe upon the legal rights of any other person or work.

No part of this book may be reproduced, stored in a retrieval system, or transmitted in any form or by any means, without expressed written permission of the author.

Edited by Lil Barcaski and Linda Hinkle

Published by: GWN Publishing
www.GWNPublishing.com

Cover Design: Aila Designs

Paperback ISBN: 978-1-959608-70-7
Hardcover ISBN: 978-1-959608-71-4

I would like to dedicate this book to the Lord Jesus, the Christ, who inspired this story. Secondly, I would like to dedicate this book to Rachel, who was the inspiration for my favorite character—Jade.

TABLE OF CONTENTS

CHAPTER ONE

SOME YEARS EARLIER...

The silhouette of an old man flickered across the walls as he drew a long deliberate breath and opened the cover of the dusty ancient manuscript. Soft tufts of light bobbed around the chamber from an old candle skirted by a thick ring of congealed candle wax. It was a large book adorned with elaborate designs; a book of histories beginning from an age long, long ago. The delicate parchments tarnished by centuries of time emanated a strong musty scent with each turn of a page. Symbols of a language long lost in eons past held firm to their silent vigil. Patiently the symbols waited to reveal their deepest secrets to seeking eyes which could decode their ancient rhymes.

The silent silhouette raised a hand casting a deep shadow across the dark chamber and dipped a stiff quill into fresh ink. A quill whose fading feathers spoke of better days long since lost to time. The room filled with soft whispers aloud as the fleeting words of a long dead language breathed again. The words came in a whisper. The hand began to write.

"Long ago, during the first age of mankind, the earth was inhabited by an unimaginable number of wondrous and exotic creatures. Strange creatures now believed to have long ago vanished, are extinct or were merely imagined. Through the eons, many of these magnificent beasts became the sources of myths and legends, religions and lore. It was an age of dragons and unicorns, dinosaurs and mythical beasts. These marvelous creatures walked the earth with humans during the first age of humankind, the age before the Great Flood.

Before the great waters filled the gentle valleys and rose above the highest hills to destroy all living creatures that breathed the air, there was a single land mass upon the face of the earth - Pangaea. The single massive super continent of Pangaea covered nearly a third of the planet. There were no vast deserts and no great mountains as they exist today. During the first age of mankind, rolling hills, soft meadows, and great forests dominated the landscapes.

As the first age passed, humankind began to populate Pangaea as they had been destined. They developed tools, and trade, and commerce as they struggled to see their civilizations come of age. But even then, as now, mankind indulged itself with corruptions of every sort. Corruptions which they had brought upon themselves through the knowledge of good and evil.

It was during this time that some of the wiser creatures began to withdraw themselves from the presence of humans. Creatures of a nobler sort preferring not to follow the pernicious paths much of mankind had chosen for themselves. Creatures equal to humans in intelligence and speech, they gathered together in the most remote regions of Pangaea. They strove to create their own civilizations free from the presence of humankind.

Over time these creature's remote civilizations flourished requiring sacred laws to be written. Laws to ensure their heritage, traditions and histories were preserved throughout the ages. Laws to preserve both their legacies and their civilizations. These laws were written with the blood of innocence and could not be broken, For to do so was to incur certain death. For centuries, there was a time of relative peace for these undisturbed creatures.

One particular species came to prosper in the most remote Northern regions of Pangaea. These creatures were gifted with the ability to shift and change their physical appearance at will. These beings could change into any physical form they wished. That is, once they possessed a complete and composite three-dimensional image of the form they chose to shape into. This ability allowed them to adapt quickly to any environment. They were to become known in the ancient common language as, "Bas-Na Eshas," *Benders of the Clay.*

And so it was that man and beasts inhabited the world. All seemed at relative peace until the day came when great clouds gathered together in the heavens and heavy rains began to fall. The torrential rains fell mercilessly for days upon days causing the oceans to rise. The swelling seas continued to climb higher and higher until Pangaea itself threatened to withdraw beneath the gathering waves. The Great Flood had come.

The Benders of the Clay waited and watched as the waters climbed higher and higher seeking to destroy their civilizations. As the waters pressed in from every side, the Clay Benders faced a desperate decision. The Great Elder decreed that all Clay Benders would take to the sea and offered each one a complete image—an air-breathing dolphin. But not all of the Clay Benders agreed with the Great Elder. A great contention quickly arose as a young Esha disputed the great Elder's decision, which would affect the very future of their survival.

The young Esha had stolen an image from the Great Archive and demanded the right to choose the form of the water-breathing shark. In the ensuing dispute, the young Esha drew nearly a third of the Clay

Benders to himself. A great rebellion arose causing war among the Clay Benders as the rains continued to fall. In the end, the Great Elder banished the legions of the rebellion and each of the two groups set out on its own.

Pangaea slowly slipped beneath the waves, to be lost forever. A handful of humankind had managed to survive and in time, set out to reclaim the earth once again. In the end, both sides of the Clay Benders survived the Great Flood as well, but they would remain divided forever.

Now, during the second age of mankind, the Esha are here among us, and they are at war. On one side of the divide stands the Order of Tryistan. The Order embraces humankind and believes it is destined to one day save and join the world of humans. On the other side of the divide stand the Tribes of the Doon Esha. The Doon Esha seethes in its hatred of mankind and is committed to enslave and ultimately destroy all of humankind. Thus, ridding the earth of its human curse forever.

It is the present day, the second age of humankind, during the sixth millennial reign of mankind. Human dominion over the earth is about to be challenged. It is all foretold in an ancient prophecy that now exists as whispers and pieces in the shadows."

Slowly and carefully, the silhouette of a hand closed the cover of the ancient book. Dropping the quill to the table, the old man reached over to snuff out the small bobbing flame from the candle. *My precious child. Jade... What have you done?...*

GLOBALCOMNEWS.NET
World Situation Report #1

"This is Michelle Galbraith. Last night in an unprecedented international move, the Russian Federation and the People's Republic of China have moved forward and approved all measures that will unite the two powers together in a final coalition now formally referred to as the United New World Coalition (UNWC). Both countries have ratified their corresponding agreements and will aggressively campaign to pursue and recruit new member states into their ranks.

Despite opposition to the coalition by numerous voices at the United Nations, particularly by the skepticism of the United States, some in the European theater are hailing this new initiative as the next step towards a more unified globalization of all nations. However, not all the representatives of the United States readily appear to support such opposition. White House Senior Advisor Daniel Richardson has reportedly said, off the record, he thinks the initiative may be a step in the right direction if all parties involved can work together in a civil manner through the right channels of global diplomacy. Some U.S. allies are speculating Richardson may be sending a signal for possible future negotiations between the world powers.

Still, there has been a growing air of stubborn skepticism within the U.S. and several of its NATO allies that could prove to be problematic regarding the future relations between standing Western alliances and the Sino-Russian UNWC. The British Prime Minister has also voiced his skepticism adding that he thinks the international economic woes that continue to plague the European states may only grow worse in the shadow of superficial and pretexted diplomacy.

The general fear is that competition for the future of global economic business with the Middle East and Gulf States will intensify exponentially. Perhaps, only time will tell. This is Michelle Galbraith, Global-ComNews.Net, reporting from our studios in London."

CHAPTER TWO

UNLIKELY ENCOUNTERS

It was late, it was dark, and it was cold. A stifling dreariness insisted on penetrating the stagnant mists as Jade carefully picked her way through the dirty cluttered backstreet alleys. The unwelcome absence of the usual dim and dingy streetlights forced Jade's knuckles to whiten as she tightened her grip on the straps of the heavy leather backpack. The usual reassurance of the noisy distractions rising from the busy city was anxiously amiss here. The course professor had kept the evening class overtime again with another mundane presentation which, unfortunately, Jade badly needed for extra credit.

Upset and irritated, she had begun the long trek home on foot to her apartment after realizing she had missed her ride. Now the smell of moldy ripe dumpsters and seeping rotting wooden crates clogged the air doing little to improve Jade's foul inner musings. Silently cursing the dismal maze of alleys, she was immediately startled. The skipping sound of a broken bottle she had accidentally kicked clattered across the alley. Jade stopped. Holding her breath, she listened to the dancing echoes of breaking glass race up and down the soulless passages. Finally, the noise faded away, trailing off into the night. The eerie silence abruptly returned.

Wincing at the stench of spoiled malt, she could sense the cold stale liquor splattered across the lower legs of her denim jeans. Fighting off a wave of nausea from the offensive fragrance, she turned and stole a nervous look back down the alley and softly sighed. *So much for a low profile...* Finally satisfied, she started walking again. Unconsciously she picked up her pace as she carefully navigated her way further on into the bleak winding labyrinth.

Placing her steps cautiously, Jade stayed to the right side of the alley and close against the faceless walls while dodging whatever clutter she could see. *This was a stupid mistake...* she thought to herself suppressing a ludicrous impulse to hum or whistle out loud. Jade reached up and instinctively clutched the small gold pendant she wore around her neck.

The shiny pendant had always been her favorite charm ever since her father had presented it to her. It was some time ago when she celebrated her coming-of-age ceremony. Over time, the pendant had become a sentimental symbol of a much simpler time, long since gone by. At the moment, it was her only source of comfort.

Rounding the next corner to the right ushered her into another even darker alley than the last as Jade continued to make her way home. After several long uneventful minutes, she finally came to the end of the alley. A dead end. It was a solid brick wall and seemed to have no beginning or end. Jade had taken a wrong turn. Reaching out, she touched the wall to be sure it was real and wishing it would vanish at her will. *Useless.* The wall remained seated like an ancient immovable monolith.

Feeling a stitch in the pit of her stomach, Jade pursed her lips and impatiently turned around to make her way back the way she'd come. The heavy backpack full of textbooks was beginning to bite into her shoulders and she was getting tired. Small beads of sweat ran down her brow and into her eyes. Wiping away the sweat with her jacket sleeve, she thought to herself, *if I wasn't so nervous, I'd laugh out loud.*

Jade was fair skinned with shoulder-length dark brown hair that curled in towards her face. Named for her green eyes, she was proud of her high cheekbone profile. At just under six feet and a bit too thin, she was considered attractive by most standards. Although fragile perhaps in appearance, having grown up with five brothers, Jade did not frighten easily. She had proven on several occasions that she could take care of herself. But for some reason, she was feeling more than a little edgy hiking around the back alleys this particular night, which was excusable given the moon's reluctance to emerge from the deep cloudy night sky.

As she made her way through the hazy darkness, Jade was glad she had chosen to wear the black leather jacket and denim jeans tonight. It made her feel more protected and invisible, which was exactly what she wanted to be at the moment. Finally, she reached the junction where she'd made the wrong turn.

Instantly, a pair of bright headlights lit up the alley. Jade stopped. Trying to shield her eyes, she squinted through her fingers to see through the blinding lights. A quick succession of bangs from slamming doors announced the arrival of what were most likely unwelcome visitors, startling her and causing her heart to skip a beat. *Police?*

Standing her ground, she remained silent as she made out one, then two, then four silhouetted figures roaming into view in front of the parked vehicle. She could feel the sweat on her palms as she fought off the urge to turn and run. The backpack was getting heavier and heavier wearing hard on her shoulders. With her heart pounding, Jade realized there was nowhere to run. She was cornered.

The middle figure took up a slow and deliberate stroll directly towards her while the other three companions remained standing in front of the headlights. *So much for the cops.*

Jade had a hard time remembering when she'd felt more vulnerable and exposed than she did right now. As her eyes began to adjust to the headlights, she could make more out of the shadowy figure approaching her. Whoever it was seemed to be in no great hurry to close the distance between them.

Her mind raced as she tried to ready herself for any possible scenario. She thought of the razor in her backpack, but quickly realized she'd never reach it in time. She wished she had that broken bottle she'd kicked earlier now but knew it probably wouldn't do her any good. The figure approaching her was nearly twice her size. She wouldn't stand a chance.

The approaching shadow figure stopped a mere three feet in front of her. Jade held her breath waiting, but said nothing, keeping her eyes trained on the figure in front of her. Suddenly, she realized she was face-to-face with a member of a local gang calling themselves The Horde.

For the first time, she began to make out the face covered in a mosaic of tattoos with the capital letter 'H' prominently displayed in the center of the figure's forehead. At least, it looked like a human being with a lot of tattoos. The eyes looked human enough, but she could not be absolutely sure.

Jade had heard of the gang but had never actually seen one of them before let alone having come face-to-face to one. The gang had a local reputation of leaning more toward petty crimes and scavenging rather than the kind of violence usually connected to any organized criminal activities.

But being outnumbered four-to-one didn't give her any comfort. None at all. She was in trouble, and she knew it, and, worse yet, there didn't look to be any easy way out of a direct confrontation. She was also keenly aware of the possibility these four figures were not exactly what or whom they appeared to be.

Jade decided to take the offensive. "Is there something..."

The man instantly threw up his right hand towards her face while slowly shaking his head. She could just make out some odd tattoos covering his palm and extending up the fingers.

Jade stood still, listening and waiting for their next move and any opportunity to end the encounter. The other three men begin to whisper back and forth as they shuffled around to the back of their vehicle from which Jade heard the distinctive sound of the trunk opening up. Feeling the adrenaline pulsing through her veins, she decided to stay quiet and let her visitor do the talking. She could no longer see the other three men hidden behind the back of their car.

Then, without warning, the figure reached in and quickly snatched Jade's necklace, ripping it from her neck in a split second and encasing it in his fist. She let out a quick gasp but remained still. The figure reached out his other hand and slowly moved forward to run a finger down her neck. *No, you don't...*

Stepping backward to avoid his reach, Jade's ankle caught the corner of an old rotting bucket throwing her off balance and over backwards into a pile of moldy palettes. The decrepit crates scattered in every direction as she landed on her back on top of her heavy backpack. The ensuing cacophony of noise caused the other three members to jump as the racket raced up and down the alleys.

Without a sound, Jade blinked and cleared her eyes. The young man was standing over her sporting a malicious set of teeth carved into a malevolent smile. Squinting through the darkness, Jade looked up into the tattooed face as it seemed to come closer and closer. She instinctively reached up to her neck even knowing the pendant was gone.

The malicious smirk smeared across her closing attacker's face instantly jumped to one of sudden surprise. Jade watched as his eyes practically bulged from their sockets, and then she gasped as two enormous and wicked black talons wrapped themselves over each one of the young man's shoulders and another up under each of his armpits.

The stunned member of the Horde glanced up and garbled something intelligible before looking back at Jade with complete horror spread across his tattooed face. Then he was gone, disappearing into the blackness of the misty moonless night as if he'd never existed. Somewhere above, in the dark skies, she thought she heard something sounding far worse than a human shriek.

She lay still and held her breath for several moments as she listened for any signs of the others. After what seemed like an eternity, she finally heard the panicked and muffled screams of her assailant's three companions. Seconds later, the alley was silent. Sucking in a long deliberate breath, she waited. Nothing. Then, the sound of footsteps. The footsteps crept closer and closer until the sight of Jade's older brother caused her to deeply exhale in relief.

"Jesse!" Jade's voice cracked.

"Jade? Jade!" Her brother jumped into the pile of scattered crates. " Are you alright?"

She struggled to sit up as her older sibling reached her.

"Jade, thank God." Jesse tried to pull the backpack over her shoulders and let it roll onto the ground without success before he finally reached down and helped his sister to her feet.

"Where have you been?" Jesse demanded. "Do you know what time it is? We've been searching for almost two hours. What are you doing in this part of town?"

Jade patted away debris and indignantly brushed her hands through her hair. Then Jesse impatiently helped her finally shrug off the heavy backpack as he checked her over, brushing away more debris and scolding her as he went. Finally, regaining her composure, she turned back around to survey where she'd fallen. Then she looked up and down the alley as Jesse grew silent.

"What took you so long," Jade finally asked.

"What took us so... I'm sorry, but you're welcome. It's dark out tonight, you know, no moon. We had a lot of trouble finding you. You didn't call. What were you thinking?"

"I know, I'm sorry," Jade continued. "I missed my ride, and my phone's dead. I thought I remembered the way."

"Well, at least you're okay," Jesse scolded. "You had us pretty worried."

"I know, I know," Jade conceded again.

"I'm not even sure how we found you," Jesse frowned.

Thinking for a moment, Jade looked down the alley towards the headlights of the abandoned car.

"Jesse, *please* tell me you didn't hurt them. They were probably drunk and just being stupid."

"Don't you think they deserved to get what they had coming? They were really going to hurt you or worse. You know we couldn't allow that to happen. Besides, were you absolutely sure they were humans?"

"Well, I'm pretty sure, otherwise they would have fought you or run," Jade answered tightly.

"That was an awfully big gamble. We couldn't tell if they were human or not until we pulled them up out of these alleys," Jesse shot.

"Jesse, *please* tell me you didn't hurt them. They were really only humans. Besides, I knew the cavalry would get here in time," she pleaded. *I was praying...*

Jesse hesitated and looked down at the ground. Jade was certainly strong willed, high spirited and young. However, she needed to learn to accept a little more responsibility. Maybe this was an opportunity to drive home the point and instill some of that very thing.

"Don't give me the here-comes-the-cavalry thing. Those guys were dead serious, and we're all better off without them. The whole world is. Really, what are four fewer sorry losers in the world? Not to mention the fact that we really don't know who or what they were and who they've been in contact with, so don't pretend you do. It just seems very strange that the one night you get lost in this forsaken maze, they suddenly show up."

Jade looked down at the pavement and felt her jaw tighten. It was all her fault. Why did she take the stupid dark alley home? Now four of the humans were most likely mentally scarred for life on her account, but she knew they would not be harmed despite Jesse's scolding. Still, the gravity of the situation began to weigh heavily on her. Fighting back her guilty anger, Jade turned away from Jesse.

"Jesse, I'm sorry. It was stupid. I know better." She waited for Jesse to berate her further knowing she deserved it. It had been a close call, and she knew it. She had made a serious and irresponsible mistake. She needed to be much more careful now, especially in light of the unfolding events over the past few months.

Softly, Jesse reached out and touched Jade's arm. "It's okay little sister. Next time, just use your head. You know what's going on. We can't afford to take chances."

"I know, I know!" Jade cried, pulling away.

Finally unable to keep up his annoyance with his sister any longer, Jesse gently reached out and tugged on Jade's arm turning her towards him. The night air was turning colder, and the headlights of the car just down the alley were beginning to dim.

"We didn't hurt them, okay? But you know that. They're probably sobering up in the river by now. Betcha they'll think twice about coming back for their wheels. We should be getting back though, Father is waiting-"

"What?" Jade's eyes flashed. "What do you mean? He's here? Now?"

"Yes, he just arrived a few hours ago, and he's not going to be pleased with all of this. We shouldn't keep him waiting. We need to go and I mean like, right now."

Jade rolled her eyes and pursed her lips. There had been no word that her father would be coming in or even a word from her three visiting brothers. This changed things. She realized her father would probably be less than pleased that she was not there to greet him. *And I know why he is here...*

Whiffs of blonde hair blew across Jesse's strong suntanned face as Jade looked into her brother's deep violet eyes accentuating their tight black vertical slits. Finally, she reached out both arms, and the two hugged each other tightly. Then they turned and walked arm-in-arm back down the alley past the freshly abandoned automobile as the headlights planted in the old beamer's front fender began to fade.

"How are you going to get me home," Jade jokingly asked. "Can you fly me there again?"

"I think we'll just walk for a while," Jesse answered. "My arms are tired."

"Oh, now they're tired," Jade shot.

"C'mon sis," Jesse pulled his sister forward.

Jade allowed her brother to tug her along as they headed towards her apartment. She knew her other two brothers would go on ahead and meet them there. *And I know, father, why you are here... Not again... Please, not again.*

CHAPTER THREE

FAMILY REUNION

Jade's father hung his large overcoat on one of the faded wooden wall pegs and strolled into the living room of Jade's third-story apartment. Squeezing his fists over and over, he sat down and began to slowly rock back and forth in the dingy oversized recliner. As he sat silently meditating in the darkness, the busy sounds of the street three stories below offered him no distraction. Neither Jade nor her three visiting brothers had yet returned, and Gharius Sol-Tryistan patiently mused over the events of the last several months.

Shortly after he had arrived at Jade's empty apartment, he had sent his three sons, now over two hours ago, to search for his daughter, instructing them to bring her home the moment she was found. He also reminded them that if anything happened to her, there would be a reckoning of his wrath which neither man nor beast could comprehend.

The generously spaced apartment was filled with second and third-hand furnishings. Both of the aging beige shades were drawn, and the room was illuminated solely by the light of a small white electric candle, "burning" on the mantle. Gharius allowed his mind to wander a bit as he watched the little electric flame playfully bob up and down as it flickered. He smiled wryly to himself watching the little flame's soft light dance across the walls.

He knew his sons would return soon. They were more than able to handle anything they might encounter. Gharius was more concerned about Jade. She was his one and only precious daughter child amidst a history of sons. Thus far, she had proven to be more trouble than all of his sons combined.

She was also his most vulnerable keep. He'd endured her high spiritedness and impulsive behavior throughout her life, but now, his long-suffering patience was beginning to wear thin.

It had gone beyond far enough when Jade had disobeyed him some years earlier and stole into the sacred archive libraries. It was late one night, long ago. Though absolutely forbidden, Jade had pulled down one of the sacred scrolls and broken the seal releasing its power, transforming her into her now permanent human form. In doing so, she had broken a sacred law, eventually forcing her to leave the safety of the Order into exile. Against her father's wishes, she transitioned to a distant city to live among the vast numbers of humans. Atlanta, Georgia, was a long way from her former home.

The gravity of the situation was further aggravated by the ongoing and escalating encounters between the Order of Tryistan and the Tribes of the Doon Esha. Within the past several months, the confrontations had grown more frequent and aggressive.

Several of the recent encounters had occurred within the region close to the city where Jade lived, and Gharius decided it was time to convince his daughter to move out of the area. Being completely human, she was his one serious weakness, and Gharius knew his enemy would certainly scheme to perpetrate events to kill her in order to get to him.

He was here, once again, to persuade Jade to relocate herself closer to the Order.

The sound of rattling keys caught Gharius' attention to the door. The lock clicked twice inviting the soft creak of the door as Gharius' children quietly began to make their way inside. Remaining silent, he made no attempt to move, choosing instead to return his attention to the little white candle flickering on the mantle. Jade quietly made her way back towards the kitchen as her brothers hung their jackets and searched for a place to stand. Jesse, the last in line, gently closed the door and quickly closed each of the four large steel bolts in order.

When the last jacket had been hung, each of Gharius' other two sons took their places against the smooth plaster wall behind Gharius' chair. Jesse found a spot close to the door and leaned against the wall as well. No one spoke a word as the tension in the room thickened like smoke. Jesse finally cleared his throat as they waited for Jade to rejoin them.

As they waited, their father spoke first.

"Thank you, Jesse. I'm pleased to see her alive and in one piece. I might have feared the worst had you not been leading your brothers to find her." said Gharius softly.

"Yes, father. She's fine, just got a little turned around in an alley. I'm sorry it took us so long, there's no moon tonight so it was more difficult."

"Yes, I know, son. I sense, however, that there is more to this tale than you're telling me. Is there anything else?" he inquired.

"No, father. We had an incident with some humans when we found her, but we took care of them. They are unharmed."

"I see..."

Gharius paused as Jade gingerly entered the room. Making her way past her other brothers, she took up a place against the wall beside her brother Jesse. Staring down at the floor, she offered nothing but her silence.

"Jade," Gharius spoke softly again. "It's good to see you again. Seems you've caused a bit of a stir tonight. Are you alright?"

She trained her stare on a dirty stain on the floor rug beneath her. "Yes, father," she mumbled. "I'm fine. I'm sorry. I-I got lost coming home. It's okay now; everything's fine."

Gharius continued to keep his attention fixed on the flittering little candle. "I'm sorry, Jade. I know this is short notice and that you didn't know I'd be coming. It was a last-minute decision. I hope that I've not intruded."

Jade looked up and stepped away from the wall maneuvering her way to a spot just in front of where her father was seated. She looked straight down into her father's eyes.

"Father, you know that you are always welcome here," she spoke softly, returning her eyes to the floor. "If I'd known you were coming, I would certainly have been here to greet you."

Gharius stood up and reached out his hands taking Jade's smaller hands into his own. Raising her head, her eyes met her father's gaze.

He looked over the face of his daughter, almost as if seeing her for the first time.

Finally, "Jade, you know what a treasure you are in my own heart? How refreshing it is that I can look upon your face to behold you. Sorely have I missed you."

Jade felt a warm tear beginning to form as it threatened to descend down her face. "Father, I, too, have missed you and how often I wish the days of old might return. Welcome, father."

Gharius wrapped his large arms around her. Jade returned his warm embrace with great relief as she buried her face into her father's shirt. The events of the evening had unnerved her and now she found herself fighting to keep it from showing.

Her father always seemed to affect her in this way. There had always been something about him that filled the air with such a strong and calm assurance. She knew at this moment she was safer than she could be anywhere else. In her mind, she reached out and latched onto that safety as tightly as she dared.

No. No, there is something wrong... Jade broke the embrace and stepped back from her father. Something was going on here. Looking over at her brothers, she searched their faces for clues, but her brothers remained quiet. Looking back to her father, she took one more step back.

"Father, if I may, why are you here?" She started. "Please tell me you're not going to try to convince me to come back to the Order."

Gharius looked down at his daughter and let out a sigh. His sons shifted nervously against the wall. Pausing for a moment, he glanced back over his shoulder and nodded his head towards the door.

Jesse immediately cleared his throat calling the attention of his two younger brothers and motioned with his eyes toward the door as he turned to quietly unlock the bolts. Anxiously all three of the young men hastily filed through the door and out of the room. Jesse gently closed the door behind him, leaving Gharius and Jade alone.

"Jade," Gharius began. "You know the conflicts have escalated over the last several months. There have been several incidents in this region alone. You are vulnerable here. I want you to reconsider your decision. You represent a..."

"Father, I know how you feel, I do, but I can't come back, and you know it. The law is very clear, and we both know that's why I'm here. It's my fault father and..."

"I know what the laws say, please don't presume to explain them to me," rumbled Gharius.

Jade sighed out loud, letting her chin fall to her chest and shrugged. "I'm sorry, father, of course, please forgive me. I just don't understand why we keep doing this. I cannot return to the Order."

Choosing his words carefully, he continued, "I know you cannot return to the Order, at least, not yet. All I'm asking is that you return to the region. With you closer to the Order, I can better protect you. It is far too dangerous for you to remain here any longer. Daughter, you are my most vulnerable link. You know if the Doon Esha discovers you, they will certainly plan an event to try to kill you in order to strike at me."

Gharius stopped to let his words sink in. Jade was truly stubborn and free-spirited, but she was not a fool. She knew full well that a human being was no match for any of the number of the possible schemes the Doon Esha could formulate. Their order possessed a powerful archive of images whose archive trust was kept in the sole possession of their obsessed leader. The Esha had become masters of manipulation, deception, coercion and corruption.

Gharius stepped closer to his daughter. "I cannot force you against your will, and you know I won't try. I am asking you as your father, pleading if you wish, for you to consider the dangers to yourself and to me. You made a mistake, but that is all in the past. You have to forgive yourself child."

Struggling to fight back her tears, Jade replied, "I am trying, father. I know I have to put it all behind me. But I'm human now. I no longer belong in your world, father. It's too late to turn back-"

"Enough, child!" The force of Gharius' voice frightened Jade, sending a wave of fear pulsing throughout her body.

Gharius' took a deep breath. His voice returned, calmer this time. "Listen to me. You are going to have to trust me. All is not known to you, child. There are forces here at work far greater than you're act of having broken a sacred law. Far more."

"I don't understand, father. What's going on?" Jade asked.

"I don't have time to explain things yet, but..."

Gharius was interrupted by a soft knock at the door. Softly, he answered, "Yes?"

The door creaked open a few inches followed by the whisper of Jesse's voice. "Father, forgive me, but I think you need to hear this."

"Hear what?" Gharius responded with a note of irritation.

"Trouble, and it's bad."

Gharius nodded silently. Jesse remained at the door while his two younger brothers filed back into the room. Gharius turned to Jesse, "Please, join me back outside. I want to know what you've found."

Jesse moved back to the door and held it open as Gharius began to leave but suddenly stopped in the doorway and turned around setting his eyes squarely on Jade. The room was dead still. He reached into his shirt pocket and produced a small necklace bearing a golden pendant.

"You dropped this in the alley, child."

Jade's hands went immediately to her neck. Her eyes grew wide as she watched the golden pendant slowly swinging from her father's hand. Swiftly crossing the room, she held out her hand into which her father dropped the shiny pendant. Slowly closing her hand into a fist, she looked up at him. Startled and surprised she stuttered, "How, where... how could you have this?"

Gharius reached out and ran his finger along Jade's cheek. "You really didn't think I'd let you walk that dark dirty alley alone, did you?"

With that, Gharius turned and strode out the door with Jesse in tow. Speechless, Jade watched her father disappear down the hallway then closed the door. She turned to her two remaining brothers, silently questioning each of them with a puzzled expression. Her brothers only shrugged, offering her no further answers. They didn't appear to have any.

She wasn't buying it. "Jonay? Turra?"

The brothers simply squirmed where they stood and shot each other quick glances while trying desperately to keep from laughing out loud. Jade stared hard at her brothers.

"There was just you two and Jesse out looking for me, right?" she demanded.

Jonay took the turn to answer, "Yes. Just the three of us. Why?"

Jade thought for a moment. "There were four of them."

This time, Turra answered, "No, there were only three of them. Jessie and the two of us took them out. That makes three. What's wrong with you, sis?"

"There were three of them at the back at the car. Who took out the one who was standing over me when I fell? That's four!"

There was complete silence for a few more moments until both brothers and their sister came to their own conclusions at the same time. Jade put her hands on her hips and threw a hard look at the front door.

Without waiting for another clue, Turra, running his hands through his hair, exhaled and said, "Unbelievable, absolutely unbelievable." Both boys started to laugh out loud avoiding Jade's burning eyes.

Finally, Jade relented, "Boys!" and retreated to the kitchen clutching the pendant tightly. Reaching the kitchen sink, she turned the hot water faucet on and waited for the water to fill the sink. She began placing some of the dirty dishes into the hot soapy water while she looked out the window over the lights of the surrounding neighborhoods. *This is not over... Not by far...*

CHAPTER FOUR

A FAIR EXCHANGE

Ivanich Rostov sat patiently waiting in the busy center lobby of the Chinese consulate in Berlin, Germany. It had taken him over two long days to travel from Moscow to Berlin due to the unexpected winter front. Most of the commercial passenger railways had temporarily closed, but Rostov had managed to catch an overnight government rail freighter that somehow had delivered him on time during the late morning. He had checked into the Brandenburg Hof hotel, managing to catch a few hours of sleep before his appointment with the Chinese ambassador.

Rostov was an official emissary from the office of the Russian Defense Ministry in Moscow. For almost a year he had been wooing the Chinese ambassador, Li Sun Chen to help him coerce the German chancellor's cabinet into joining the United New World Coalition (UNWC). Just two weeks prior, France, under harsh protest by the U.N., had agreed to launch a committee seeking how best to become the newest member of the coalition while retaining membership in both NATO and the U.N. Of the two, Germany continued to demonstrate the most resistance.

Part of Rostov's mission was to ensure that all parties involved understood that Russia and China had recently formed the organization to answer rising international global threats to their access to the Middle East oil fields; the same precious oil fields that supplied fuel to their war machines and helped to drive their economies.

The fact that all three of the coalition's targeted nations, Germany, France and Italy, belonged to the NATO alliance further complicated matters on an international scale. The United New World Coalition represented a purely financial alliance of cooperative economic opportunity, which in turn raised stark international concerns that NATO's allied nations would be vulnerable to different levels of conflicting interests. Given that the United States was still in the infancy stages of developing its local energy resources, and political and environmental obstacles continued to ensure the nation's energy dependency lay outside of its national borders. With the financial weakening of the European Union and rising fears of catastrophic economic destabilizations, friction between the NATO nations of the E.U. and the U.S. continued to mount.

Further frictions were fueled by the fact that both Russia and China were engaged in aggressive campaigns to expand each of their military capabilities and international influence. Coming at a time when the U.S. was engaged in a pinpointed military reduction of its deployed forces worldwide, the U.S. faced a decline in both its global presence and influence. Tensions were unavoidable, and as the increase in joint military operations and training between the UNWC parties seemed to indicate, further tensions appeared unstoppable.

Rostov, a man in his mid-fifties, was a bit too short for a standard Russian diplomat. Sporting a pair of sixties-style black-rimmed glasses, his well-worn black leather shoes and drab gray suit gave him the appearance of a classically somber old school New York detective. Odd as he might appear, however, Ivanich Rostov sported a reputation as a keen negotiator and carried his own sense of persuasive charm.

The trip was just one of many that Rostov had taken to Berlin over the past 12 months. This trip, however, was going to be a little different. Rostov drummed his fingers on the compact briefcase beside him. Inside the case nestled a small item Rostov had been told would certainly thrill the Chinese ambassador. He was counting on it.

The appearance of a sharply uniformed Chinese Marine caught Rostov's attention. Rostov's patience was rewarded as the young man came to attention in front of him. "Sir, the ambassador will see you now."

The soldier did a snappy right-face, waiting for Rostov to gather his coat and briefcase. Without any further word, the Marine led Rostov up two flights of stairs and down a dimly lit but lushly carpeted hall way to a black door at the very end of the passage. Rostov struggled to keep up with the young man. Upon reaching the studded heavy door, the soldier gave two sharp raps to announce Rostov's appointment.

Without waiting for a response, the soldier stiffly opened the door and motioned Rostov inside. Nodding to the Marine, Rostov made his way through the door, laying his coat over his left arm to cover the briefcase and extending his right hand.

Li Sun Chen stood up from behind his desk. "Counselor Rostov! How good it is to see you again. I trust your trip went well?"

Gripping the Chinese ambassador's hand firmly, Rostov smiled. "Ambassador, as always, you are looking well. Yes, my trip was fine, thank you."

Releasing his grasp, the ambassador motioned Rostov to a large burgundy French leather chair adjacent to his own desk. Rostov took his seat, setting his drab overcoat across his lap and softly setting the brief case down on the floor beside him.

The ambassador returned to his oversized executive chair and reached down into a desk drawer. "Perhaps you would care for a spirit? It's some of the best vodka right from your own city."

Rostov shifted in his chair. "Thank you, Mr. Ambassador, but no thank you. I don't drink."

Li Sun Chen stopped, looking a little puzzled. Putting the small flask back into the drawer, he sat back into his chair. "You didn't seem to mind a good spirit during your last visit, counselor."

Caught off guard, Rostov stiffened up in his chair. Clearing his throat, he answered, "I'm sorry, Mr. Ambassador, I simply meant that I don't drink anymore. I've been experiencing some significant life changes lately."

Smiling, the Ambassador replied, "No need to explain, counselor, I understand fully, really, I've been trying to make some changes my-self." Patting his stomach, the Chinese Ambassador continued, "I am getting older, counselor but, unfortunately, not any thinner."

Both men chuckled for a moment until Rostov cleared his throat again, "If it is appropriate, Mr. Ambassador, may I suggest we get down to business?"

Ambassador Chen stroked his tightly trimmed dark goatee. "Yes, counselor, I think it is most appropriate. I understand that you have something for me?"

Rostov smiled, "Yes, of course, Mr. Ambassador." Rostov reached down and retrieved the compact briefcase. He briefly punched in the key codes and opened the locks with two slight clicks. Laying the briefcase on the desk, he slowly pushed the case across the desk into the waiting hands of Li Sun Chen. The Chinese Ambassador positioned the case in front of him and switched on the small desk lamp. Slowly he opened it and stared down at the delicate silk-covered object for several long moments.

Finally, the Chinese Ambassador reached down into the case and pulled out a small bundle of black silk. Carefully unwinding the silk band, he produced a small, exquisite ring. Turning it over to read the inscriptions, Ambassador Chin felt the warm glow of ancient gold embracing his fingers. Looking to Rostov, he asked, "You are sure it is authentic?"

"It is authentic, Mr. Ambassador. You are holding the Royal Emperor signet ring worn by Emperor Kangxi during the sixteenth century dynasty. You will, of course, wish to independently verify its authenticity."

"Of course, counselor." Ambassador Chin spent several more moments examining the ancient treasure. "This piece has been missing from the Imperial Collection in Beijing for over 50 years. It is virtually priceless. I would think it a most interesting tale as to how you have come about it."

"A most interesting tale indeed, Ambassador," Rostov replied as he shifted in his seat. Actually, Rostov had no idea where it had come from. He was simply here to complete the delivery details of his mission. He hadn't even known what was in the briefcase until he had been quickly briefed before leaving Moscow. He had been instructed the Ambassador would be eagerly awaiting its delivery. The Ambassador's cooperation was critical to help convince the German government to join the newly formed Russian-Chinese union of the UNWC.

Finally, Rostov spoke, "Mr. Ambassador, we are very concerned as to how the negotiations are going with your German contacts. As you know…"

"There is no need, counselor, for your government's concern." Wrapping the ring back into the silk handkerchief, Li Sun Chen gently placed it back into its case and snapped the lid shut. "I have very reliable information that by this day next week, the German cabinet will most likely vote in favor of committing to an interim position with our coalition."

Rostov relaxed and rubbed the back of his neck. "That is very good news, Mr. Ambassador. My government will be most pleased to see this happen. I trust you approve of this act of good faith?"

"Most assured, counselor. I, of course, will do my part." The buzzer rang. Answering in Chinese, Ambassador Chen engaged in a short conversation and then clicked the buzzer off. "I'm sorry, counselor, but it seems I have another appointment waiting. Please tell your superiors that everything is according to schedule." The Ambassador rose to his feet.

Rostov rose with him and offered his hand, which the Ambassador shook firmly. "Thank you for seeing me, Mr. Ambassador."

"You are most welcome, counselor." Ambassador Chen escorted Rostov to the door. Stopping a few steps from the exit, the Chinese Ambassador continued, "You know, the Americans have filed another security complaint with the United Nations. They are most unhappy to see this coalition between our countries. There are fears and rumors of rising tensions within the U.N. and I fear it may come to the serious attention of the U.N. Security Council.

Rostov glanced at the door and replied in a hushed voice, "It will not matter, Mr. Ambassador. The coalition will be too strong for the UN to mount any threat to us. My government and yours are the backbone of this coalition. Combined, we are greater in force than the Americans, especially since we have successfully all but dismantled the NATO alliance's real influence in Europe. Soon it will only be a matter of time until we, the coalition, have complete and absolute control of the Middle Eastern oil fields. Then we will see what the Americans will say."

Again, the Ambassador stroked his dark goatee. Narrowing his eyes, "Such a situation could easily lead to war. Should the Americans ever perceive what we are really doing, I do not think they will choose diplomacy for very long."

"It makes no difference, Mr. Ambassador. By such a time, should it occur, and it will, we will have full territorial control of our mutual interests, and there will be nothing they can do but negotiate with us if they wish to keep their country running."

"Yes, I believe you are right. Well then, to the future of our coalition." With that, the Ambassador reached out and pressed a button on the side of the door. Immediately, the door crept open as the young Marine outside came to full attention. "Perhaps your next visit will allow you to see some of the finer sights Berlin has to offer, counselor." Retrieving the key lock codes for the briefcase from his pocket, Rostov handed the slip of paper to the Ambassador.

"Perhaps, Ambassador," Rostov smiled as he replied. *Except there won't be a next visit.*

Rostov bowed slightly to the Ambassador, turned and followed the soldier back down the hallway. Moving down the stairs and back into the busy main lobby, Rostov quickly checked out with the security office and headed out to the street. He stood on the curb several minutes until a taxi finally answered his hail. Having instructed the driver to return to the hotel, Rostov leaned back to let out a sigh of relief. Everything seemed to have gone very well, and he was pleased.

A 15-minute drive brought Rostov near his hotel. As he exited the taxi, he fumbled through his pocket for the correct currency. Frustrated, he finally handed a small wad of bills to the driver who appeared to be very grateful, calling after him in German for several moments as he walked away towards the hotel. It was time to check out.

As he neared his hotel, Rostov spied several police vehicles and an ambulance parked near the main entrance with lights flashing furiously. He stopped at a distance to watch what was transpiring.

After several minutes, a group of paramedics and police officers emerged from the entrance of the hotel pushing a gurney loaded with a body roughly covered in a dark blanket. Rostov watched the procession as it approached the ambulance. Suddenly, he noticed the two worn black leather shoes poking out from beneath the blanket. Looking down, he studied the worn back leather shoes he was wearing. *They found him...*

Taking a deep breath and pursing his lips, Rostov turned and began to quickly work his way back down the crowded busy street away from the hotel. *Time to go...*

He turned down two side streets until he finally found an old back alley and stopped. He did not want to attract any undue attention. Casually looking around the street and then back into the alley, he waited for several moments before quickly sliding into the alley and continuing to make his way into the darkness.

When Rostov was satisfied, he was far enough away from any prying eyes and the busy main street, he ducked behind an empty rusted waste dumpster. Realizing he couldn't return to the hotel; he sat down on the cold pavement and rested his head against an old brick wall. The cold winter clouds darkened the sky as the evening began to settle in.

Almost an hour passed, and a small flurry of light snow began to fall. Quoros, an elder member of the Third Tribe of the Doon Esha got up to his feet and leaned against the old waste dumpster. Brushing the light snow from his drab gray jacket, he studied the coming night sky. Satisfied, he began to slowly walk further into the dark alley and further away from the still bustling noises of the streets.

He had spent the last hour going over his mission details one last time recalling how he had befriended Ivanich Rostov over some late evening drinks in the hotel's lounge two days prior. Rostov had drunk too much, talked too much and later hastily agreed with Quoros to take the six flights of stairs back to his room to avoid being noticed by hotel foot security or the ever-present news journalists with cameras who frequented the hotel.

Quoros had merely followed quietly behind at a good distance as the ill-fated Russian emissary stumbled up the last set of steps to meet his fate, He had finally managed to reach the sixth floor's top step when human hands suddenly threw the man back down the stairs. Rostov's neck had snapped like a twig, and Quoros merely watched and waited in the shadows as a pair of human hands eagerly retrieved Rostov's money belt and quickly fled away back up the stairs. After making sure he had a true 3D image of the stricken man, Quoros had waited until all was clear and then quickly stashed the body in a janitor's closet unobserved. He then retrieved the key to Rostov's room and entered the room to grab the black briefcase from under Rostov's bed. All had gone according to plan.

Taking one last look back up the alley towards the distant main street, he began to stride further and further into the dismal corridor. He quickened his pace for several steps and began to run. Concentrating deeply, Quoros closed his eyes and spread his arms. An instant later, a large furry winged reptilian silhouette quickly sailed up and out of the alley, beating its wings fiercely as it fought for altitude and disappeared into the wintry night sky.

The snow was falling heavier now than before. It would be a long flight. And there still remained much to do if the timetables were to remain intact and on schedule.

GLOBALCOMNEWS.NET
World Situation Report #2

"Once again, just in from our news correspondent in Iran, there are several fires burning out of control at three major Iranian oil refineries in Khuzestan, Chabahar, and another blaze at the Kharg Island Terminal facilities. Again, first witness reports appear to indicate that some sort of lightning or a fiery event phenomenon was observed dropping down from local low-level clouds at the Kharg Island facility, but we have no further confirmation as to what may have caused any of these blazes or whether or not they are related. We will be bringing you live coverage as soon as it is available. This is Deidra O'Hare with Global-ComNews.Net, live from our studio in Tel Aviv."

CHAPTER FIVE

REVELATIONS

Standing on the steps outside of Jade's apartment, Jesse closed the cover of his phone and placed it back into his coat pocket. "I don't know, father... it could be anything. Maybe terrorists or maybe a missile strike. Or it may be..."

"Yes, son," Gharius answered. "Or it just may be something more. It's not much information to go on, but it would seem to confirm our suspicions. Whatever has happened, this will surely escalate tensions between Europe, Asia and the Americas."

"You think it has something to do with the prophecy?" Jesse asked.

"Who is to say, son? It may well be, but it may not." Gharius replied.

Jesse sighed and looked down at the empty street.

"I'm sorry, Jesse, you must think me a bit crazy to speak in riddles all the time."

"Forgive me, father, but sometimes I just don't understand what you're saying. I don't understand how we're supposed to understand the prophecy when we have so little of it. Just so many pages, and it seems to me the really important pieces to the puzzle seem to be, excuse me for saying, conveniently missing. If we just knew what parts of the prophecy the Doon Esha possessed."

"Jesse, there is no use in wishful thinking. You must have faith that what we have is enough. It is never as much as we want, but it is enough."

"There, you see, I don't understand. I've studied the prophecy. There isn't enough to tell us when exactly it will be fulfilled or even exactly how. Just a few pages in the ancient language, which I don't understand all that well either. With all this, what I really don't understand is how you always seem to know the things you do."

Gharius stared up into the late-night sky as though searching the heavens for more stars. A light wind lifted his white hair just above his jacket collar. "Jesse, you are my eldest son. When I leave, the responsibility of the Order will fall to you and your brothers and sister. In all these years I have been with you and taught our ways, how is it you still try to see with only your eyes?"

Jesse rocked back on his heels and looked up into the sky with his father. "My eyes are your eyes, father. Maybe I just don't see things the way you see them."

Several moments passed before Gharius turned to Jesse. "My son, can you recall any time that I have ever misled you?"

Jesse thought for a second, then, "No, father, except that sometimes I get the feeling you haven't exactly told me everything."

Gharius grunted and smiled. "No, I haven't always told you everything. I will tell you what I believe you need to know when you're ready to know it. Too much information at the wrong time can be as dangerous as too little information at the right time. Take the image library for example. Within our sacred archives are images of great power. Could you have handled the power of being the great leviathan beast when you were younger?"

Jesse looked back down to the ground. "No, father. It would have been too much for me to control."

"Yes, son, it most certainly would have been beyond your control because you were not ready then. It is in these things that I must decide how to best teach you, and, to bring the Order along. The true power of the sacred scrolls lies in their truths contained in all the sacred laws and the prophecy. It all works together in its own time."

"But, father," Jesse interrupted, "I still don't understand where the laws get their power. We have our histories, stories and even legends that show us how the power of the sacred laws binds us and the Doon Esha together. Even your own daughter was exiled according to the sacred law at the demands of the Doon Esha. I still cannot believe she was forced to leave the Order. Surely..."

"The power of the sacred laws cannot be broken, Jesse," said Gharius firmly. "No one is exempt from obeying them or suffering certain consequences. To disobey them is certain to bring consequences, even death. It was so from the beginning and so to this day. The sacred laws were written and sealed in the blood of an innocent to preserve our kind."

"What do you mean sealed in blood, father? How does that give the laws the power to bind us?"

"Because the blood used to seal the laws and the prophecy was innocent blood taken from a prophesied newborn Esha at birth."

"Wait a minute. That is not in the history. How do you know all this?"

"I know, Jesse, because it was *my* father who wrote them, the father of us all. The blood used to seal them was *my* own."

Jesse's eyes bulged as he stepped back away from his father. Then, he pursed his lips and tried not to smile as he looked away. Gharius said nothing for several moments letting his son flip the words over in his own mind to sort them out.

"Son, I've been waiting for the right time to speak to you about these things, and it appears the time is now. It's time that you knew the whole truth as I believe my time is getting short, and I must begin to prepare you for what is coming."

Shaking his head slightly, Jesse turned back to face his father. "Father, I know that I am yet a youngling, even for my knowledge, but this doesn't make any sense. What you say is impossible! That would make you almost five thousand of the human years old."

"Well, I don't know about five thousand years. The humans have changed their calendars from time to time, so that would be hard for me to say."

"Hard for you to say? Please tell me you're joking. You've never spoken of these things before. Are you saying that your father wrote the sacred laws?"

"Jesse!" Gharius rumbled.

Jesse stepped back, bowing slightly and apologized, "Forgive me, father, please, I did not wish to offend you."

Gharius moved gently to his eldest son's side and put an arm around his shoulders. "No, son, you have not offended me. I expected worse. I know it's hard to believe, but I can explain all of it to you if you wish to listen." Gharius dropped his arm. "It is your decision, son."

Jesse rubbed his hands through his thick blonde hair and looked at his father. There was something in the older man's eyes, a reflection of the truth. He had known for a long time that his father's age was the source of many rumors, but this was a stretch he could not reach alone. Wiping his forehead with his sleeve, he straightened his shoulders and faced his father. "Tell me everything, father. I want to know everything. I believe I'm ready."

Gharius sized up his eldest son and took a deep breath. "Then, so be it. Come, walk with me, son. There are a few things we need to go over first so the rest will make more sense to you."

Jesse fell in step with his father, and the two made their way up the deserted sidewalk. The time had come and he wanted to know more. *I need to know it all, father...*

CHAPTER SIX

FATHER AND SON

After a little over an hour, they returned to Jade's apartment, Gharius looked up and down the street, which had quieted substantially with little traffic. "Perhaps we should sit."

They both took a seat on the cold steps leading up to Jade's apartment. Gharius cleared his throat and began. "So, yes, I have believed you were ready for some time now. Jesse, do you remember our history of the great waters?"

"Yes, father, I know it. Our history scrolls say that our kind divided into two factions. We both survived the great waters never to be reunited. All we have ever known is war."

"That is a small part of it. The truth is that the decision was made by my father for our kind to take the form of dolphins to survive the great waters. It was a young Esha who divided our ranks during the last days when he disagreed with my father and decided for himself to take the form of the shark. The conflict was a bitter one, but in the end, this young Esha took a third of our kind with him. He was once one of my father's most trusted, an upcoming Esha with a promising future."

Jesse interrupted. "I know this may sound somewhat trivial, but I have never understood why there was so much dissension over what form to take. I mean, what real difference did it make to form a dolphin or a shark?"

"In one sense, it meant nothing; in another sense, it meant all the difference in the world," replied Gharius. "You have to understand that no one had any idea how long we would have had to maintain those forms. You know quite well that the longer an Esha occupies any given assumed form, the more danger there is that the transformation becomes a permanent effect. That was at the very heart of the disagreement. However, even though neither side suffered the permanence effect, the damage from the rebellion was already done."

Jesse said nothing for a moment, taking in his father's words. Gharius continued.

"When the great waters subsided and the lands began to repopulate, there was a dispute over a mountain region where myself and our kind had set upon to make our new civilization come to pass. The young Esha, leading the rebellion of the Doon Esha came to our region and wished to claim our established territory for their very own."

"There was a bitter war, but in the end, the young Esha and his followers were fully expelled and scattered. As a result, there has been only war through the ages as the Doon Esha expanded and established their tribes on all the world's continents. It is from this mountain region in which we live that we have continued to fight the Doon Esha who swore ages ago to take it from us."

Gharius hesitated, waiting for any questions from his son. Receiving none, Gharius again continued. "As the second age of the humans came into its own, we formed the Order of Tryistan. Throughout time as we watched the humans dominate the earth and realized it was always meant to be theirs, we began to seek a way to join with humankind. It was my father's wish. He left us the very scroll that transformed Jade into her permanent human form, and it is the only one of its kind. The Doon Esha has tried many times to obtain and destroy it."

Jesse spoke, "But father, why does the Doon Esha hate the humans so much? The humans are so very weak and frail. They don't really represent a threat to us at all."

Gharius replied, "The Doon Esha holds the humans responsible for the great waters and the terrible destruction that happened back in those terrible times. They also blame my father for his increasing interest in humans over time.

Further, the Doon Esha believe the prophecy foretells that the evil things the humans are doing and continue to do will bring about another calamity, ultimately destroying the whole earth completely. They are aware that we value the humans and wish for a bridge to be built between the humans and ourselves. It is to this end that the Doon Esha hates humanity and craves to either destroy mankind or enslave it. This is the battle we have been fighting since the second rise of humankind."

Jesse put his hands in his pockets and exhaled. "Father, do you know what happened to the young Esha who divided our kind?"

Gharius hesitated and pursed his lips as though calculating an answer. After several moments, he leaned forward and rubbed his hands together. "He inhabits the underground cavern regions of the Galapagos Islands. He is their leader and has great abilities and an image archive that is truly powerful. He is to be respected, Jesse, and you must not ever underestimate him."

Jesse exhaled again and said, "But I thought the histories say he died a long time ago. They read that the Doon Esha are governed by an Elder Council, not a single leader. How do you know he is still alive, father?"

"I know because he comes to see me from time to time."

"What!" Jesse jumped. "This Esha has actually been within the borders of the Order? That's impossible! Surely, we would have detected..."

"No, you would not. He is a master of images. He could be beside you, and you would never know it. Trust me, son and know that he is alive and well."

"Father, what is his name?"

"He has gone by many names over time. You may be familiar with his more current and direct title, Celetin."

Jesse silently repeated the name to himself. "I thought that name was a myth."

"Well, as I said, he has gone by many names as have I. He has many faces and has used them throughout mankind's history to interfere in the affairs of humanity. Wherever, throughout history, you find humans destroying each other, you will find one of his faces and a name."

Jesse said nothing for several moments trying to take everything in. Much of it made no sense. "Father, I still don't understand. It is against the sacred laws to kill a human. How can he get away with what you're saying? I thought all Bas-Na Esha were bound to the sacred laws and prophecy. You said there were no exceptions."

"It's true that no Esha is above or beyond the sacred laws. Celetin knows the laws as well as I do. I did not say that he actually takes a physical part in mankind's history of death and destruction as far as personally killing them. He merely plays the catalyst, and advocates if you will, by providing fuel for the fire. Celetin and the Doon Esha have instigated war after war pitting men against men, brother against brother, children against their parents, but they never actually participate in the killing. To do so would violate the sacred laws and bring instant death to any Esha."

Jesse shook his head. "It's very hard to put it all together. How do you cause the humans to go to war and not participate?"

Gharius answered, "By simply being in the right place at the right time. Here, let me try to explain. You know of the human, Adolph Hitler?"

"Yes, father, he was the human leader who caused much death and destruction in the mid-twentieth century on the European continent."

"That's right. History shows that before the human Hitler rose to power, he was powerfully influenced by a man named Dietrich Eckhart, his mentor in the early 1930's. It was this mentor who gave Hitler the ideas, confidence and support to rise to power, consequently costing humanity tens of millions of dead in the second great human war."

"I understand that part, but what does that have to do with the Doon Esha?"

"One of the tribal Elders of the Doon Esha was that very mentor. Do you understand?"

"No, I do not understand. If Hitler's mentor was a factual character, how can he have been an Esha at the same time?" Jesse asked.

"It was an assimilation," Gharius answered flatly.

"Assimilation?" Jesse exclaimed. "But that is impossible. Well, not impossible, but rather it is absolutely forbidden, father. How can that be?"

"It is forbidden as you say, son. However, it is only forbidden to us, not to the Doon Esha. They have mastered the art, and they use it when it suits their purposes," Gharius replied.

"Then all Esha are capable of doing it," Jesse continued.

"Capable, yes," Gharius explained. "But the how of the whole thing is a mystery. A mystery that means that one must possess the knowledge to accomplish it."

"Do you have this knowledge, father?" Jesse asked.

"Yes, Jesse, I do. But it will never be used by any member of our order. I am the only one who possesses the knowledge, and one day, when I am gone, that knowledge will go with me."

"But wouldn't it be to our advantage to use it as the Doon Esha have done?" Jesse asked with a hint of cynicism.

"No!" replied Gharius sharply. "Jesse, you don't understand. To initiate assimilation of a human actually harms them far more than it might help us. The Doon Esha care little of the harm they inflict on a human as long as the assimilation does not cause death to the human they assimilate. We never have and never will use assimilation, ever. That, Jesse, is not open for any discussion. It must simply suffice to say that the Doon Esha have used it throughout human history when it was deemed convenient to their causes. Hitler's mentor was, again, but one example."

"Father?" Jesse asked. "What happens to a human who has been assimilated, I mean, when the assimilation is completed and the Doon Esha leaves the human?"

"Usually, the human is left unconscious for varying periods of time, which can range from a few hours to several days. There will be lapses in memory, dehydration, malnutrition, and so forth. It all depends on how long the assimilation lasts."

Jesse mulled it over in his mind. It was incredible! How could it all have happened? Even more disturbing was the notion of where else the Doon Esha might have interfered within human history. Was it happening now?

"Father, where else in human history has the Doon Esha influenced the outcome of events?"

Gharius let out a sigh and reached back to rub his neck. "Jesse, there is not enough time to try to explain them all to you. I'll give you only some of the more obvious: Genghis Khan, the Caesars of Rome, the Third Reich, and Joseph Stalin just to name a few."

Jesse's eyes went wide. "They were all Doon Esha?"

Gharius shook his head. "No, but they were all powerfully influenced and guided at precise moments in their lives in many of the same ways Hitler was guided. Power, Jesse, is always the common denominator, but you must remember that power must be taken. Such power can come in many forms, say, in the form of ideas and deceptions. It is this art of persuasion which the Doon Esha has mastered, and they then use that knowledge on any willing human they choose to work their craft on as long as it is in their own interests."

Jesse had more questions than answers. "So, I can only guess that all this goes back to the Doon Esha's hatred for the humans..."

"And also the reason why we of the Order of Tryistan have not yet permanently formed to humankind. As long as the Doon Esha lives on, the humans are in danger. We have resisted joining the humans because of the ongoing war with our common enemy."

Jesse shook his head. "Then where will it all end, father? A war five millenniums long and with no end in sight? We may never unite with mankind."

Gharius slowly stood up and stepped back down onto the sidewalk stretching his back. He turned to face his son who sat looking down at the pebbles on the step. "This is where the prophecy comes into play. The prophecy as we know it, what we have of it, foretells an end. The question is whether the end refers to us, The Doon Esha, the war between our kinds, or of the world itself."

"So, the Doon Esha believes the prophecy refers to the end of the world itself?"

"Yes, I believe they do." Gharius answered.

"But, father, you don't believe the prophecy refers to the end of the world, do you?"

"No, Jesse, I do not."

Jesse thought for several moments. "Then what do you believe the end does refer to?"

"I believe that that the prophecy refers to a mixture of all other possibilities."

"But how can that be, father? There can only be one end."

"That is as true as saying there can only be one beginning, which you know is not true. In a real sense, humankind has had two beginnings as we also have."

"But father..."

"That is enough for now, Jesse. My legs are getting stiff." Gharius looked up and down the empty street stretching backward again just a bit. "Come, walk with me again, my son. There are some additional details I want to talk to you about before I leave."

Gharius began to steadily make his way down the dark deserted sidewalk. Jesse jumped up and hurried to catch his father. A local church bell sang out its solemn midnight chimes through the dark cloudy night.

I just don't know father... I can believe some of it, but all of it, I just don't know...

CHAPTER SEVEN

THE "ADVISOR"

A very long hour had passed since Senior Presidential Advisor Daniel Richardson had arrived at the White House. It was not like the President to keep him waiting. He knew there was an emergency meeting of the Joint Chiefs of Staff in session and strongly felt he should have been included in that meeting.

As one of the President's senior advisors, Richardson believed that he *needed* to be in that meeting. How else was he going to advise the President on the recent events in Europe and the Middle East if he was kept out of the loop and out of the ongoing part of the bigger picture?

As Richardson sat silently musing, his attention was caught by the broadcast on the small HDTV monitor mounted on the dove white wall across from him. Frowning, he reached over two chairs and retrieved the unit's remote control to turn up the volume to hear the GlobalComNews.Net report:

"As you well know, the German chancellor has so far resisted the mounting pressures of China and Russia to join the newly formed United New World Council. This morning, the German cabinet voted unanimously to approve Germany's induction into this emerging global organization. The United States is calling for an emergency session in New York City with the United Nations Security Council, calling Germany's actions a grave mistake."

Richardson leaned forward in his chair turning the volume up.

"Mounting pressures within the United Nations have resulted in a temporary lapse in negotiations between the United States, and members of the UNWC over oil distributions coming from the OPEC nations of the Middle East. We have received no official position from the White House. The latest information we have is that President Wesley has called an emergency cabinet meeting in response to this new development. For now, it appears the United States may try to continue or utilize diplomacy in wake of today's events. Stay tuned for an update on the fiery blasts that rocked three Iranian refineries two weeks ago. This is Heather Tierney, reporting live..."

Richardson muted the volume and tossed the remote control down on the chair beside him. He had been waiting for this news. Now there was an unspecified yet viable threat to the United States from the economic coalition union between China, Russia, their newest members, and most likely Germany in the coming weeks. The ongoing meeting, in which he was currently excluded and in session in the President's office, was certainly called in light of the events covered in the broadcast he had just watched. Richardson could not think of any other reason the emergency meeting had been called.

Suddenly, it occurred to him that maybe it was better he wasn't involved in the meeting after all. Perhaps this would provide him the opportunity to advise the President in a more private setting. *Change of plan...*

Richardson suddenly became aware that he knew exactly how he would proceed in advising the President on these recent events.

The members of the Joint Chiefs of Staff (JCS) suddenly burst through the President's doors, all talking and arguing at the same time as they filed out of the President's office. Richardson quietly sat staring at the floor as the group of senior officers and advisors filled the small lobby with the loud buzz of a dozen tense conversations. The group slowly rolled past Richardson failing to notice or acknowledge him. The commotion continued to drift down the hall until finally disappearing around the corners. Then, the strange sterile quiet abruptly returned.

Richardson cleared his throat audibly reminding the President's secretary that he was still waiting to see the Commander-in-Chief. The older woman reached down and slowly picked up a phone. Richardson stared as she conversed with someone on the other end. Finally, the secretary got up from her chair and walked over to where the senior advisor was seated.

"Sir, the President will see you now."

"Thank you," replied Richardson tersely as he rose and followed her to the door.

The secretary led the way to the door and knocked three times before opening the large wood-paneled door. Richardson waited while she announced him to the President and heard the President utter something unintelligible. Then, the secretary stepped aside returning to her desk.

Richardson strode into the President's office smiling and offering his greeting as was his usual manner. "Mr. President, thank you for seeing me, sir."

President John D. Wesley sat at his desk staring at a television as Globalnetcom continued to broadcast world events across its screen. "Have you seen the news, Richardson?" The President was obviously irritated.

"Yes, sir, I have."

"Well," The President motioned Richardson to sit down, "What do you make of it?"

"It's a little hard to say for sure, Mr. President. We've known for some time that the Chinese and the Russians have been working hard to recruit a number of various nations into their economic coalition. It comes as no real surprise."

The President rubbed his face with his hands for several moments. Then, putting both hands on his desk, "Daniel, I don't pay you for the information I already know. I pay you to tell me things I don't know or haven't thought of yet. Is that the best you can give me?"

Exhaling, Richardson laced his fingers and leaned forward in his chair. "Mr. President, I believe we have to look at a bigger picture. We know where this is heading. China's economy is growing at a phenomenal rate. As an unofficial superpower, China needs energy to keep both her economy and her war machine moving as do the Russians, but the Russians have large energy resources.

However, Russia and China want support from key European allies connected to the Middle East. A number of European nations primarily get a large portion of their energy from the same country, mainly Russia, which seems to point to a common denominator - energy. But Russian energy cannot supply them all for a sustained period of time into the foreseeable future.

The only thing in the way of their going in and taking control of the Middle East oil supply is time and us. That, Mr. President, is how I see things."

"Unfortunately, Daniel, the JCS agrees with you. They want to begin to form plans for military options, but I am still not convinced it has come to that. I still believe diplomacy can work here. We've appealed to the U.N. Security Council. Personally, I think we can work the U.N. to our advantage here."

Richardson hesitated. "Mr. President, there is something else to consider here."

"What else?"

Clearing his throat, Richardson continued, "There are rumors, sir, unofficially, of course, that those refinery fires that occurred in Iran two weeks ago may have been the work of U.S. Special Forces in an attempt to undermine Germany's confidence in voting to join the union."

"What?" The President jumped up from his chair. "What are you talking about? We had nothing to do with those events. There has been no official word from the international investigations into those events. I would have had to personally authorize any such actions, so I would certainly know."

"Mr. President, I said the stories are unofficial. My own personal sources, however, tell me that this rumor may have actually been used to influence the German cabinet to join the union. Sir, they get approximately 40 percent of their oil from Iranian refineries. Of course, it would be in their best interest to move to protect their assets in the interest of their own national security."

"I'm not sure I follow you, Daniel. If the rumor was meant to undermine German confidence, how could it have served to encourage the Germans to join?"

"Because the Russians are conducting the investigations at the request of the U.N.. As you know, the Russians and the Iranians have been entertaining a mutually generous economic relationship for some time. It's very possible someone started the rumor for one purpose, and the Russians grabbed it and used it to their advantage to encourage the Germans to sign on."

"Do we know who that someone, whoever, might be?"

"No, Mr. President, we do not know as of yet, but we are working on it."

"And we still don't know who started those oilfield fires, do we?"

Richardson shook his head. "No, Mr. President. For all we know, the Iranians set the fires themselves to support their Russian friends regarding Germany's vote."

"That's absurd, Daniel, but you said there was an ongoing investigation. My understanding is that various members of the U.N. have been appointed to the investigating panel."

"Yes, Mr. President, that is certainly true. However, the U.N. representatives appointed to the investigating committee are from China, Russia, France and Germany."

"Well, that figures."

President Wesley rose from his chair and began to pace silently from one side of the room to the other. Turning to Richardson, "Why is it that no one else has informed me about the rumor that we were involved in the Iranian incident? You know, Daniel, three years ago, when I took office, you came highly recommended by a very close associate of mine. It's funny how, thus far, you've proven to be very informative. It's almost like you've got a sixth sense."

"Mr. President, I am only trying to fill this position you appointed me to do as best I can. This is my country too. I'm as concerned as anyone about the possible ramifications of these unfolding events. I think it might be wise to start considering all options at this point in the interests of national security including a military option should it become necessary based on the results of further investigations. Investigations, Mr. President, that we can be almost sure will not paint us in a positive light."

The President continued to pace the room. "The Joint Chiefs agree with you; however, military options are at the back of the line here. I refuse to believe that we would have to..."

"Have to what, Mr. President? Consider the possibility that a military option may ultimately be the answer? I am not sure that in the long run I can see any other way. The world must be shown that we will not tolerate any threats to our national security or be held hostage by our demands for oil. Whatever it takes, we must make the world understand that we will not be badgered into submission by the whims and will of any union or organization that chooses to threaten us. National security demands that we stand ready to meet any such threat to our sovereignty with whatever options we determine, regardless of how severe they may be."

The President stopped. "You are not suggesting any sort of nuclear option?"

"I'm not going to necessarily advocate any such option. I'm only saying that we must be prepared to do whatever it takes to protect our national interests. If it were ever to come down to a small demonstration of our fortitude through the use of limited nuclear means, then perhaps the world will once again understand that we are willing to do whatever it takes to protect American lives and our way of life."

"You're preaching, Daniel. Do you seriously think it could come down to a nuclear option? The world would never accept this. We got away with it during WWII, but we're talking about something completely different here."

"Are we, sir? We have the means to counter threats to our security by any number of means. Diplomacy may work, but I wouldn't completely count on it in light of recent events. They are trying to force us into a defensive posture. May I submit, sir, we might start to think more offensively? Let's start flexing our muscles and rattling some swords and start sending a message. Mr. President, you are the Commander-in-Chief of the most powerful arsenal in the history of the world. What do you really have to fear?"

President Wesley had stopped to stare out of a window overlooking the city of Washington, D.C. *He's right,* the President thought. *I do command the world's most powerful military force. Why am I just sitting here confused and indecisive? After all, I am the President of America, the world's number one recognized superpower.* The President turned and returned to his chair.

After several quiet thoughtful moments, he straightened up in his seat and said, "You know, the Vice President would argue strongly against taking such a bold position. He believes we can resolve this whole thing through proper diplomacy. At this stage, I must admit, I am still inclined to believe him. Rattling our swords now, as you put it, might send the wrong message and start something worse than we already have on the table."

Richardson looked down at the floor. "Mr. President, I know the Vice President is a good man. He believes in diplomacy and has a long and distinguished background of service to this country, particularly in overseas policy. But I'm looking at all of this from a historical and economic point of view. We've been stalled in the past on numerous occasions by diplomacy while in the meantime, nothing was accomplished. Look at the events prior to WWII. The whole world turned a blind eye while diplomacy raged on and on and what did it accomplish? Nothing but the start of a major world war which killed tens of millions."

Richardson paused to let it sink in. "Look at the history of the Middle East. Diplomacy has been used there for longer than we can count. Has it really solved anything? No. We know from our own history of involvement in this volatile region of the world that diplomacy does not often work. We fought two wars there because diplomacy failed. Diplomacy has failed to renegotiate our oil supplies, and now we're paying well over five dollars a gallon at the pumps. Why?"

Drumming his fingers on his desk, the President answered, "You believe diplomacy doesn't work. I understand your position. Your record throughout my administration has been one of taking solid action. I must admit that your advice has proven to be very effective, but this is a very serious situation. What you're suggesting could very easily escalate the situation into a full-scale war. So, this is what you are advising me?"

Richardson looked hard at the President. "No, Mr. President, again, I'm only suggesting that we make a carefully planned and visible show of power to signal to the world that we are prepared to protect our interests and that we are fully ready to do so. I believe it will cause this emerging union to think twice and very hard about taking any steps in the wrong direction."

Richardson stopped again. The President seemed somehow distracted in thought. Richardson decided to continue his press.

"Mr. President, the hard facts are these: First, the Chinese economy has grossly expanded. Their middle class is expanding faster than their resources can keep up with. This means more homes, cars and businesses that need fuel to run them, and again, the Chinese do not have those resources. They have to get them from somewhere. Next, we know the Chinese are buying up Russian military hardware at a phenomenal rate with American consumer monies, and they are expanding their military at an alarming rate. We also know that the Russian economy now depends very heavily on its arms exports and more so from the revenue from their energy development. Next, France and Germany represent two of the top three economic powers of the 10 European nations. And last, Germany will most certainly vote to join their new economic union. It is only a matter of time before the other European economic powers join this union, and Italy looks to be next."

Richardson paused and then continued, "And finally, Mr. President, it comes down to this. If you look at the combined military and economic potential represented in this new union, we can only conclude, in the final analysis, we are looking at a force that we are not equipped to handle financially, economically or militarily. They will, in fact, control much of an Eastern bloc and virtually the road to all of Asia.

They will have a combination of more money, oil and tanks than we do Mr. President. A whole lot more."

Richardson exhaled signaling he was done. The President sat silently trying to piece the whole picture together as Richardson had laid it out. The silence continued for several minutes. Then, the President stood up and leaned over his desk, setting both hands firmly down on the polished cherry wood finish. In a low voice, he spoke, "Daniel, do you realize that what you're saying might seem to come across as some sort of global conspiracy? Do you understand what you've just said?"

Richardson looked up from his seat unwavering, "I know, Mr. President, it sounds almost ludicrous. Maybe it's my background speaking, or maybe I'm a little paranoid. I am your advisor, sir, and I am looking at all the facts we have at this time. When you put them all together, it just seems a little too bizarre to write off so much information as a mere coincidence. Reality, sir, is that America has set a standard of living the rest of the world wants, and there are simply not enough resources in the end to make everyone happy. You said it yourself; you pay me to tell you things you may not have thought of yet." Richardson stopped on purpose waiting for the President to respond.

The President stood up straight and strolled back over to the window looking down on Pennsylvania Avenue. After several long moments, he turned to Richardson. "Thank you, Daniel. You've given me something interesting to think about. I'm not saying I buy it, but I will give it some consideration. Ah, one more thing, didn't you once say you have a background in history?"

Richardson perked up, "Yes, sir, I have what you might consider an extensive background in the history of world civilizations and development as well as anthropology."

The President smiled, "I was never a big fan of world history. Law was always my passion. It's good to know you've got my weaknesses covered."

"Thank you, Mr. President."

The President turned his attention to the window again. "Would you please ask my secretary to step into my office on your way out?"

Richardson took his cue and immediately stood up from his chair. "Yes sir, thank you, Mr. President." Realizing the conversation was over, Richardson turned and walked to the door trying to ensure that each step of his pricey European loafers resounded loudly off the hardwood floor. He grasped the doorknob and stepped out of the office, turning to close the door firmly.

Stepping to the counter of the desk, Richardson informed the secretary that the President had asked for her to come to his office immediately. She quickly locked her computer terminal and snatched up a pair of slim frameless glasses. Richardson turned and headed for the door leading out of the small lobby and began to make his way to the security office. He could hardly keep a persistent smirk from dominating his face.

Mezlash, fourth Elder of the Doon Esha in the Americas, felt good about his private meeting with the American President. He knew he had not quite convinced the President completely, but that was not his immediate intention. He knew enough about humans to know that most often a seed need only be planted. Reaching the security office, Richardson unclasped his security pass from his lapel and handed it to the attendant. It was time to go. Celetin would most certainly be looking for an end-of-the-day progress report.

The President's secretary knocked three times and opened the door to the President's office, "You wanted to see me, sir?"

The President turned away from the window, walked to his desk, and sat down. "Yes, Stephanie. Would you please get me General McMillan at NORAD on the phone? I'd like to speak to him directly. Tell his secretary that there are some concerns I need to discuss with him. Use the secure phone."

"Yes, Mr. President, right away." The secretary vanished. Several minutes later, a light began to blink on the President's secure encrypted land phone. President Wesley rubbed his chin thoughtfully as he stared at the blinking light for a moment before picking up the handset.

"General McMillan? Yes, this is Wesley. Well, thank you and you, also. What? No, no there's no problem. Actually Mac, I just had a couple of quick questions about the operational status of our mobile missile defense grid. Do you have a minute? Great."

CHAPTER 8

ESCALATIONS

Soundlessly, the two translucent forms glided through the air at 300 feet some 50 miles northwest of the Boston mountains section of the Ozark Mountain range. The only visible evidence of the two opaque forms was the internal intermittent soft blue bolts traversing their bodies and the moonlight reflecting the outlines of the beasts as they twisted and turned in flight. Their 20-foot wingspans made virtually no noise as they effortlessly sliced through the air. To the casual observer, the pair of beasts might appear to be more at play as they gracefully commanded the sky, slipping this way and that. However, the casual observer would be mistaken. The pair of Guardians of the Order of Tryistan was not playing; they were on patrol.

The pair communicated constantly between both themselves and the main hold of the Order. Tightly focused bands of invisible electrostatic pulses fired back and forth to the receivers manned by the Order's watch operating 24 hours a day. It had become necessary to initiate day and night patrols due to the upscale encounters with the Doon Esha. Twice the borders of the Order of Tryistan had been crossed by various parties of the enemy. Twice the Guardians had been dispatched to meet the threat only to find nothing.

The Guardians of the Order were something of an enigma. During the Great Waters, a small element of the dolphin form, destined to become the Order of Tryistan, simply disappeared. They had chosen to dive deep into the waters in search of more abundant food and had vanished. It would be almost a 100 years after the Great Waters had subsided that the first of the Guardians had appeared to Gharius' father. They had changed into forms previously unseen by any of the Esha. Gharius' father took them in.

No one had ever been able to determine how or why the Guardians had assumed their mysterious forms, or why the forms were permanent. Through time, they had proven themselves to be fiercely loyal and a powerful ally. In time, they were chosen and dedicated as the Guardians of the Tryistan Order, and the archives of the sacred scrolls.

The Guardians had, in fact, taken on the forms of some of the most bizarre and strange creatures living in the deepest darkest regions of the oceans. The creatures were virtually invisible to the naked eye, becoming momentarily visible only as they moved out of their normal flight maneuvers. In the dark, they were especially difficult to detect depending on the level of light present. This made them excellent candidates as first line Guardians of the Order and especially suited for night patrols.

Tonight, the two Guardians patrolled the skies literally undetected under a full pale moon. Their bodies traced arcs in the air as an occasional blur of soft electric blue streaks barely reflected the pale moonlight off their opaque bodies. The pair continued their patrol as usual both undetected and unnoticed.

Suddenly, out of what seemed nowhere, a blinding burst of orange-red fire traced across their paths like a red-hot careening comet. Caught completely unaware, both Guardians abruptly stopped in midair and hovered side-by-side, as they scanned the horizon. Immediately, their invisible electrical pulses fired off in the direction of the Order as the Guardians reported this unexpected phenomenon. The Guardians, Neeash and his mate, Nezfur, waited for instructions. They quickly searched the skies while instinctively beginning to widen the gap between themselves to form a circular sweep pattern taking care to keep a distance of only 50 yards apart.

The attack came from above. Three red-brown, steel-scaled dragons of the Doon Esha screamed down on the Guardians, picking their targets carefully. Neeash turned to his mate just in time to see her engulfed in an immense ball of red fire. The attackers sliced through the air, diving between the Guardians while the closest dragon dove by the stricken Guardian raking her body with its hind claws as it passed.

Nezfur, on fire and bearing deep gashes along her side and neck, began a sickening and erratic descent back down to the ground. Neeash could only watch as his mate silently burned while she spiraled to the earth. A trail of dancing red embers traced her descent.

Neeash gathered himself together and furiously began to climb for altitude. Processing his energy forces, he concentrated hard, pushing his internal energies back past his hind quarters. Sensing the attackers were in pursuit, he beat the air more furiously to gain as much altitude he could reach while sending electric pleas to the Order. He searched the skies to determine where the next attack might come. *There.*

The three dragons rose up calling out to each other. Neeash couldn't understand their language, but he understood their intentions. The lead dragon was larger than the other two and quickly became Neeash's preferred target. Neeash slowed his speeding ascent to a crawl, turned and stretched out his wings waiting as the attackers closed the distance to him.

Neeash knew too well the same fate of his mate also awaited him, who was now rushing straight towards him at high speed. The lead dragon was coming in first as the other two covered its flanks just behind.

With a powerful flick of his scorpion-like tail, Neeash unleashed a frightening barrage of electricity much like the tongues of lightning in a thunderstorm. The blue-pink bolts leaped out towards the attacking dragons in multiple layers. The lead dragon suddenly dropped out of formation leaving its two comrades to take the full brunt of the electric storm.

The bolts leapt out slamming one of the smaller dragons full in the face and disintegrating the young dragon's skull. Another bolt caught the other young dragon straight through the chest erupting through the back of the beast, spewing blood and chunks of bones in every direction.

Both of the fourth-rank dragons began the sickening long descent back to landfall, burned to death by the decisive lighting storm unleashed by the Guardian Neeash. The Guardian had no time to watch as the two corpses descended, burning to ashes until finally disappearing in a cloud of vapor before hitting the surface. Searching the heavens for the elusive lead dragon, Neeash detected nothing. He began to cautiously descend in search for his mate's body to return her to the Order. *Nezfur.* With a stricken cry of grief, Neeash flipped his wings over and began a dive to the ground.

Coming to a spot about a 100 yards above the earth, Neeash spotted Nezfur's body and slowly descended to where she lay. He could see that at least she was still alive but only barely. Suddenly, Neeash instinctively shot upward into the sky just in time to avoid a single reddish-orange ball of fire. He barely missed the brunt of the fireball but felt the heat searing his hind quarters. Letting out a furious shriek,

Neeash pushed the remainder of his energies into his tail and came to a hover 50 feet above a cluster of small trees.

The dragon slowly dropped down to meet Neeash a mere 20 yards away. Face-to-face, both creatures sized the other up. Finally, the dragon spoke.

"Guardian, I am an Elder of the Doon Esha. I demand that you yield."

The Guardian's opaque form began to generate strong gyrating streaks of red, blue and pink light in a fit of agitation. In a flowing but uneven tone Neeash replied, "I am Neeash, Guardian of the Order of Tryistan, and I demand that you yield."

The dragon also appeared to be agitated. "Guardian, I am a ranking Elder of the Doon Esha. You are outranked, and I again demand that you yield."

The Guardian's streaks of light began to alternate between purple, blue and red racing through its body in a startling array and betraying Neeash's agitations. "I know that you are an Elder. I demand that you yield in the name of Gharius of the Order of Tryistan."

Both creatures stared at each other, sizing up their opponent while beating the air with their powerful wings. Suddenly, Neeash let loose another layered burst of powerful bolts of electricity. Taken aback, the dragon quickly drew his wings together deflecting the powerful onslaught. Then, relaxing his wings just enough to peer through them and still keep in flight, he said, "I see, Guardian, that you are indeed worthy of your task. I know the name that you speak. I will not yield. You are outranked and you are compelled to give way to me. Give way, Guardian, or you force me to..."

"To do what?" A powerful voice trumpeted somewhere above and behind the dragon.

Both Guardian and dragon were startled and cautiously moved around each other to see where the voice had come from.

"I asked you a question, Esha. I asked you what you intend to do to one of my Guardians?"

Guardian Neeash dropped quietly to the ground and stood still. He knew that strong voice intimately. He also knew that he would do well to keep still and be quiet.

The dragon landed as well, eyes darting around the landscape looking for the source of the power voice. The voice was familiar. "I'm afraid you have me at an advantage. Might you show yourself that we might make known of our ranks?"

"Your rank is of no importance to me, Esha. Your attack upon my Guardians, however, is another matter."

"*Your* Guardians?" The dragon rasped.

The wind began to pick up. Neeash spotted the silhouette first, but the dragon caught the Guardian's gaze as well, and they both stared into the sky together. Whatever it was, it was very large and came in quickly.

The hind feet landed first followed by the enormous fore claws. In an instant, the dragon found itself face to face with an enormous scarlet Griffith with a lush thick mane surrounding a lion's head and eyes lit like the embers of a fire. There was no mistaking the great crimson creature. Both Guardian and dragon shivered in its presence.

The Griffith turned slightly and nodded to the Guardian who responded with a modest bow. Then, the crimson creature turned into the dragon.

"I am Gharius, of the Order of Tryistan. What is your name?"

The dragon fought to find the words until finally, "I am solo, for I am one."

"Very well, solo. What business do you have with my Guardian?"

"Th... they attacked us, your Guardians did," the dragon sputtered.

"I am sure they did. Why, did you say us?" Gharius demanded.

"We were three, but now I am one," The dragon replied.

"Yes, well, dragon, my Guardians were two, and now there is one. This cannot pass away, dragon."

"Surely you will not destroy me. I know who you are, Son of the Great Elder. I will yield."

"Stay your ground, dragon," Gharius commanded. *How are they so close to our borders...*

Gharius turned and walked a short distance to where the stricken Nezfur lay. Gently, he picked the opaque body up with his large fore claw and inspected the stricken Guardian. Neeash stared down at the ground until he noticed the dragon began to slightly move its head back and forth. The Guardian quickly glanced at Gharius who seemed to be completely engrossed with his inspection of the fallen Guardian.

Without warning, Neeash fired a violent storm of electric light at the dragon. A bolt tore through the dragon's wing and struck the creature in the chest, knocking it backward and bringing it to the ground. Gharius let out a tremendous roar as did the dragon as its thick, scaled head slammed hard into the earth. Neeash stumbled forward and took to the air ready to fire again.

Slowly the dragon shakily raised itself back up to its full measure. Without another word, it quickly spread its wings and violently launched itself screaming into the sky. Then it was gone.

Neeash hesitated, trying to decide whether to pursue the escaping Esha until Gharius shook his head, "No, it is enough. Come now, Neeash. We will take her back to the Order."

The Guardian settled to the ground, but Gharius could tell the creature was in pain. "Guardian, can you make it back to the hold?"

Neeash began to fire bursts of green and blue light over his body signaling he could fly.

Gharius reached down and gently took Nezfur up into both of his fore claws. Turning to Neeash, Gharius' voice strained, "She's dead, Guardian."

A moment later, carrying the body of Nezfur, Gharius launched into the air escorted by a grief-stricken Guardian back to the Order. There would be a price to be paid for sure, but for now, the Order would grieve its senseless loss.

CHAPTER NINE

HOMECOMING

Petrawnus stared up into the brilliant unfolding morning sky, searching the horizon. The sun, just cresting over the eastern ridges of the Ozark Boston Range, threw an array of magnificent light and shadows across the massive rock formations. The deep mist drifted up from the valley as the warmth of the morning sun softly began to awaken the land. Feeling the gentle western wind across his back and neck, Petrawnus often embraced these few early precious moments of the dawn while he relished in the feeling of a sense of freedom these isolated mountains brought with them.

Petrawnus, however, was not standing his vigil watch this morning just to enjoy the beauty of the moment or stretch his wings to soak up the warmth of the sun. Gharius was returning, and Petrawnus, a senior Elder of the Council of Twelve and commander of the Order's garrison stood at the center of the entrance peak waiting for his master's return.

The majestic scarlet and white Griffith's powerful wings effortlessly beat the air as it descended down onto the peak's center plateau. Gharius, along with Neeash, landed directly in front of the awaiting Petrawnus, who bowed down on his assumed form's forelegs bringing his head towards the ground.

"Gharius, welcome. Your servant awaits your orders."

Casting a glance around the peak, Gharius tucked his enormous wings back and looked down upon his faithful companion. "Petrawnus, good morning. It's good to be home, old friend. I trust all is well?"

Petrawnus rose up. "All is well here and in order, my Lord,"

Petrawnus' eyes fell upon the Guardian Nezfur as Gharius gently laid her body on the smooth rock. Gharius took a step forward into his human form and looked up at his long-time friend.

Petrawnus stepped into his human form and shook his head. "My Lord, we only had one incident to report last night. It appears you have all the details. I was afraid we'd lost her."

Leaning in towards Petrawnus, Gharius whispered, "She is dead, my friend." Petrawnus stepped closer to Gharius and without a sound mouthed the word, "Dead?"

Gharius nodded and motioned to the peak's entrance. "Neeash, would you please summon a call and have her taken to the inner chambers?"

Immediately, the distraught and exhausted Guardian limped off towards the peak's entrance rift to retrieve a detail to help carry his mate's body into the mountain.

Gharius grimaced and turned to look out over the ranges. "That was a little too close."

Petrawnus stood beside his master. "Do you know who attacked them, my Lord?"

"It was an Elder along with two of his followers of the fourth ranks. Neeash managed to dispense of the two followers, but the Elder outranked him and would not yield. It's a good thing that I went out there last night personally. Only one of you of the Twelve would have had the rank to force him to yield."

Gharius continued, "Neeash is to be commended, and I intend to do it myself. This is the third time in as many months. I think it's about time..." Gharius stopped and looked down at the body of the fallen Guardian for a moment. Petrawnus waited and watched until Gharius finally sighed heavily and began to walk to the edge of the peak.

Several moments later, the sound of whirring and chirps descended on the peak as six Guardians under the direction of Neeash gently landed where the dead Guardian lay. Gharius and Petrawnus turned to watch as the Guardians quickly maneuvered themselves into position around the body of their fallen comrade. On Neeash's command, they carefully lifted Nezfur's body into the air and carried her to the mouth of the entrance to the peak while Neeash followed behind. Suddenly, Neeash collapsed to the ground in a crumpled heap. Without a word, two of the Guardians fell back from the others and carefully lifted the struggling Neeash up. The detail proceeded to gently carry both stricken Guardians into the open rift on the side of the mountain.

When they had disappeared inside, Gharius motioned to Petrawnus to accompany him to the edge of the peak. Together, they watched the sun as it rose above the last crest illuminating the entire range.

Gharius spoke first, "Have you received any more information about the Europeans and their intentions concerning joining the coalition?"

"No, my Lord. Except that the Italian government intends to vote on the issue by week's end. It looks to us like they may well vote in favor of joining the coalition. However, like their European allies, the membership would most likely begin as a sort of interim agreement."

Gharius rubbed his chin thoughtfully. "I believe they will as well. And I believe that the Doon Esha have a powerful hand in all of this. It's all starting to add up and come together. This will not be good news for our American hosts. I'll call a meeting of the Twelve. We will need to discuss these recent events."

"Of course, my Lord." Petrawnus lowered his voice, "Not to change the subject, but I see that you've returned alone. Jade has again refused to return I assume?"

"For the moment," Gharius answered. "I believe that in time she will change her mind. I left three of my sons with her for the time being. She will need their protection now, more than ever."

Glancing around the peak, Petrawnus continued. "It is most unfortunate she cannot return to the Order, my Lord. If only she'd not..."

"Broken the law? Yes, my old friend, I know. Don't worry; I am working even now to take care of that. It will not be a problem much longer."

Curious, Petrawnus cautiously pursued the subject. "Yes, but since she broke the law, the Doon Esha can claim the right to her execution rather directly, human or not. Although you chose to exile her as a temporary stay in place of carrying out her sentence, the Doon Esha only needs to use a human agent or arrange for any accident to befall her. No doubt they would even sacrifice a low rank under the law to get to her and still claim justice. It would seem that she would want to at least relocate closer to this region for her own safety."

Gharius looked hard at his old friend for a moment. "Petrawnus, you're fishing."

"No, my Lord, I, I just ..." Petrawnus stopped and bowed his head slightly. "I'm sorry, perhaps I was. After all the time I've known you, there are still moments when I feel as if I really don't know you much at all."

Putting a hand on Petrawnus' shoulder, Gharius started to smile. "It's alright, old friend. But you don't have to worry about Jade. I have left three of my best sons to watch over her. They're more than capable of keeping her safe, and that is what is important at the moment." Gharius dropped his hand and gently shook his head.

Petrawnus sighed. "Of course, my Lord. It's just that she represents a real vulnerability and an opportunity for the Doon Esha to strike at you. As a senior Elder of the council, I wish to recommend placing two of my guardians closer to her if it would please my Lord."

Gharius pursed his lips looking up at the enormous spiraling wall of rock supporting the upper peaks. Finally, "No. Not yet. I believe Jade is safe for now, and I need your resources here for the moment. Last night's attack can only mean the Doon Esha are getting bolder and will continue to escalate their activity. Let's keep the Guardians close to home until otherwise necessary. I believe we most certainly will need them." *All of them...*

Bowing his head again, Petrawnus replied, "Yes, my Lord. It is as you say."

Gharius turned from his old friend a moment to survey the morning sky one more time. He marveled at the brilliance of the sun as its light touched everything around him, giving fresh life to the mountain valley. He never tired of seeing it.

Petrawnus, hesitant to interrupt again, said softly, "My Lord, your hosts are waiting to receive you, when you are ready, of course."

Gharius turned back to his council Elder. "You're right. We should be getting inside." With that, Gharius gestured towards the passage, and the two walked to the entrance rift and through the small carved access door carefully tucked into the mountain's side.

Having traveled the short access tunnel, they entered a small entrance chamber. Petrawnus waved his hand over a small rocky pylon just inside the chamber, prompting the sliding plate of rock into motion, which slid its way across the chamber's entrance, sealing them inside the chamber.

The small chamber was illuminated well enough for Petrawnus to easily cross to the other side and wave his hand over a second rocky pylon next to the opposite wall. The chamber vibrated slightly as it descended deeper into the mountain. After a minute, the vibrations stopped and Petrawnus again waved his hand over the rock pylon. Silently, the smooth rock door slid away to the side and out of sight as the chamber filled with bright illuminating light.

Gharius proceeded through the opening with Petrawnus dutifully following behind his master. The host was welcoming Tryistans, all in human form, and bowed as Gharius proceeded down the huge carved light blue and gray marbled steps. The immense ceilings sported stellar cathedral heights, which went straight up almost disappearing into the cavern towers. A lush beautiful scarlet rug dressed with white edging was laid at length from the bottom of the wide carved staircase, across the receiving room, stopping just short of the far entrance door. Hesitating at the bottom of the steps, Gharius waited as Petrawnus drew up beside him. It was good to be home. *But there is something missing...*

CHAPTER TEN

NEEASH

Petrawnus called for order and made his herald, "To the host of the Order of Tryistan, I, Petrawnus, senior Elder to the Council of Tryistan say to you - rise up and bid our Lord Gharius welcome home."

For a moment, no one moved. Then suddenly, Gharius found himself surrounded by the excited host of his fellow Tryistans, each trying to get near enough to greet him with a hug or a heartfelt handshake. Tired as he was, he made sure he hugged or shook the hand of everyone who approached him until the welcoming host was later dismissed.

Happy as he was to be home, and despite the joyous welcome, Gharius realized there was something missing that bore deep into his heart—Jade. He suddenly missed how she used to welcome him home among the hosts.

She would over-exaggerate her bow, playfully rolling her eyes at Petrawnus' often lengthy introductions. It was her way of standing out to get her father's attention. Sometimes it was annoying and other times Gharius found himself masking a smile or suppressing an urge to laugh. He dearly missed her right now.

As the last of the attending hosts wandered out of the hall, Gharius walked over to where Petrawnus was standing watch at the entrance doors and motioned him to follow. Petrawnus immediately fell into step as they left the hall together.

"Petrawnus, where have you sent the Guardian Neeash?" Gharius asked as they walked down the long lit carpeted corridor.

"He is being cared for in the south wing of the colony tunnels."

"And his mate?"

"It was Neeash's wish that she be buried in the East gardens with honors as a Guardian, my Lord."

There was silence as the two continued through the corridor. Finally, Gharius asked, "How many know about last night's attack and Nezfur's death?"

"Only a small handful, my Lord. Also, there have been two reports by the local media stations related to UFO sightings last night in the same area, but little else worth noting. Is there a problem?"

"You are sure, old friend?" Gharius asked.

"Yes, my Lord. The affairs of the Guardians are known only to yourself and the Council and not for all to know, but of course you know that my Lord; they are completely loyal to you."

"Of course, Petrawnus. Thank you."

As they neared the last section of the corridor leading into the enormous underground fortress' capital courtyard, Gharius stopped. Petrawnus took several more steps before realizing he'd strayed ahead and turned around with an embarrassed expression, "My Lord?"

"No, old friend, quite alright." Gharius suddenly became all business. "Petrawnus, please go check in with your watches and let me know if any new developments occur. Double your Guardian patrols tonight as well. I want a full fortress lockdown by sunset. Call a meeting of the Council of Twelve, say, in about four hours, and make sure Zelotus is there. I know several of the Council are already here. Employ the usual encrypted portals for the others. There is something I need to do first, and then I will join you. "

Petrawnus bowed, "It is as you say, my Lord," and hurried off down the west wing corridor taking him past the gardens in the main court-yard.

Gharius rubbed his eyes for a moment and then followed behind Pe-trawnus down the west wing corridor, back into the capital courtyard and then towards the south colony tunnels. After several long min-utes, he arrived to find the tunnels were alive with Tryistans, mostly in human form, going about their assigned tasks, each presenting a slight bow as they became aware of his presence.

Passing the south command control center, the heart of the colony tunnels, he paused slightly to note who was on watch duty before continuing deeper into the chambers of the south colony. Gharius suddenly stopped as he sensed the colony's Watch Commander ap-proaching him. Simotas, the on-duty Watch Commander, bowed waiting for Gharius to greet her.

"Simotas, I trust all is well?"

Simotas answered apologetically, "Lord Gharius, we received word you'd returned. Please forgive me, my Lord. We delayed our attendance as we thought it might have been possible to have the Guardian Neeash up and ready for your arrival. We failed, my Lord." Simotas dropped her chin slightly to her chest.

Gharius looked closely at his faithful watch ward. Reaching out, he clasped Simota's shoulder, "There's no need to explain, my friend. I know the Guardian survived the brutal attack. I've come to see him, if I may?"

Simota's eyes widened, "Yes, my Lord, of course. He suffered only minor injuries, but he is very weak. I honestly don't know how he managed to fly back to the Order. My Lord, Nezfur... she is dead."

Gharius nodded slightly and softly said, "I know, commander. If Neeash is strong enough, I'd like to see him."

Turning and gesturing to one of the adjacent chambers, Simotas beckoned Gharius, "Yes, my Lord, please. This way."

Simotas led the way as Gharius followed behind through the labyrinth of the service tunnels. They arrived at the section where numerous rooms had been precisely cut out of the rock to make up the main infirmary. Simotas turned a corner down an open passageway until reaching the third room on the right. The door was partially open and inside lie Neeash curled up on a large table in a corner at the back of the dimly lit room. Wires and leads ran from the Guardian to a number of blinking medical monitors on an adjacent table.

Gharius paused at the door and surveyed the room.

"Simotas, I would speak to Neeash alone, if you would please."

"Simotas straightened to attention. "Of course, my Lord. He is sleeping, but I'm sure he will come around shortly. If I'm not mistaken, it will soon be almost time for his next scheduled evaluation and treatment."

"Thank you, Simotas." With that, Gharius slid quietly into the room, shutting the door firmly behind him leaving the watch officer to return to her station and assume her duties.

Gharius stepped gently across the floor noting the monitoring equipment and the wires running along the ground between the tables. Reaching for a side chair, he slid it up to a corner of the table where the Guardian lay. Gharius sat staring at his faithful sleeping Guardian for some time. Finally, he closed his own eyes and began to speak softly to the Guardian in the ancient language of his father, the Elder. Gently, Gharius laid his right hand on the sleeping Guardian's shoulder.

Several minutes passed as Gharius continued to recite in the ancient language until small and intermittent streaks of pale blue lights began to pulse erratically in slightly noticeable waves throughout the Guardian's body. Gharius continued in the old tongue as the emanations became more pronounced. After several more minutes, Neeash slowly opened his eyes.

It took a few moments for Neeash's eyes to clear enough to reveal the presence of the Master of the Order. At first, Neeash tried to utter some sounds in a barely audible scratchy voice. Gharius continued to speak in the old tongue seemingly unaware that the Guardian's audible life signs began to evolve into more familiar rumbling purrs. Suddenly, in a moment of pure frustration, Neeash tried to move his wings to which Gharius instantly reached over and touched the Guardian's neck, calming the creature.

"Be still, Guardian, I am here with you," said Gharius gently. "Take your rest."

An hour passed as Neeash regained his strength until at last he could raise his head a few inches above the table. Gharius had stopped speaking, giving the Guardian time to recover. Pulses of bluish green light flashed in rhythmic patterns over the Guardian's opaque body as he began to rumble his apologies to the Order's master. As the Guardian continued to muse, the pulses of light became stronger and more erratic as he spoke.

Gharius reached out and touched the Guardian once more, "No need, mighty Guardian. It is I who should bow to you."

Neeash began to protest appearing more agitated as faint splashes of reds begin to intermingle with the blue light pulses pouring over his body.

Gharius moved his hand to the Guardian's shoulder wing, "Yes, Neeash, I know of the loss of Nezfur. She was truly a Guardian of honor. She died defending us. I know your loss, my friend. I knew her well through the many nights she stood watch while I studied in the old archives. She spoke so much about you. I miss her deeply as well."

The Guardian's light emanations slowed to small bluish intermittent patterns again. Rumbling softly, Neeash laid his head back down.

Softly stroking the Guardian's exposed wing, Gharius felt his eyes moisten. "Mighty Neeash, you have done me a great service."

The Guardian had fallen asleep again. Gharius stood up and spoke in a whisper, "I know your pain and your loss, my friend. I tell you this;

your pain will falter, and your heart will be filled once again. I tell you the truth."

Gharius rose slowly and moved quietly to the door where he paused to look back at the sleeping Guardian. He closed the door and made his way out of the southern colony towards the capital chambers. It was time to call the other missing members of the Council from their continents to conference with the Order for an immediate session. Taking the west wing corridor, Gharius headed for his sacred archives struggling with the gnawing feeling he had missed something. *Something or someone is not right here...*

CHAPTER ELEVEN

AN ACCOUNTING

Fiomass, Elder of the Doon Esha, was exhausted from his long flight. It had taken two days with a damaged wing to make the long trek across the great oceans to one of the remote islands of the Galapagos. The burn hole in his right wing had made the flight more difficult, but it was the burn to his chest that hurt him the most. The Guardian had caught him by surprise. *It will not happen again...*

Fiomass had underestimated a Guardian's resolve for the second time during his life span. He had vowed during the flight back that it would surely be the last. Smoke from a neighboring island drifted lazily up from its small semi-active crater. The winds were calm and much warmer as was the ocean that softly stroked the dark volcanic beaches surrounding the main island, which housed the fortress of Tribes of the Doon Esha.

Dropping down to a 100 feet, the Doon Esha Elder hardly noticed he had been joined by two third-rank dragon-type escorts. The trio descended slowly until coming to rest on the outer rim of the old decaying volcanic rim. Small whiffs of sulfur popped up and out of the rocky grounds to be whisked away by the gentle wind. Pools of black mud bubbled here and there, freely releasing their minute traces of toxic gases into the near still air.

To the outside world, this island was virtually dead and inhospitable. The semi-dormant volcano had served as the headquarters of the Doon Esha for almost two millenniums. Once a powerful force of nature, it had been silenced long, long ago by the waters of the Great Flood. Now it served as the main hold for the powerful leader of the Doon Esha, Celetin. Fiomass knew Celetin would be expecting him.

Having landed, the two third ranks walked several paces behind him as the trio made its way along the outer ridge to where a vertical jagged ledge met the side of sheer rock cliff. Fiomass stopped and waited as two unnoticeable stone-still rocky figures posted on each side of the entrance emerged from the ledge as if suddenly coming to life. The two figures silently looked the Elder over carefully without a sound. Satisfied, they returned to their unmoving foundations, blending in perfectly with the volcanic rock surrounding them. A 12-foot slab of rock slid sideways noisily until one of the statue-still figures rumbled, signaling to Fiomass that the Elder was cleared to enter.

Stepping in through the entrance, Fiomass changed into wolf form. The two third ranks changed their forms to pack dogs as they followed the Elder's lead as best they could. The small pack headed down the dark corridor toward the central hold. The burns Fiomass had sustained in battle were obvious even through the thick fur that covered his frame.

Changing to a human form was forbidden here. Celetin had developed such a hatred of humans that the sight of one would send him into a frenzied rage. He had ordered a decree and added it to his own laws that for any Doon Esha to be found in the form of a human within the fortress was punishable by an excruciating death.

Through time, the Doon Esha had learned to form strange and unrecognizable creatures by deliberately inter-mixing naturally pure images with one another under the direction of Celetin. As the Eshas advanced through the ranks, the stranger and stronger images they were provided access to were literally the twisted creations of Celetin himself. The mixing had advanced so far that now, only the Elders themselves had the ability to form to the pure and the complete previously unaltered natural images.

The fact that Fiomass was completely wolf appeared strange to many within the fortress and held by many to be somewhat of an enigma as with all the Elders. Even the two third ranks escorting him were unable to form *completely* to a pack dog. Instead, they had formed a hybrid of the spotted body of a pack dog, sporting leopard's legs and paws with a jackal's head.

This was also the reason why the fourth-rank dragons killed during their encounter with the Guardian had fallen rather easily. They were not pure and complete dragon forms dressed with the armored scales a true dragon needs for protection. Instead, they bore the image of a dragon mixed with the image of a vulture's skin leaving their hides thin and vulnerable. It was one of the unpredictable features that eons of Celetin's image tampering had produced, though none would have ever dared to challenge him.

Fiomass, limping slightly, and his two escorts reached the main hall at the end of another dark entrance tunnel. Two creatures, scorpulas, formed of the mixed images of a scorpion and a tarantula, stood guard at the entrance. Their powerful tails complete with lethal spear-point stingers were held high to signify they were standing watch.

Fiomass stopped as the two creatures moved towards him on eight legs with large pincers raised and ready as they closed in to inspect Fiomass and his escort party. After several moments, apparently satisfied, the scorpula in charge challenged the Elder.

"Elder Fiomass, welcome back from your task. Lord Celetin is expecting you."

Fiomass nodded and looked about the huge hall as many small fires burned from crudely cut pits illuminating the hall in an abysmal sort of flickering shadow dances.

"Thank you, sentinel. I ask to pass through to see our Lord Celetin."

The scorpula stepped back and away. Gesturing with its massive tail, "You may pass, Elder Fiomass."

Fiomass stepped through the tunnel entrance. His two escorts turned and retreated back down the passage. They were forbidden from entering any further.

The fetid and putrid smell of sulfur immediately filled and assaulted his lungs. Creatures unimaginable filled the dome's main hall, going in, over and throughout the many temple-like structures and stone structures filling the massive dome.

Fiomass continued across the central courtyard, hesitating to give a slight bow to an enormous statue dedicated to Celetin as was the law. Finally, he passed the market area and headed for the north chambers. It was there that Celetin kept himself virtually locked up and away from the masses. Celetin rarely ventured out of his chambers. Fiomass could not remember the last time Celetin had been seen outside of them.

There were dark rumors underground that Celetin had gone mad; rumors that were heard in the vapors of sulfur and wind that blew through the dome and whispered only in the darkest shadows. Fiomass cared little for such rumors. He reported directly to Celetin as an

Elder of Celetin's order. The images Celetin had bestowed upon the Elder had granted him access to more power than most of the other members of the Doon Esha.

It was not a privilege necessarily granted by trust, but more through necessity. This was because Celetin was, beyond any doubt, the most powerful creature of the order. He guarded his complete authority and control absolutely and would not conceivably share it with any other Eshas. This was the very reason why Celetin kept the scrolls and the image archives within his own personal chambers, and the reason why he almost never left them.

Fiomass reached the entrance of the north chambers. Carefully picking his way through the jagged rock way, he continued through into a small dimly lit cavern. The distant howls of the pits caught his ears as he went.

The pits held those poor creatures of the Doon Esha who had been permanently warped by the failed image distortions and twisted tampering of Celetin's designs. They were failed experiments who had gone completely mad attempting to assimilate image transformations they were unable to handle or control. These doomed Esha now occupied specially designed pits and were kept in chains because they had taken on especially hideous forms almost beyond the control of even Celetin himself. They were especially dangerous and could not be trusted among Esha or humankind alike. Many of the Doon Esha wondered why Celetin had not killed them off, but Fiomass knew that Celetin had a good reason to keep them alive and enchained in the darkness of the pits. The time for their release would come soon enough.

Finally, Fiomass came to the spot where the cavern divided into two large corridors. The corridor to the right was dimly lit and filled with the strong smell of sulfur lingering throughout its expanse leading right towards the pits. The other corridor to the left was cut out of molten glass decorated with jewels, gold and silver and other precious metals while bathed in a soft shimmering light.

Hesitating to glance down the tunnel towards the pits, Fiomass shook his head as he entered in the left corridor and proceeded down the beautifully arrayed passageway. This corridor, of course clearly announced the way to Celetin's chambers. The Elder continued down the corridor until finally as Fiomass approached the entrance to the chambers, two of Celetin's personal guards unwrapped themselves from their marble guard posts up among the walls and planted themselves in front of the beautifully adorned doors. The two-winged serpents stared down at the Elder.

"Stay you fast. Who are you to approach the master's chambers?"

Fiomass instinctively tucked his tail and flattened his ears back. "Elder Fiomass to see Lord Celetin as commanded."

One of the winged serpents approached him and proceeded to inspect him from nose to tail. After several moments, both winged serpents took their position back on each side of the doors. The larger serpent hissed, "Very well, Elder Fiomass. Enter. Master Celetin is expecting you."

With barely a nod, Fiomass stepped forward and formed into a light gray unicorn. He knew that Celetin would be more receptive to this particular form by experience. He had managed to complete his mission, but only partially. Despite the obvious wounds he'd received, he had, in fact, failed to destroy both Guardians. Keeping his head bowed low, the Elder tried in vain to hide his limp as he entered the chambers of Celetin.

As he slowly made his way into the chamber, Fiomass raised an eye and noticed the perfect geometric arrangement of jewels and precious stones set into the molten glass walls. Pieces of scrolls and old parchment neatly lined the many shelves of artifacts both old and new. Set across the shimmering white walls all around the chamber were displays of uniforms, weapons, and body armor used by humans over the last thousand years. The armored helmets on display alone were worth a small fortune, but here served as mere trophies. The few large furnishings were arranged in geometric perfect order in the center of the chamber. To Fiomass, the whole chamber looked absurd in its perfection compared to what lay outside of Celetin's chambers. It was always most unsettling, even distasteful to Fiomass to be here.

Fiomass proceeded down the center of the chamber between the center furnishings and on towards the secluded back chamber Celetin used as a study. Reaching out with a hoof, the Elder pressed a large circular marble stone mounted on the wall to the right of a set of elaborately carved double doors. He waited while the low and deep drone of distant bells drifted out from the other side of the doors. The doors suddenly opened into Celetin's study chamber, and Fiomass waited to be acknowledged.

"Enter," a voice beckoned as if from a distance. But it was more. The voice was like the sound of many voices pitched in perfect harmony calling out to each other. Celetin's voice sounded almost orchestral, as if many voices were talking, yet singing at the same time, each in perfect harmony with all the others. To a human, it might have been likened to a perfectly tuned choir.

Stiffening, Fiomass limped past the doors into the chamber and hardly noticed the double doors closing behind him. The chamber was smaller than the main chamber, but much more richly lavished with precious decor. At the back of the chamber, Celetin reclined on a large couch of rich purple fabrics fitted with scarlet and gold trim. The walls of the oval chamber were lined from floor to ceiling with books varying from the most ancient to the most recent fare.

"Mighty Fiomass, I am most pleased to see you return alive and well. Welcome, Elder." The multi-harmony voice continued, "I have most anxiously awaited your report."

Fiomass lowered his head and approached a large gold and silver circle set in the center of the chamber's marble floor. Once inside the ring, the Elder bowed down on both of his forelegs.

"My Lord and master, almighty Celetin, I thank you for the privilege of serving you. Your servant has come at your bidding. If it pleases my master, I have a report."

"Very well, mighty Fiomass, rise, and give me your report," the voices answered.

Fiomass rose from his bow, standing up straight, but keeping his head slightly bowed. He allowed his eyes to slowly behold his master but carefully avoiding staring into Celetin's eyes. Celetin reclined easily upon his large couch. The master of the Doon Esha was formed into a large complete one-and-only snow-white dragon purer than any other form a Doon Esha could possess.

The white dragon's gold crested wings and silver streaked mane bore him up as the most beautiful images among the Doon Esha tribes. Piercing blue eyes complimented the high cheek bones and soft facial features dominating the dragon's face. The creature bore no horns but only scales that seemed more composed of velvet than armor. The lights in the chamber shone down on the velvety coat giving the ivory white creature an almost halo-like aura.

Fiomass, however, knew better than to succumb to the allure of Celetin's appearance. He had known the master a long time. He had learned the hard way on a number of occurrences that appearances could often be most deceiving.

"My Lord, the probe into the Tryistan borders was successful. One Guardian was destroyed, the other mortally wounded. I did, however, lose two fourth ranks and suffered personal injuries in the process."

Celetin waited several moments as if reflecting on the information. "I am aware of the loss of the two fourth ranks. They died doing their duty in my service. I fail, however, to understand how or why you allowed the second Guardian to live."

Fiomass hesitated, "My Lord, I delivered a blow the Guardian surely could not survive. I believe it is dead even now. That brings the count of Guardians destroyed to three, as you continue to will."

Celetin rose and sat straight up on his massive perch. Stepping off, he said nothing as he walked several steps towards the bookcases, seeming to inspect several ancient volumes.

"I am disappointed, mighty Fiomass, that you failed to destroy the second Guardian. And from your wounds I see, it appears a Guardian dealt with you well. You are aware that I have decreed the destruction of four Guardians. I see only the destruction of two."

Fiomass shifted and replied, "My Lord, I believe the second Guardian is surely dead. There is no way it could have survived the encounter. It could not outrank me."

Without any warning, Celetin's whip-like tail snapped, cutting a four-inch gash into Fiomass' left cheek just below his eye. The unicorn let out a shill scream and shook his head violently from the blow. But the Elder held his place. A small trail of blue blood began to run down the unicorn's cheek, falling as droplets to the marble floor.

"Mighty Fiomass, why do you bring me lies and deceit? You have been one of my most trusted agents for a very, very long time. You were my instrument when I taught the humans to make war. I sent you to guide the Alexander human to conquer the known world. I sent you yet again to the human Ghangis Khan. Did I not choose you above all to go to the Caesars to show them the way to their destiny? And it was you whom I entrusted the highest honor to go and to lead the human Hitler to achieve his dreams?"

Fiomass shifted again and kept silent.

Celetin continued, "It was I who provided you with the knowledge to help the humans reach their greatest goal of their precious nuclear power and yes, those wonderful weapons. And it is I, yes, I, who even now am working to orchestrate the final war between the humans and grant us our greatest victory which we have waited for so very long. I have given you great power, position and opportunities to demonstrate your loyalty to me, yet you reward me with lies about a simple mission?"

Fiomass realized Celetin knew all the details of his mission or at least most of them. As the blood from his cheek continued to drop to the floor, all he could do was stand still staring down at the circle encompassing him and remain silent.

Coming closer, Celetin's eyes narrowed, "Come now, Elder, might there be anything else you would like to add to your report?"

Fiomass spoke hoarsely, "It is as you say, my Lord. I stand ready to atone for my failure. I will return and destroy the second Guardian." *You're fishing, master...*

Celetin turned and returned to the couch, settling himself in. "No, mighty Fiomass. That will not be necessary. The Guardian, though not dead, is not a factor anymore. I am almost pleased with your report, but not quite.

Fiomass again bowed down on both forelegs, "I await your bidding, my master." *He doesn't know about Gharius being there...*

Celetin's face twisted into a sort of contorted smile as the white dragon reached out and pressed a small marble pylon adjacent to his couch. Immediately, the two large-winged serpentines entered through the opening doorway. Fiomass glanced over his shoulder to see the sentinels approach.

"Mighty Fiomass, though partially successful, I do not believe that you fully understand or appreciate the full meaning of the prophecy that is upon us."

Turning to the sentinels, Celetin commanded, "Take him to the pit chambers and give him 20 lashes. When you are finished, release him. Then send for Haxiss. I have need of someone I can *trust*."

The two-winged serpents immediately took positions on each side of Fiomass. The Elder glanced at the white dragon for a moment sarcastically noticing the emphasis on the word *trust*.

"It is as you wish, my Lord," the Elder croaked. With that, Fiomass bowed his head once more and rose, wheeled about and limped towards the exit from the inner chamber escorted by the two-winged serpents. He had gotten off easy, this time. The light lashes would heal in time.

CHAPTER TWELVE

THE COUNCIL

Deep down inside the Tryistan Order's mountain fortress, the attending and present members of the Council of Twelve sat waiting patiently for Gharius to arrive. Seated around an elegant and greatly aged deep brown mahogany round table, they debated with each other in sharp whispers over the possible different reasons why Gharius had called for the council meeting. Video monitors were placed in front of the empty chairs of the Council members who could not be physically present. All 12 members were physically present or online.

Petrawnus, the most vocal of the 12, stood heatedly debating with Johhanicus and Jasmetricus, their voices carrying throughout the chamber. Several other members sat listening to the exchange while Zelotus, having arrived only an hour prior, sat quietly listening to the other various issues discussed around the Great Room. Each Elder wore an elaborate adornment of layered white robes dashed from shoulder to hip with a specific sash of color signifying their office and their continent assignment. Each of the members present had assumed their human form.

The Great Room chamber served as the official meeting place of the Council of Twelve. Thirteen elegant, oversized sixteenth-century Victorian chairs rounded the huge dark mahogany table of eighteenth-century Italian vintage. Massive, clawed legs elaborately adorned with the finest craftsmanship supported the huge table. A blonde sash, cut and polished, lazily crafted across the center of the table from one end to the other, beautifully accented the natural tones of the wood. The chamber itself was sparsely furnished save the table and chairs and two serving tables set adjacent to the east walls, which held all the electronics needed for video conferencing and media presentations.

The only other notable feature was the enormous fireplace carved into the wall of rock set directly behind the seat Gharius occupied at the head of the table. The fireplace measured 10 feet wide by 6 feet high. Supporting an elaborately carved mantle were two massive dark marbled columns that accentuated the mahogany table centerpiece. This room was where the Order of Tryistan made its most important and crucial decisions.

Echoes of whispers and debates resounded off the rocky walls and drifted upward into the cathedrals until without warning, the two huge mahogany entrance doors into the chamber burst open. Gharius, dressed in his white ruffled and layered Elder robes, strode into the room. Immediately all 12 of the Elders rose from their chairs and bowed their heads, chin to chest while offering their cupped hands up. The room remained silent as Gharius's footsteps echoed across the chamber. Coming to his place at the Great Table, he paused to look at each Elder in turn. Finally, he pulled out his chair and sat down, adjusting his robes.

"My friends of the Council welcome. Please, sit." Gharius commanded.

Immediately the Elders dropped their hands and set themselves around the table in each of their assigned seats, adjusting their robes.

Petrawnus spoke first, "My Lord, we are most happy to see you've returned safely. Welcome back from your task. I have assembled the council according to your wishes, Lord Gharius, long may you live."

"And you, Petrawnus. I wished I could have taken you with me, but again, it was a personal matter concerning Jade."

"I understand," injected Petrawnus. "I'd like to accompany you on your next task. It's getting a little closed in around here these days."

Gharius let out a chuckle as did the other members of the Council. "I understand, Petrawnus. It's just that for now, it is better that we be very careful. Once this is all over, we can again return to roam as freely as we once did."

Turning to Johhanicus, Gharius asked, "Johhanicus, what is the news from the European regions? What do we know?"

Johhanicus sat up placing his hands on the table. "My Lord, the news is bad. The United New World Coalition, or the UNWC if you prefer, has all but been fully established. The United Nations is raising a lot of noise, but I don't believe they have the power or means to stop it. The NATO alliance is virtually beginning to unravel. The disasters at the refineries in Iran and the plant in Alaska have put the European international community on edge. I'm afraid our hosts, the Americas, are at a loss as to what to do."

Gharius rubbed his chin for a moment. "Then it is as I have believed." Turning to Zelotus, "Who do we have in D.C. to advise the Presidency?"

Zelotus shifted in his chair. "My Lord, we tried to place Ploruvus in as an advisor, but I'm afraid he hasn't been able to get close. At the moment, we believe a Doon Esha Elder has somehow managed to infiltrate their ranks as one of the senior advisors to the President. Of course, that is only speculation at the moment."

The brow of their leader furrowed. "Zelotus, I specifically placed you in charge of organizing our counter efforts in North America. This is not the report I was hoping to hear. Tell me, what do you plan to do at this point?"

Shifting again in his chair, Zelotus answered, "My Lord, we will double our efforts to influence the right people to get Ploruvus into the inner circles. I had originally planned to bring him in as an aid to the Joint Chiefs of Staff, but the humans proved to be too cynically suspicious. I am currently attempting to establish him as a successful law graduate intern. I believe this will get him into the circles we wish to influence, my Lord."

Gharius seemed to be deep in thought. The room remained silent. Finally, "Zelotus, I want you to go to D.C. personally to oversee our operations there." Quiet murmurs began to make their way around the table.

Gharius turned to address the council, "I know I gave orders for all of you to remain either here or where you are currently for a short time during the escalations before you return, but the situation warrants this action. Zelotus, it is crucial that you complete your task. What you do, you must go and do quickly!"

Without any further words, Zelotus pushed back from the table and rose from his chair, giving a slight bow. With that, he hurriedly turned and strode out of the great room. The 11 other Elders looked at each other in confusion. Gharius waited until the closing doors announced Zelotus' departure.

"My friends, please. This is necessary. Zelotus knows what he must do. Don't trouble yourselves. Everything is working as the prophecy speaks."

Philocus raised his hand. "My Lord, I know that you know the prophecy as no other. I and my brethren do not understand what this is that you do. If Zelotus is absent, how then shall the Council meet?"

Gharius placed both his hands on the table and pushed back his chair. Rising from the chair, he stood straight up to his full stature. "My friends, the prophecy is clear from what we know of it. There will be a betrayal. Believe me, each of us has our part. We must all play the part which we have been tasked. I am no different from each of you. You all have your part in the times to come. I have my own part, which I must fulfill. Zelotus has his part as well. Everything is working according to the prophecy. All is as it should be."

Petrawnus interjected, "My Lord, we don't have all the prophecy. How can you know for certain what will be the final end? The Doon Esha possesses parts of the prophecy as well, and we are seeing their interpretation as events are unfolding. How do we know what is to be the final outcome?"

"Faith, Petrawnus. Faith. You must have faith." Gharius lightly replied.

"It is as you say, my Lord, but what do we do in the meantime?" Petrawnus asked.

"We do our part," replied Gharius.

Philocus interjected again, "My Lord, what will we do with North America? They are already beginning to conduct their own war game exercises. If Zelotus is unable to put someone close to the President, events could lead to an all-out war if things are not handled properly."

Gharius paused a moment, then looked around the room at each of his Elders. "I have planned for the possibility that Zelotus may fail. I have managed to gain the ear of the Vice President through a personal source. He is persuaded that a peaceful diplomacy is the path to take given the current situation. I have taken this task on myself personally."

Again, more murmurs around the table. "My friends," Gharius stepped away from his seat and began to circle the table opening his arms out wide.

"Throughout the human's history, how often have we interceded? How many times have we gone to extreme measures to counter the terror and horrors that Doon Esha would ignite among them? For over 2,000 years, The Doon Esha has sought every opportunity to set the humans against each other. They have brought war against war, civilization against civilization, and brother against brother. Do I need to remind each of you of the cruelty and hatred Celetin holds against the humans? He has delighted for two millenniums in their wars and their killings and their inhumanity against each other. We have sought at every opportunity to intercede when and where we could to prevent more wars and to help the humans recover and rebuild."

Gharius waited a moment before going on to let his words sink in.

"It was long ago decided that we would add ourselves to humanity when the time was right. We would join the humans who dominate this planet and live our lives peacefully among them. But that has never been possible because we are the only thing that stands between humanity and their ultimate slavery or destruction by the Doon Esha.

It has always been our duty to intercede whenever and wherever the Doon Esha would cause the humans to make war or use their abilities to destroy each other. It was the will of my father, our father. Now, what shall we do? The Doon Esha is obviously convinced the prophecy is fulfilling itself even now. They interpret the prophecy in their own ways which makes them all the more dangerous."

Gharius paused again. No one in the room moved a muscle.

"Celetin and his priests believe they have uncovered a secret code embedded within the writings. They are using this code system to fill in the blanks. I know that each of you believe that we only have fragments of the prophecy, but you must understand that my father wrote the prophecy. There is no secret code; nothing of the kind. I was there when he wrote it. I beg of each of you to believe that."

His speech concluded, Gharius dropped his arms, turned and walked towards the fireplace. Taking a stoker, he poked at the flickering flame gently crackling in the fireplace. He continued to work at the fire for several moments as the Council Elders silently watched on. Finally, he set the stoker down turning to the table, "My friends, I need for each of you present here now to tarry a day before you return to your lands and continue to watch over your regions. Time is of the essence. All the details of the prophecy will be fulfilled soon. Please keep me updated of any news you receive and go in peace."

The present members of the Elders slowly rose from their seats and began to quietly file out of the chamber whispering among themselves. One by one, the video monitors went blank. When the last Elder had left and shut the door, Gharius returned to gently stir the small crackling fire. A tiny creak from the entrance doors drew his attention away from the flame. Petrawnus came back in through the doors and softly bowed. Gharius smiled, as Petrawnus approached him. "My Lord, may I have a council with you?"

Gharius returned a slight bow, "Of course, Petrawnus. What is it that troubles you, my old friend?"

"My Lord, you are the son and the only direct descendant of the father of us all. I am concerned as to your safety. Why did you let Zelotus go? He is the latest and most junior Elder elected to the Council. I did not detect in your voice any assurance as to the task you assigned him. I suddenly find that I am not sure that I trust him."

Gharius looked into Petrawnus' face. "I know your concern, old friend, but don't worry. He will do exactly what he believes he is supposed to do. I'm counting on it." *Yes, Zelotus, go and do what you must...*

CHAPTER THIRTEEN

TIMES AND A TIME

"I can't believe it," Jade gasped. "That can't be true. Jesse, do you really expect me to believe that?" She put both hands on her hips. It had been over three weeks since her father, Gharius, had come to see her before returning to the Order. Since then, Jesse and their brothers had lived out of Jade's apartment, shadowing her wherever she went. She felt more like a prisoner than a tenant.

Still, cramped as the apartment had become, Jade had to admit she enjoyed having her brothers around, and she longed to see her other two brothers still stationed at the Order in time. She was still a little skittish after the incident with the four humans that dark night in the alley. She knew the Doon Esha was still looking for her.

Jesse sat rigidly in the dingy, oversized recliner with his hands clasped together behind his head. "I know it's hard to believe, but father was very specific. Agents of the Doon Esha are slowly closing in on this city and it's only a matter of time until they find you. He asked me to talk to you about it. I think he thought my influence might help you reconsider moving back closer to the Order."

Jade, sitting on an old adjacent couch, craned her neck trying to relieve the tension in her shoulders. "It's just so hard to believe all of this is coming out now. I mean, c'mon, Jesse, we never thought this would happen during this time in our lives. It just doesn't seem real, I mean, it's just something that should still be way down the road." Jade rose and started restlessly pacing the room.

Suddenly, Jesse got up from the recliner. "Let's go for a walk. I think we could use the fresh air. Besides, it's starting to feel a little cramped in here. I'll let the others know we're going out for a bit."

Jade hesitated, then acquiesced, "Okay, I guess I'm up for a walk."

Jesse disappeared down the hallway for a few moments then re-emerged and retrieved his loafers as Jade tied up her boots. Grabbing their jackets, they left the apartment and made their way down the stairs and out to the busy street. Jade locked her left arm around her brother's right arm, and they walked. The wind was light but chilly as they went. Little was said until they reached a side street four blocks down from Jade's apartment. Turning down onto a less busy side street, they resumed their conversation.

Brushing away the hair from her face, Jade looked up and into the thick cumulous clouds spiraling across the sky. "I love rainy days. I wish it would rain right now although it feels more like it could snow."

Jesse glanced up, "It would be cold either way. I like the warm rain of the summer. And, speaking of summer, I have a feeling there is some-thing you've been hiding, little sister."

Jade slowed her pace and eyed her brother curiously. "What's that sup-posed to mean?"

Jesse looked away, keeping her waiting for a moment. Then, "What if I was to tell you that there's a rumor that you were spending a lot of time last summer with a certain male human? I believe Michael is his name."

Jade stopped. Jesse winced slightly as that familiar flash crossed his sister's eyes. Pulling away and putting her hands on her hips, she stepped closer to her brother. "Great, so now you're spying on me too? What do you expect me to say? I'm fully human now. I met him last year in a class I was taking. He's in Europe right now studying art in Paris. He's nice and I like him but don't worry, we only went to the movies a couple times before he left. There, are you happy?"

Jesse looked down at the ground. Taking a deep breath, he looked up at her, "You know I'm not spying on you. We just have to take every precaution. I'm sure you of all people would understand. Besides, Father is concerned. I don't think he's ready to think about you and a human getting involved yet." Grinning, he reached out and tugged at Jade's jacket, "C'mon."

She shrugged and slipped her arm around her brother's arm again and they began walking in silence, each lost in their own thoughts. They walked for several minutes down the sidewalk until Jade's curiosity got the better of her. "Jesse, do you think that when we permanently form to humans, we will have their kind of souls?"

Jesse pulled his sister's arm and continued to walk for several moments. "I don't know, Jade," he replied. "No Esha has ever permanently formed a human besides you. I don't know if that makes a difference, but I do know that every Esha carries a flicker of the flame of life, each within ourselves. You know that which makes us sentient beings. Beyond this, that's a question you would have to ask father."

Jade pursed her lips, "I wish it were all simpler than that. The humans live their lives and die. Then there are those who believe in a soul, and there is another life they go onto except for the ones who don't believe there is another life. They have so many different ideas about how things actually are, and each of them seems to have their own views of how things work and how things are going to work out in the end."

"I don't think it's good to worry about that right now. We are what we are. It has been so since the beginning. You cannot change that which has always been, well... except for you apparently." He smiled at her wryly. "We each have emerged from our own kind, the humans from their own. There's no use in trying to make a lot of sense of what the humans believe and do, much less why they do it."

Jade answered, somewhat perturbed, "But this is different. There has been a change. I am now fully human. So, do I have a human soul now or not? If I do, according to many of the humans, this is something very important."

"You're asking questions I can't answer. Many of the humans are serious about their next life and some are not, or at least they don't live like it. One thing is sure; they are very much divided on how everything works. The other thing is that they have no idea who we are and the lives we live. That much I do know."

Jade smirked, "I don't suppose they'd be very happy to know about us anyway. Humans have a very hard time accepting things they can't explain. They'd rather believe a lie than to live with conflicting realities. I mean, look at their history. It's pretty awful."

Jesse grinned, "Well, that might be true, but think about how their theories of evolution would be upset if they suddenly bumped into us. I wonder how they would try to explain us away?"

"Aliens, Jesse, aliens. Don't you ever read their literature?" Jade giggled.

Laughing, Jesse shook his head, "Well, technically I could become a little green man from Mars, but I don't think father would be amused. We all know where he stands on that issue."

As the pair continued to walk, the street shops slowly gave way to residential homes. The clouds began to clear as brother and sister walked in silence, each contemplating Jade's questions. Such questions had rarely been raised in all the time the Tryistan Order had committed to the day when they would join the human race. Jade represented an enigma and presented even more questions that had yet to be answered.

A few light beams of the sun's rays penetrated through the puffy cloud cover as the two continued to amble down the sidewalk. Spotting a small park, Jade tugged on her brother's arm and led him through the soft grass to a well-worn bench overlooking a small and tranquil pond. They sat together and watched a pair of gray ducks hobble along the bank on the far side. Just beyond the pond, a small group of parents and their young children had just arrived and were beginning to spread out around a fenced playground, laughing and shouting as they went.

It was Jade who broke the silence nodding at the parents who stood clustered together in conversation while watching over their children. "It's still not fair, you know. I mean, look at the way they live. Some of them have no clue or don't care what happens to them after they die. We are taught to cherish every moment of life. We spend our lives protecting them from the Doon Esha, and they have no idea what's going on. It's just not fair!"

Jesse leaned forward clasping his hands together. "Maybe that's why we live such long lives. Look at father. You still don't believe half of what I've told you. But, according to him, he's been around for a very long time."

Jade leaned forward beside her brother. "It's impossible to begin to imagine all he has seen and done."

"I know. I can hardly grasp it myself."

"I still don't understand why our Order ever got the idea to assimilate to the humans. Now that I've been one for some time, I'm beginning to think it might not be such a great idea."

Jesse looked down at the still grass, "Do you ever miss being an Esha?"

"I miss being able to fly the most. I used to love to form as a falcon and make passes through the canyons of our fortress, especially at dusk when the sun set. Sometimes father would chase me through the valleys, and we would race for the highest peak above the Order. I miss that the most—and you and my other brothers of course."

"Father misses you very much." Jesse said softly. "I can see it in his eyes, especially at the welcoming ceremonies when he has been away. He looks for you even though he knows you're not there. Everyone can tell, but he never speaks about it. All I know is that he has some kind of plan to make things right again so you can come home."

Jade sat back against the bench and stretched her legs as she reflected, "Home. I'm not sure what that means anymore. I'm not even sure who or what I am, let alone, where I belong."

They continued to stare out across the small pond. The group of children were laughing and playing around the playground under the watchful eyes of their parents. Brother and sister watched in curious and enviable silence as the laughter and excited cries of the children emanated from the playground and echoed through a grove of pine trees just outside of the park.

Finally, Jade spoke, "Look at them. All these things are going on right now under their noses, and they have no idea what's really going on at all. There's a war raging on and on, and they can't even see it. They have no clue who I am, who you are, or what you can do. They have no idea what I've done, how I got here or what I really am. It's almost laughable."

Jesse put his hand on Jade's knee. "Somehow this is all going to work out. Jade, we must have faith in our father's way. I believe in him, and I wish I could be more helpful. I'm afraid I just don't have very many answers."

Jade put her hand on top of Jesse's. "I know. It's okay." She rose up from the bench, "I'm ready to go. We can cut through crazy dog alley again to get back to save time."

Jesse hesitated. "You're joking! You want to walk past that crazy insane mutt again? He's huge! I don't mind taking the long way back."

Starting off towards the street, Jade looked back over her shoulder, "C'mon *big* brother, besides, he's on a chain."

Sighing with feigned hesitance, Jesse got up and followed his sister towards the street and into an adjacent backstreet alley which served as a backyards to the residential houses on both sides. They walked without uttering a word. As they reached the third block, Jesse nudged

Jade's shoulder, and they scanned the large, fenced backyard behind a large brick house on the right side of the street. They peered over the fence searching for the canine behemoth. Strangely, there was only silence.

"Huh. I guess he's not out rooting up the yard. Oh well, no running for our lives today."

"Good. I hope he's at the vet getting a mental health checkup. That thing's a monster." Jesse said.

They had barely gone 10 yards beyond the dreaded fenced-in yard when they heard the ear-splitting sound of splintering wood. They looked back just in time to see the fully grown Rottweiler explode through the wooden fence, foaming at the mouth. It was loose and coming at them as fast as its legs could carry it, barking furiously.

Jesse reached out grabbing Jade's arm and began to run. They raced up the alley with the maniacal animal in hot pursuit. Jesse realized that the dog was gaining on them. Two blocks further down the alley, Jesse stopped, reaching out to push Jade behind him as he wheeled around to face the oncoming canine's fury of teeth.

Jade, out of breath, put her hands on her brother's back. Jesse waited until the animal closed to 10 yards away. As the dog rushed in, Jesse formed a Tyrannosaur's head from his neck up, dropping the lower jaw down to nearly ground level. With an earsplitting roar, the five-foot-long head of a Tyrannosaur opened its massive salivating jaws wide to receive the oncoming canine.

The astonished Rottweiler suddenly began to furiously backpeddle as it lost its balance skidding across the gravel and broken pavement towards the ominous jaws directly in its path. The dog slid across the road coming to a dead stop mere inches from the massive cavern of the Tyrannosaur's eight-inch serrated teeth. Several seconds of absolute silence ensued until finally the massive jaws of the reptilian head slammed together in a loud sickening snap, spitting out a blast of heat and saliva the terrified dog felt throughout its whole body.

Time stood still as the Rottweiler licked its lips and softly whined while inching its way backwards. With a sharp whelp, the hysterical canine hurriedly turned its tail and tore off headed back to the safety of its fenced domain. The head of the Tyrannosaur returned to Jesse's human form.

Jade released her hold on Jesse's jacket as he turned to her.

With a smirk Jade could not resist, "Um, you're not supposed to do that," she said flatly.

Feigning his surprise, "What? It just kinda came to me."

Putting her hands on her hips and cocked her head to the side, "Well, just see that it doesn't happen again. You probably gave the poor thing a complex."

Jade could barely keep the tears of laughter from welling up in her eyes as she fought to keep her scolding composure straight.

Shooting a smirk back, Jesse answered, "Maybe you'd have preferred a rat?"

Finally, Jade's laughter won out. "You could have been a little more subtle. Did you see the look on his little face?"

Stretching his neck, Jesse tried to keep his teeth clenched as he led Jade further up the alley. Neither could hardly speak a word through all the laughter as they made their way back to Jade's apartment.

Not everyone in the alley was laughing as a watchful pair of orange vertical-striped eyes kept track of the brother and sister duo making their way back to their apartment. Exactly which apartment was going to be very important information to some very interested parties—information which would surely fetch a hefty price for the asking.

CHAPTER FOURTEEN

THE ALASKAN PROJECT

The bitter cold sliced through the melancholy moonlight shining down through a high thin layer of light clouds to illuminate the snow-covered landscape in deep contrast to the vast night sky bristling with innumerable stars. Haxiss, second Elder to Celetin of the Doon Esha looked back over his party. Three third ranks and two second ranks followed him in close formation in their winged forms.

Despite the increased wind chill of the flight, their thick fur kept them warm having formed a Pterodactyl-wolf escaping the scaly reptilian skin the winged form normally offered. They flew steadily at about a 100 yards above the massive pipeline following it for miles to reach their intended destination. The steady aurora shimmering across the Alaskan night sky was hardly noticed by the group as they silently sailed on their way through the night.

Finally, Haxiss began to descend. The location he had decided on put their touchdown was less than five miles north of the Alaskan port of Valdez. Haxiss had assembled his team, and the flight had taken nearly 26 hours with only four stops. There was very little time to lose. Haxiss calculated 60 minutes on the ground and another 26 hours back to the Galapagos fortress. It was a long and grueling mission, and Haxiss had personally selected his team for this purpose.

Settling on the snow-covered ground, Haxiss waited as the other ranks landed. Without a word, the three third ranks formed wooly mammoth-rhinoceros. The two second ranks formed eagle-lizards that took high to the sky again to serve as lookouts. Haxiss formed to a red dragon-serpent and motioned for the mammoth forms to take up their positions against a support stanchion on which the pipeline rested. Once Haxiss was satisfied, he let out a soft rumble.

The three mammoths immediately steadied their positions against one of the pipeline support stanchions. Haxiss looked over their positioning, calculating their combined strength for maximum effect. Satisfied, he rumbled again, and the three mammoths began to push against the stanchion in unison. The mammoths strained as their combined weight exerted tremendous forces against the pipeline support struts.

The plan was to push the stanchion until the pipeline was partially severed. Haxiss knew that oil would not be flowing through the pipeline at this time according to the company's schedule. He was counting on it. The current receiving station would be nearly abandoned; therefore, no humans would be in immediate danger. The mammoths continued to push against the stanchion, which was beginning to make creaking noises under the strain. After a couple of minutes, Haxiss rumbled for the mammoths to stop. This was going to take some time. He was pleased that he had factored in 60 minutes to break the pipeline open enough to suit his purposes. *Thirty minutes would have been better.*

After allowing the mammoths five minutes to rest, he grunted for them to take their positions. The mammoths immediately obeyed and took their positions against the stanchion supports again. At the sound of Haxiss rumbling, the mammoths put their shoulders into the support and pushed. The slow low creaking of straining metal came faster this time as the enormous creatures put all their weight into their task. After two more minutes, Haxiss called for a halt, and kept an eye on his sentinels in the air.

This time, he allowed the mammoths 10 minutes to rest. The cold was beginning to sink into Haxiss, and he violently flapped his wings to gain some warmth. For a moment, he was tempted to start a fire, but thought better of it. He searched the skies again but received nothing from his sentinels. A hint of light snow had begun to fall again, the semi-full moon overhead reflecting its light through and off the tiny crystal flakes.

Grunting again, Haxiss signaled the mammoths to take their stations. He moved in behind the mammoths, getting close to them. Rumbling, he signaled them to once again begin pushing against the stanchion. The three mammoths put their weight against the support, straining to the limit of their capacities. Slowly but steadily, the stanchion began to give way as the sound of metallic distress increased in volume. Drawing himself up quietly, Haxiss drew in a deep breath and then blew a narrow, dark red flame across the backsides of the mammoths.

The fire lightly seared the hind sides of the mammoths all at once. The sudden extra "motivation" caused the beasts to startle as they pushed against the stanchion even harder until finally the steel pipeline stanchion bowed and cracked at the bolts. With a final push, the mammoths moved the broken stanchion forward straining the pipeline support structure until it twisted loose and fell with surprisingly little noise into the snow-covered ground, leaving the remaining pipeline running towards the pumping station horribly twisted but intact and wide open.

Rumbling the mammoths away, Haxiss stepped down and looked deep into the open pipeline that headed towards the pumping station at Valdez. Looking over his shoulder, he made sure the other toppled pipe section lying on the adjacent ground was well clear. Grunting, he again ordered the three mammoths to get clear. The mammoths, relieved, formed back to pterodactyl-wolves. They took to the sky and joined the other sentinels who had already formed back to their thick furred-winged creatures as well.

Haxiss continued to peer down the enormous steel tunnel. The sickening smell of residual oil filled his lungs. This was exactly what he was counting on. He drew himself up with a deep breath. He would have to perform this blast perfectly. Feeling the gases build within him, he opened his mouth as wide as he could, and belched a red fire blast into the pipeline headed south toward the Port of Valdez. Immediately, he launched himself into the sky fighting for altitude.

His superheated fireball shot into the massive pipeline near instantaneously igniting a large backdraft blast careening south through the maze of pipeline. Superheating the oil residue as it sped down the southbound pipe, the fireball quickly picked up momentum, igniting more and more of the residual oil along its way. The maelstrom gathered enormous force as it raced toward the pumping station at Valdez. His mission over, Haxiss screeched out his orders, His team followed him as they hurriedly gained enough altitude to begin the long trek back to Galapagos.

The fireball continued to roar down the pipeline, picking up more speed as it went. It bore down faster and faster towards its destination until finally, in the middle of the quiet still night, it reached its target.

Without any warning, the pumping station's four port fueling stations of the Alaskan pipeline at Valdez simultaneously exploded with incredible violence, wreaking immense destruction. Mournful sirens began to ring as station maintenance personnel housed some distance outside of the station were almost immediately rousted from their beds. It was going to be a very long night.

The explosions were later reported to have been heard over a radius of almost 15 miles. Fortunately, there were only a few minor firefighting injuries as the pumping stations themselves were unmanned for the night. The fires would rage for over 24 hours before the main pipeline break-site carnage was discovered. By sheer luck, the valve station had shut down all of the associated access pipe routes only four hours prior to the explosion before a scheduled limited fuel flow shipment destined for the Valdez station was to have been initiated. Later, an official statement would list the cause of the blast under an indigenous geographical anomaly.

CHAPTER FIFTEEN

A MEETING AT THE U.N.

On the 10th floor of the United Nations building in New York City, a hushed top-secret conference was about to begin. Vice President Stephen J. Monaham, along with Defense Secretary Robert F. Kurtz and General George V. Reynolds, Chairman to the Joint Chiefs of Staff, sat on one side of the massive conference table. The Ambassadors representing the UNWC consisting of China, Russia, Germany, Italy and France sat on the other side of the elongated conference table. Camille Marcion, the Canadian Ambassador to the U.N. had been selected to mediate the meeting. Jypinga Seiti, Chairman of the U.N. Security Council, sat at the far end of the table with his secretary.

As the whispering from each side of the table grew louder, she sat herself at the end of the table closest to the attendants. Clearing her throat, she nodded to the secretary of the Security Council to begin taking her minutes. Everyone on both sides of the table took immediate notice and the whispering ceased. Ambassador Marcion reached over and pressed the "on" button on a small recorder.

Rubbing her hands together, Ambassador Marcion cleared her throat again. "Gentlemen, I would like, at this time, to call this meeting to order. I take this time to remind all in attendance that this meeting is confidential and informal in nature. I further remind all in attendance that anything and everything that is said here is being recorded for the archives of the Security Council and may be used in the event that the Security Council deems it necessary. The United States has called for this emergency meeting with the newly formed UNWC, otherwise known as the Unified New World Coalition. As you know, Security Council Chairman Jypinga Seiti is sitting in as an observer only. He will not be participating in these talks. If there are no objections, I call on the Vice President of the United States to make his opening statement."

Sporting a crewcut and exhibiting all the attributes of the marine he once was, the Vice President took a moment to look each of the UN-WC's Ambassadors in the eye. "Ambassador Rosnivich, I was expecting to see Ambassador Rostov."

The Russian Ambassador leaned forward addressing the Vice President, "I'm sorry, Mr. Vice President, unfortunately, Ambassador Rostov recently passed away. I was selected to replace him for this conference. I hope this is not a problem."

"No, Mr. Ambassador. I'm sorry, please accept my condolences. I'd known Ambassador Rostov for some time. I am sure he will be sorely missed."

"Of course, Mr. Vice President," Ambassador Rosnivich flatly replied.

"Well, then, I will proceed."

The Vice President turned his attention to the rest of the Ambassadors seated on the opposite side of the table.

"It has come to our attention that the newly formed UNWC represents a significant threat to our oil supplies in the Middle East. We have sought to successfully negotiate through peaceful diplomatic means but have not reached any meaningful agreements with this new coalition. It is hoped that this meeting can be of use in setting some middle ground upon which we may begin to open a peaceful dialogue with this change on the world stage."

Ambassador Marcion nodded her head and spoke again, "At this time, the designated representative of the UNWC will speak."

The Ambassador from Russia, Boris Rosnivich, leaned forward to address the Vice President's remarks in his thick Slovakian accent. "Mr. Vice President, we realize your concerns, but we can assure you that there are no reasons for such concerns. Come now, there is plenty of oil for the world. We of the UNWC offer no threat whatsoever regarding your concerns over your precious national security."

The Russian ambassador sat back in his chair away from the table and casually crossed his arms choosing to fix his gaze on the documents in front of him on the table.

Ambassador Marcion paused, and then motioned, "Defense Secretary Kurtz will now speak."

"Thank you, Madam Ambassador. Ambassadors, if what you are saying is true, then we would have no good reason to have felt it necessary to convene this meeting. It is the official position of the United States that we consider this new coalition to be a real and present threat to our national security. Ambassador Rosnivich, I am surprised at the rather nonchalant manner of your comments. It is common knowledge that the Middle East Oil Coalition has made public the fact that their oil reserves have passed their peak optimal limits. They are, in fact, tapping deeper into the earth, meaning that the fat days of oil production in the Middle East are getting leaner as we speak. That is all, Madam Ambassador, I yield the floor."

Several moments passed without further word as several of the Ambassadors took notes and shuffled their paperwork through their folders nervously. Ambassador Marcion finally nodded and looked over to the UNWC ambassadors signaling their opportunity to respond.

The Chinese Ambassador leaned over and whispered to the Russian Ambassador. Nodding, the Russian Ambassador turned to their Canadian mediator. "At this time, I wish to yield my reply to my Chinese associate."

The Canadian Ambassador looked over at the American representatives who each gave a nod of consent. The Chinese Ambassador, formerly of the Chinese Consulate in Australia, spoke in perfect English.

"Gentlemen, I applaud your willingness to sit down and discuss with us options in which we can peacefully resolve our differences. There is, however, the matter which I believe we are really here for. It concerns allegations that parties of, or in league with the United States, did knowingly and deliberately attempt to sabotage oil refineries and production plants in Iran. These incidents involve refineries that produce and supply a large majority of oil to Russia, Germany and substantially to China itself. Further..."

"There has been no evidence of our involvement with those *accidents!*" General Reynolds vehemently interjected jumping up from his chair. "You have no..."

"Gentlemen!" Ambassador Marcion shouted. "We are not here to toss these serious accusations like mud across this table. We are here to open a peaceful dialogue between the parties represented here today. We must have order!"

General Reynolds fell back into his chair and took a deep breath but remained silent. The tension in the room began to thicken like an early morning fog rolling in off the ocean.

The Chinese Ambassador hesitated a few moments to diffuse the tension and raised his hands, "I apologize, General for the accusations. I merely meant allegations, which are still under investigations of course." Putting his hands down on the table, he continued, "Allegations, which would bear serious consequences, should they be found to be true."

The Chinese Ambassador stopped and nodded to the Canadian mediator. Ambassador Marcion turned to the Vice President. "Mister Vice President, you have the floor to respond."

Clasping his hands together on the table, the Vice President leaned forward. "It would indeed be unfortunate to discover that sabotage played a part in the Iranian oil disasters. It would also be most unfortunate to discover that sabotage contributed to our Alaskan refinery disaster as well, which, I remind you all, is still under investigation."

The UNWC ambassadors looked at each other. Ambassador Rosnivich leaned forward planting his hands palms firmly on the table. "Mr. Vice President, are you accusing us of something here? Your own news outlets have reported the cause of the incident to be nothing more than some sort of geographic phenomenon. What does a random earthquake, shall we say, have to do with what we are discussing here?" The Russian Ambassadors ears were turning red.

The Vice President leaned in further. "Mister Ambassador, we're not accusing anyone specifically, at least not yet. You must admit however, that the turn of events almost defies the possibility of coincidence. We remain unconvinced about the cause of the pipeline incident and are close to turning all of the evidence and our defense department's final investigations over to the U.N. Security Council in the interests of the security of the international community."

The Chinese Ambassador spoke up, "It will be interesting to see what evidence you turn over to the Council concerning your pipeline, however, Mister Vice President, do you believe it is a coincidence that American paramilitary items were found at all three of the Iranian disaster sites? How do you intend to explain that?"

Ambassador Marcion stepped in, "Gentlemen, please. Let us keep this meeting in order by speaking in turn. Mr. Vice President, you have the floor to respond."

Vice President Monaham leaned back in his chair keeping his eyes on the Chinese ambassador while waving his hand towards his General.

"Very well, Mr. Vice President, Ambassador Marcion noted. "General, you have the floor."

General Reynolds faced the Chinese Ambassador, "The so-called evidence you're referring to could have been planted by any number of the active terrorist groups operating in the Middle East and around the world, and you know that."

Defense Secretary Kurtz jumped in, "I don't think we fully understand the gravity of this situation. Are we really going to sit here and point fingers all day long?"

"Gentlemen!" Ambassador Marcion interjected. "May I remind you this is an informal conference? Please, we must proceed in order!"

Defense Secretary Kurtz sat back, dropping his pen on the table and began rubbing his chin. General Reynolds followed suit. *This is getting nowhere...*

The Vice President loosened his tie a bit, noticing that the room seemed to be getting warm and stuffy. Tensions were rising substantially. The other members of the conference relaxed back into their seats staring around the room or at the floor. Ambassador Marcion hesitated to allow the tension to ease. The Canadian Ambassador took a sip of water from her glass noticing the warm stuffy feeling in the room. The U.N. Security's secretary removed her glasses and was rubbing her nose between her eyes. This was going nowhere fast.

Ambassador Marcion picked up some documents and looked around the room. "At this time, I am calling a short recess, say, 15 minutes for us all to get of breath of fresh air. I know I could use some."

There was noticeable enthusiasm at the call to recess upon which all of the attending representatives seemed more than happy to vacate the table. The room was quickly emptied, and the doors shut and locked.

Twenty minutes later, the doors were reopened, and the attending representatives slowly filed into the room and took their seats once again at the table. Ambassador Marcion had sent a courier to let the conference attendees know that she would be several minutes late.

The JCS Chairman and the Defense Secretary were whispering to each other in an intense conversation. Each Ambassador of the UNWC sat with their hands crossed on their laps waiting for talks to resume. Finally, Ambassador Marcion arrived and apologized to the attendees as she took her seat, laying her documents on the table.

"Gentlemen, at this time, we should move this conference forward. I believe we need to move towards more productive talks concerning the initiation of an outline for a unilateral agreement in which we can all agree upon considering the futures of oil supply and demand. We must begin to look at taking steps that will pave the way for the Americas and the UNWC to work together for a more peaceful and prosperous future."

"Well said," spoke the Chinese Ambassador with a wide-open smile. "In the end, what we all really want is peace. I am sure, given the present situation, this can be achieved."

Defense Secretary Kurtz leaned over the table. "I agree with the Ambassador from China. Except, I don't see how we can even talk about peace when, at this very moment, joint military forces of China, Russia, and Germany are conducting extensive exercises near several Middle East borders."

Ambassador Marcion cleared her throat, "Again, we must proceed in order. Does the Chinese Ambassador wish to address Secretary Kurtz at this time?"

Shifting in his chair, the Chinese Ambassador nodded and replied, "Mister Secretary, these exercises are conducted on a pre-planned schedule according to the agreements of the UNWC. Does not your military, even now, conduct your own exercises off the Persian Gulf and several other Middle East seaways?"

"Your response, Mr. Vice President," Ambassador Marcion injected.

The Vice President nodded to his General.

General Reynolds stepped in, "Those exercises have been a routine part of our presence in the Middle East for the past decade. Your people can predict our schedules better than we can stick to them. It would be a very unfortunate day should these exercises come into contact with each other. Given the area your forces are operating in, this is a problematic possibility. It's difficult for us to understand why you've chosen to conduct your exercises so close to ours.

The Ambassador from France, who had remained silent throughout the conference, finally cleared his throat and sat up to lean over the table. With a furrowed brow, he addressed the Americans without interruption.

"Madam Ambassador and Gentlemen. We are not here to throw about accusations and point fingers. We are here to find a way to exist peacefully in a world of chaos. We want to bring order to that chaos. We want to build a better world. Can we not agree that America is no longer the sole supreme superpower on earth? It is now time that America finally realizes that we of the UNWC are equal. The 'biggest bully on the block,' idea died with the conclusion of the Cold War. We are not your enemy. We only want the same way of life for our people that you Americans have enjoyed for so long. Is that too much to ask in the interests of peace?"

Vice President Monaham rubbed the back of his neck. His two associates offered no reply to the French Ambassador. He took a moment to consider the French Ambassador's words, but something didn't seem right. Then, he realized what it was.

"Madam Ambassador, if I may respond?"

Ambassador Marcion nodded her head.

"I applaud the Ambassador from France on his position. But at this point, I am going to make the position of the United States of America quite clear. We will not tolerate any threat whatsoever to our national security concerning our nation's oil supplies. We are America, the sole superpower on this planet, and we do not recognize any other. We defeated the former Soviet Union, with respect to the Russian Ambassador. We will continue to conduct our military exercises as we have done for some time, and I am going to caution you of this new UNWC that should there be an incident of any kind, it will fall on your heads. I am absolutely convinced we can reach a diplomatic solution, but I..."

"You cannot tell us what we can and cannot do!" The Chinese Ambassador sharply interjected. "Who are you to decide our future?"

General Reynolds jumped up from his chair, "We're not doing anything about your future. We are protecting ours, and that means we'll do whatever is necessary," he stopped. The room was suddenly very quiet. Looking around the table, he slowly sat down.

After several moments, Ambassador Marcion cleared her throat. "Gentlemen, I recommend we take a five-minute recess. We can resume these talks after..."

Vice President Monaham raised his hand to get some attention. Ambassador Marcion nodded to him to speak. Vice President Monaham rose to his feet. His other two associates rose with him.

"I'm afraid that won't be necessary, Ambassador Marcion. I've heard enough. It's obvious this conference is not going to accomplish anything. I have no other choice than to advise the President. To the Ambassadors of the UNWC, I would like to thank you for the opportunity to sit down and work out our differences. Unfortunately, at this point, I can see no other recourse than to submit to the Security Council a new set of grievances against the UNWC."

Looking each of the UNWC ambassadors in the face as he spoke, he then turned to the Canadian Ambassador, "I will advise the President on our next course of action based upon my analysis of the results of this conference."

The Chinese ambassador rose to his feet signaling his colleagues to rise with him. Locking eyes with the Vice President, he spoke in a low, menacing tone. "I hope the Vice President will advise your President of the urgency to continue on this diplomatic course of action."

Matching the Chinese ambassador's tone, Vice President Monaham kept his eyes locked on his adversary, "I will advise the President that all options are on the table."

The Chinese ambassador did not flinch, "Well, there it is. You have said it yourself, Mister Vice President. *All* options are now on the table. We will return to our governments and report our findings as well."

The Vice President broke off the engagement. He hastily reached down for his briefcase, placing it on the table and loudly snapped the locks with a firm finality. Then, he addressed the Canadian ambassador, "Madam Ambassador, I believe we're finished here. Thank you for your services." The Canadian ambassador glanced at the UNWC ambassadors who sat quietly staring at the table. She received no reaction.

"Very well gentlemen, this meeting is adjourned." The Canadian ambassador rose to her feet.

The Vice President turned to the Chairman of the Security Council, "Mister Chairman, thank you for attending this conference. I formally request to please have your secretary forward her minutes to my staff as soon as they are completed." Chairman Jypinga Seiti gave a slight nod but said nothing.

Addressing the five UNWC ambassadors, the Vice President said, "Gentlemen, always a pleasure, you'll be hearing from us." With that, he wheeled about and led the way out of the conference room with both of his associates in tow.

The meeting was over.

The representatives of the UNWC quietly gathered their documents and filed out of the conference room one by one. As they moved down the hallway towards the elevators, the Chinese Ambassador tapped his German counterpart on the shoulder signaling him to slow down a bit.

When the two had fallen behind the others at a distance, the Chinese Ambassador quietly spoke to his German associate, "You did not speak much during the conference. I was sure you would have something more significant to add to the discussion, no?"

The German Ambassador stopped as did his Chinese counterpart. Keeping his voice down, the German Ambassador said, "No, Mr. Ambassador. I had nothing much to add to the discussion. I believe you and our Russian associate did an excellent job aggravating the Americans. I simply watched and listened as I wanted to make sure that my report to my government is absolutely accurate."

"I see," the Chinese Ambassador replied stroking his chin. "Well then, we should get going. Our flights leave in a couple of hours."

"Of course, Mr. Ambassador," the German Ambassador replied. "Please, go on ahead. I need a quick visit to the men's lavatory."

The Chinese ambassador smiled and offered a slight bow to his associate, "Very well then, Mr. Ambassador. I will look forward to seeing you again,"

With that, the Chinese Ambassador turned and strode back down the hallway towards the elevator. The men's lavatory was right across from where the two men had just been conversing. The German Ambassador quickly crossed to the lavatory, and stepping inside, he laid his briefcase on the counter.

He looked into the mirror for a few moments before placing his hand under a spigot, which immediately gushed out a stream of cold water. He took a moment to pat his face with the water then, taking a few sheets from a paper dispenser, wiped his face dry.

Atuvola looked into the mirror again studying the face staring at him. Having been recently promoted as a first rank in the third tribe of the Doon Esha, he had been eager for an assignment to prove himself to Celetin. It was his first assimilation, and as Atuvola studied the face in the mirror, he decided to agree with his master; humans were just plain ugly.

Suppressing the urge to immediately break contact with the human, Atuvola stepped back and adjusted his tie. Reaching down to retrieve his briefcase, he glanced one more time in the mirror and turned to make his exit out of the dormitory. It would be a long flight back to Germany, but he was looking forward to the day he could go home to the warm tropics of the islands. For the time being, he needed to continue to play his part and complete his assignment.

Atuvola stepped out into the semi-busy hallway and made his way towards the elevators. Yes, his flight would be a long one, but he realized how much he also enjoyed flying first class. He could almost picture in his mind... *The Doomsday clock located at the University of Chicago clicked one second closer to midnight.*

GLOBALCOMNEWS.NET
World Situation Report #3

"This is Jeremy Parker reporting from New York. There has been little word coming out of the United Nations concerning an important meeting that took place between the American members of the U.N. Security Council and representatives of the UNWC.

"An anonymous source has told us that apparently there were tensions present during the meeting but so far, we can only speculate as to the exact nature of the conference itself. We are still waiting to learn if any mention of the accident involving the Alaskan pipeline project was discussed during the conference and if there could be any connections between the Alaskan incident and the refinery fires in Iran.

"The official word from the American government concerning the Alaskan pipeline accident is that a small earthquake in the region may have been responsible for the accident itself, but other sources close to GlobalComNews.Net are questioning the validity of the explanation offered by the American press.

We will continue to follow this story and bring you any further information as it becomes available. This is Jeremy Parker, GlobalComNews.Net, reporting from our studio in New York."

CHAPTER SIXTEEN

BETRAYAL AND DISBELIEF

Ploruvus did not resist as the two Scorpulas escorted him through the deep central chamber of the Doon Esha fortress. He had been deliberately ordered to human form by his captors and was being escorted to Celetin's chamber. The Doon Esha fortress was oddly all but deserted with only an occasional fifth rank Esha laborer pausing to notice the quiet trio somberly passing through the central chamber courtyard. Ploruvus barely lifted his eyes to behold the enormous statue of Celetin that dominated the center of the underground fortress' courtyard square.

Rubbing the back of his neck, Ploruvus tried again to concentrate on the last thing he remembered. It had been late in the night. He'd spent nearly four hours researching the internet for world events at the Cafe de Francois eight blocks from the Capitol. He was preparing for his introduction to an aide serving one of the defense secretary's advisors the next morning. The meeting had been arranged by one of the Tryistan Elders according to his information. At about 1 a.m. in the morning, he remembered getting into his car and a sudden stinging pain through his right shoulder. Then, nothing. Whatever had happened next was a complete blank.

Ploruvus blinked his eyes rapidly to clear the bit of fogginess still plaguing his vision. He wasn't quite sure what day it was or how long he'd been out. He was quite sure, however, that he was not in Washington, D.C. anymore.

The scorpula nudged Ploruvus again to pick up his pace. Having crossed the main underground courtyard chamber, they proceeded towards Celetin's tunnel wing. As they neared Celetin's chambers, Ploruvus paused at the intersection casting a glance down the right tunnel. The echoes of wailing and pitiful cries faintly reverberated through the rocky passage. The scorpula harshly pushed Ploruvus into the left tunnel. They walked in silence until finally, at the chamber entrance, they were met by Celetin's personal guard. Both winged serpents came forward away from the sides of the doors to take possession of the prisoner. Without a sound, the scorpulas moved away, turned around and headed back down the tunnel.

The two large doors slowly swung open into Celetin's chambers, and Ploruvus felt himself nudged by the whip tail of a winged serpentine. He knew that he outranked the two-winged Esha but realized he could never make it out of the Doon Esha fortress alive. He couldn't even remember how he'd gotten to this point through the labyrinths of the fortress. As he cautiously entered into Celetin's chambers, he was instantly mesmerized by the incredible adornment. No member of the Tryistan Order had ever seen the personal chamber of Celetin and returned to talk about it. This sudden realization saddened Ploruvus. He had failed.

As the Tryistan wandered into the chamber towards the lavishly furnished center floor, he detected the audible click of the doors closing behind him. Though tempted to look back over his shoulder, he fought the urge thinking the act would appear weak. He was well aware that the eyes of the Doon Esha leader followed his every step.

He could feel the sensation on the back of his neck that he was being watched.

As he reached the center of the enormous chamber, a voice unlike any Ploruvus had ever heard spoke. "Ploruvus. Mighty warrior and servant of the Tryistans. Welcome."

Ploruvus carefully searched the room, unable to locate the source of such a sweet harmonious choir of voices. He'd never heard such beauty of speech, and he fought hard in his mind to resist the temptation to accept the allure of the beauty and harmony the voices offered him.

"You are impressed by my abode, yes?" Celetin's voice orchestrated throughout the chamber. "It is my prison. My freedom. My life, and my death. It represents absolute order and total chaos. It is my design and my copy. I love it, and I hate it."

Ploruvus hesitated to answer. Finally, he decided to keep his silence. He fought within his mind to resist the alluring melodious voices that spoke to him in such beauty and perfection.

"You know that I and your precious leader, Gharius, once walked together long, long ago. We are not so different, mighty Ploruvus. I can see as I watch you that even now you are fighting to understand how such a voice as mine can be so evil. I ask you, mighty Ploruvus, is this truly a voice of evil? Ah, but I'm not being fair. Stand where you are and raise your eyes."

With that, Ploruvus stopped and slowly looked up. Fifty feet above him, from a heavily jeweled and carved rocky loft, he watched as a beautiful white dragon opened its gold fringed wings and gracefully descended to a spot 10 feet from where he stood. Ploruvus could only stare as he looked upon the beautiful form folding its wings and facing him in a less than intimidating manner. As each beheld the other, there was a strange sense of hope that encouraged Ploruvus. Before him was not a horrible abomination which repulsed him. It was nothing like he'd been expecting. Not this.

Celetin slowly cocked his head to the side. "You were expecting a monster?"

Ploruvus could hardly speak, captivated by the incredible warmth of the harmonious voices that seemed to fill the chamber in layers of soft whispers. Blinking his eyes as he struggled to clear his clouded mind, "May I assume you are Celetin himself whom I might address?"

Celetin rose up to his full stature and slightly tilted his head in a modest bow. "I am Celetin, whom you shall address."

Ploruvus gave a slight nod in a show of respectful acknowledgement. "Very well. I am Ploruvus of the Order of Tryistan. I am outranked by you, and to you I must submit. I assume that you have reason to bring me to your own hold for purposes not known to me. I submit humbly to your rank and make a request of you to return me to my own Order. I have no place here with you."

The seamless white dragon looked Ploruvus over from head to toe. After several moments, Celetin said, "Mighty Ploruvus, I do not seek for you. Tis not your own self I seek, but merely to send you as my own messenger back into your own Order. Detest you, not my company. Consider it yourself, how in our presence, we might find truth between us. A peculiar truth between enemies that I might find rare even among my own servants."

Ploruvus paused to consider these words. *Very strange, not like I'd expected...* Still, Ploruvus was not a fool. He had studied long and well in the Order's libraries. The war between the Tryistans and the Doon Esha was historically more than well documented. References to Celetin himself were small in number, but clearly translated that Celetin was to be considered dangerously powerful and to be respected for that power.

Ploruvus continued, "A messenger of yours might I be if for the very reason I am here. I would know your message and return to my Order all the sooner if it be within your power to grant to me."

Celetin backed away from Ploruvus, setting himself in an enormous and lavishly jewel-plated enthroned pedestal. When he had settled, he gazed at Ploruvus. Finally, "I am curious, mighty Ploruvus. Tell me what you know of the prophecies. You surely know that even now there is a height of escalation between us. I wish that you would speak to me what you think the times may be."

Caught off guard, Ploruvus glanced around the chamber. This was not what he'd expected. Why was Celetin himself asking a fourth rank Tryistan about prophecy? Something was clearly wrong here. Ploruvus decided to choose his words carefully to try to decipher what the Doon Esha leader was looking for.

"I am not sure I can accommodate you, Celetin. Prophecy is an issue of the learned and the student of the same. I am versed in law, particularly of the Order and of the humans. Prophecy is not a comfort for my knowledge."

Celetin sensed Ploruvus was skirting the issue. "Come, mighty Ploruvus. You are a fourth rank chosen to set upon an important task for your own order. You are not even curious how your task was discovered and by what means you were delivered to me?"

Ploruvus stared at the floor considering Celetin's words. He realized how curious he was that he'd been discovered. How could they have known? Zelotus of the Council had assured him of complete autonomy. Esha possessed no known ability to sense each other from a distance despite whatever form they assumed. Yet, here he was, and it didn't make any sense.

If he could find an answer, and Celetin would send him home to the Order with some twisted message, it might have some intelligence value. Such intelligence would be very valuable especially in light of the current escalations between the Doon Esha and the Tryistan Order.

Ploruvus replied, "I admit to you that I am curious as to your revelation. It would seem that you had the upper hand in your translation of the escalations you speak of."

Celetin managed a slight smile. "Mighty Ploruvus, my eyes and ears are everywhere. I have agents in every corner of the world. It is my own business to know who and what is passing along at any time I may refer. Upon occasion, it becomes necessary for me to travel myself over the earth in order that I might know that which is and what may be to come."

Ploruvus hesitated, then said, "I have my own reservations as to why you might inquire as to what I might know of prophecy."

Celetin leaned forward, "The prophecies are the root of that which I seek. Surely you know that which serves as the foundation of your own Order. What would you think to know that the prophecies you studied were written by me?"

The idea startled Ploruvus. This was completely contrary to what he'd been taught throughout his learning. It was not possible. Celetin wrote the prophecies? Now Ploruvus knew that Celetin was lying to him. *But why...*

Ploruvus felt a surge of indignation, giving him a sense of confidence before he finally straightened his shoulders up and spoke, "Do you truly think me a fool? Gharius forbid. I am fourth rank, but I know that the father of the Esha wrote the prophecies, which father you are not."

The tension rose within the chamber, and Celetin seemed obviously irritated. After several moments, Celetin replied, "Mighty Ploruvus, do you not know well the copies of the prophecy, which you most astutely studied?"

"Yea, Celetin, the copies of the prophecy are quite clear. What we have left of them we commit to our own understanding. But I repeat, I am not a student of the prophecies."

Celetin smiled, "The copies of your own prophecy are in error. They err because they are not of that which our father wrote. They have been deceived through time by me. A word here, a word there. Once, I managed to destroy and rewrite an entire passage, long ago. Your precious Gharius knew not, for he has never mentioned any incident to me, and I have spoken with him many times through the ages."

The prophecies altered... Ploruvus could not accept it. How could the prophecies be altered? Of course, the original manuscripts had long since disintegrated, but of course, the words had been preserved. *Right?*

Ploruvus looked straight into Celetin's face, "You would make me to believe that you had a hand in the defamation of the Order's own prophecy? Our very word? Forgive me, but I find that a belief which I am taxed to accept."

Again, Celetin smiled. "Would you seek yet the very proof? Perhaps your own eyes set upon the original writ would convince you, yes?" *Original writ? How is that possible?*

Ploruvus shuddered. A chance to see the originals of the prophecy as the father of Gharius had written himself. He could hardly refuse such an offer but knew the possibility of Celetin possessing the original texts had to be impossible. The Tryistan Order itself possessed copies of copies preserved and handed down throughout several thousand years.

"I would much like to see these originals that you allege to possess. I am versed fair enough to know the difference if you will present them."

"Very well, mighty Ploruvus," the dragon replied. "Come then, see for your own self."

With that, Celetin rose from the pedestal, turned and led Ploruvus towards an adjoining chamber at the back of the Celetin's main chamber. As they walked, Ploruvus chewed on the idea in his mind. He was strongly skeptical he was actually about to see the true original writings of the prophecy and not the copies as he had studied which were being called into question.

Celetin stopped short of a golden scepter standing in front of the smooth rock covering the entrance to the adjoining chamber. Ploruvus looked at Celetin, waiting for the Leader of the Doon Esha to produce this claim. Celetin waved a clawed hand over a small rock formation on the wall and looked up. Slowly creaking upward, a 10 foot by 20 foot slab of rock slowly rose until coming to rest 10 feet above the floor.

The chamber revealed a dim light illuminating the chamber within. It was a small inner chamber dimly lit by thick beige candles adding to its antique and almost ancient atmosphere. Dusty bookshelves stood filled with ancient looking books, maps, and drawings, which looked to be in no apparent order.

Ploruvus stepped through the door and slowly approached the center silver table upon which a short sturdy and elaborately crafted mahogany book pedestal supported what looked to be a very, very old open manuscript. The book itself rivaled the Book of Kells, looking greatly aged and beautifully adorned with pure gold bindings and elaborate illustrations. It was opened to what appeared to be freshly read pages.

Ploruvus struggled with the ancient language of the open page, silently mouthing the words.

Celetin watched the Tryistan for several long moments. "Have you found that which you seek?"

Ploruvus startled and turned to see Celetin's head through the doorway. "I... I don't understand some of these writings. They don't make sense. I can read a little of it, but most of this looks nothing like what I've seen from the Order's libraries or read like these."

Celetin slowly smiled, "I'm quite sure they don't. Your Order does not possess the knowledge required to reconstruct the full text as I have done. Once I discovered the key, it was all quite simple to reestablish the text in whole. Come now, mighty Ploruvus." With that, Celetin withdrew his head from the chamber. Ploruvus turned to leave and hesitated, glancing back at the pedestal table. Pursing his lips, he turned away and came out of the small chamber.

With a wave, Celetin waited while the door sealed the chamber. Turning to Ploruvus, "I imagine you might have questions? Please, walk with me."

Ploruvus followed Celetin to a well-lit tunnel shaft that led to another large chamber. As they walked in silence, Ploruvus fought to understand what he'd just witnessed and how to reconcile what he'd just heard. It didn't make sense. Gharius would never intentionally deceive anyone. It was common knowledge that Celetin was no match for Gharius' power. Yet, here, the leader of the Doon Esha seemed to have all the pieces of the puzzle.

What really upset Ploruvus was the first passage he'd been able to translate, which revealed the fall of a great leader as a great griffin brought down to the ground. Gharius often assumed a great griffin when he traveled. The Tryistan's libraries contained no such reference to a griffin, or any other form for that matter. As they walked, Ploruvus did not notice the occasional glances from Celetin's eyes as they made their way through the tunnel.

Finally, they came to the end of the tunnel, which suddenly opened up into a large circular chamber. Celetin waved a hand over a small rocky outcrop causing the rocks on both sides of the chamber to begin to slide in opposite directions. Ploruvus stood still and watched as the rocks silently opened up two enormous entrances on each side of the chamber giving him full access to the outside world with a stunning view of the ocean.

Once the doors came to a rest, the chamber offered a nearly unhindered view of the island and the ocean on two opposing sides of the chamber. A warm island breeze suddenly filled the chamber whispering back up the entrance tunnel. The smell and sounds of the ocean resounded off the chamber walls. It was a breathtaking view that was not lost on Ploruvus.

Celetin hesitated to allow his prisoner to take in the view. The sun was just setting off to the west highlighting the golden sky laced with the mournful cries of distant seagulls. The scene was truly stunning.

"I come here often to study," Celetin whispered. "This setting sun signals the arrival of my most cherished time of the day. Do you not think it beautiful?"

Ploruvus nodded his head as he took in the sights and smells of the fresh evening air. The sight before him momentarily distracted him from his questions and his dilemma. Standing there, looking out at the vast ocean, he suddenly felt a strange peace. Like things weren't as bad as they seemed, and maybe it was going to work out for him after all.

His questions seemed to lose their urgency as if the answers were somehow out there somewhere to be found whenever he was ready. Surely there was a rational explanation for everything that had happened to him up to now. Then, from the back of his mind, Ploruvus had a thought. Then, he had a question.

Turning around, Ploruvus faced Celetin who was set on all fours. He noticed that there was a good 10 yards between them now. Inwardly shrugging, Ploruvus cleared his throat. "I was just wondering..."

"Yes, mighty, Ploruvus?"

"As I was reading, I noticed that a great leader is prophesied to fall by fire. Forgive me, but I didn't get far enough. Can you tell me by what flame does the prophecy say will cause the great leader to fall?"

Celetin glanced out towards the ocean for several moments. Finally, "The prophecy reveals that the great leader shall fall to crimson flame, mighty Ploruvus."

Ploruvus looked down at the floor for a moment, running his hand through his hair. But prophecy I have learned of says that a great leader shall be pierced by a purified blade of light. It says nothing of any crimson flame. Your text also refers to another leader as having the greater power to decide. Our texts reveal nothing of this. I don't understand..."

Celetin lightly licked his lips. "Mighty Ploruvus, I would be most willing to share whatever knowledge I have with you. You would be most welcome to stay and study the texts for yourself. Perhaps, in time, you would come to see for yourself that the volume I possess is the true one. Have you not seen it for yourself?"

Ploruvus glanced at the floor again, then back to Celetin. "I'm sorry. What you offer me is most tempting; however, I must decline."

Celetin's eyes flashed as small charges of gray-silver flashed through his wings. "Mighty Ploruvus come, let's be reasonable. I only offer you the truth. I'm afraid I am somewhat baffled by your rejection."

Ploruvus stood straighter now. Looking Celetin in the eyes, "I might have fallen for your offer except that I am remembering that you told me yourself that you have infiltrated our Order upon occasion to alter our own texts. It seems unlikely that you would go to so much trouble when you believe that the prophecy you possess is the only true one. If that were so, then why the deception? If our texts had been truly wrong to begin with, why would you have needed to attempt to change them? It doesn't make sense. If in fact, your text is true, then there would be no reason for you to offer me such an opportunity. I realize that you outrank me, but I do not believe you. I would return to Gharius at once."

The cracking of Celetin's knuckled front claws echoed up into the ceiling. The white dragon was obviously agitated as the pulses of silver-gray charges danced erratically over his wings. Keeping his voice low and even, Celetin addressed his prisoner in a slight dissonance of voices, "Very well. If you wish to stay a puppet servant to your Order, then so be it. But I will not return you to your Order. I have other plans for you, my new servant rank."

Stepping forward, Ploruvus clenched his hands, "When Gharius learns of what has happened to me, he will come..."

"Let him come!" The white dragon's voice began to lose its melodic harmony. "What do you know of power, servant rank? If your precious leader is so powerful, then tell me, why am I not destroyed? Answer me!"

Ploruvus refused to back down. With his jaw set, Ploruvus firmly replied, "Everything has its time. All is foretold. It is true you are not destroyed - *not yet.*"

The sound of sickened cackling seemed to work itself into the chamber from both the walls and the ceiling. Through the dissonant orchestra of the cackling laugher, Celetin's voice came again, "Foolish child! What do you know of destruction? What do you know of power? And you shall tell me, Celetin, that I am not *yet* destroyed? You are a fool!" The cackling grew into a symphony of sonic chaos. Ploruvus put his hands over his ears tightly shutting his eyes.

After what seemed many moments, Ploruvus slowly lowered his hands, opening his eyes. He blinked as the white dragon appeared to have completely regained its composure. Ploruvus glanced around and noticed that he was standing near the edge of the chamber with his back to the enormous window overlooking the ocean. Celetin had moved to the center of the chamber a mere 20 feet directly in front of the Tryistan.

Celetin finally lowered his head to face his prisoner. In a perfect unison of melody, the voices spoke, "I see that there is no chance of turning you. That is unfortunate. You have no idea the power I could have given to you. I might have made you as powerful as any of my elders. It is of no matter. Whether you believe it or not, your great leader will go down under the fury of crimson flame, my crimson flame."

Ploruvus' eyes narrowed, "I do not believe you possess any such power."

Celetin's own eyes narrowed while several small drops of fetid acid slipped from his mouth boiling into the floor where they hit. With barely an audible whisper, "Oh? I see..."

Fiomass, an Elder of the Doon Esha, lay quietly on the white sandy beach as the fresh cool seawater cascaded up the beach and over his front paws. Fresh gashes across his back still oozed traces of blood. He watched as the fading light of the dying sun slowly turned the breezy dusk into a beautiful richly colored evening sky. Casually looking back over his shoulder, he suddenly winced as two red napalm-like blasts of fire shot out of the high upper ridge of the ancient volcano. Turning back to the darkening sky, he closed his eyes and concentrated on the cool saltwater between his claws. The ashes of the stricken Tryistan would float on the ocean breeze for days until finding places to rest.

CHAPTER SEVENTEEN

FIRE AND SMOKE

Jypinga Seiti, Chairman of the Security Council, stepped up to the formidable array of microphones scattered around the podium. He was flanked by three of his advisors. The announcement was to be made at an outdoor event at the top of the steps of the U.N. conference building. Scores of reporters, writers, and news correspondents crowded the steps waiting for Seiti to speak, hoping for a chance to throw up a question. Security was tight with both mounted and foot police, along with private security officers, creating a very visible presence.

The Chairman softly cleared his throat as he tugged at his necktie. Glancing at his advisors, he finally put his hands on the podium and leaned into the microphones.

"If I may have your attention... First, I'd like to thank the delegation of the UNWC for their cooperation and patience concerning the turn of events over the last several weeks. I'd like to thank the President and the White House staff for their cooperation as well. I am here today to announce the United Nations formal acceptance of the UNWC as an established political entity. Despite strong opposition, the voting results have been established and recorded."

The Chairman waited a few seconds before continuing.

"Unfortunately, the Chinese Ambassador, who was to be here today, passed away in the tragic events of three days ago when his ocean passage vessel encountered tragic circumstances, the details of which are not yet fully known. We offer our condolences to the Chinese government and to the Ambassador's family. It is a major loss to the ongoing diplomatic process between the UNWC and the United States, and his presence will be sorely missed. The President has assured me personally that a full investigation will be made of this most tragic event. Thank you all for coming."

Stepping back from the podium, the Chairman tensed for the onslaught of questions he knew was coming. He was not disappointed. The crowd of correspondents immediately pressed forward. Pointing at a tall correspondent woman he recognized, he took her first question.

The whole scene was not lost to Petrawnus. He stood watching the event from a distance of 40 or 50 yards away from the attending crowd and further back from the central courtyard. The audio system had clearly conveyed the Chairman's words, and Petrawnus stood watching as Chairman Seiti fought to answer the aggressive reporters vying for attention.

This was not the news Petrawnus had been hoping to hear. The Chairman's announcement along with the recent turn of events could only add to the friction between the East and the West. Petrawnus reached up and rubbed the tense spot between his eyes, squinting as he looked to his right while trying to evaluate the outcome. *There.* Petrawnus froze. Blinking, he focused on the crowds mulling about the street corner across the far side of the main street just to his right. *There it is again.*

Two figures haunted an old out-of-order telephone booth on the far side of an adjacent street corner. Petrawnus watched the couple. One was oddly inside the booth speaking on a cell phone and looking out at his companion, who had his back turned to Petrawnus. *There, again.* Petrawnus felt a surge of adrenaline. He tensed up as he continued to focus on the two men at the phone booth. This time there was no mistaking the man inside the booth. His eyes. They flashed again. The man's yellow-gold eyes with dark vertical slits for pupils flashed several times more. Petrawnus instinctively knew humans did not possess such exotic optics.

Petrawnus looked back over at the podium area where the Chairman continued to field a barrage of questions from the crowd of reporters. He looked over at the phone booth again where the two strange men continued to loiter. The one in the booth was still speaking into his cell phone.

Suddenly, an ear-splitting blast immediately was followed by a hot burst of wind, which literally forced Petrawnus to jump backwards over the short hedge row behind him. Landing on his back, he instantly realized what had happened. He could feel his pulse racing through his eardrums over the intense ringing in his ears.

Shaking his head, he sat up and feeling somewhat disorientated. Petrawnus pivoted on his right arm and raised himself up until he was standing. He could barely make out the scene now enshrouded in smoke and heavily armed security officers running from every direction.

Petrawnus realized the limited scope of the detonation pointed to a small explosive device, but it looked like it had done its job. *It was in the podium...*

The attending crowd of reporters, journalists, and camera crews who were not among the injured broke up and were running helter-skelter. Some of them were bravely attempting to reposition themselves to report what was happening. The podium was mostly destroyed with no sight of the Chairman of the U.N. Security Council. The cries and screams of the injured began to rise to a feverish pitch as the acrid smell of smoke from the bomb slowly drifted away from the center of the target.

Petrawnus glanced over at the phone booth. Nothing. The two figures were gone. He immediately realized that if the pair were Doon Esha, they had certainly managed to involve human agents in the bombing. He also knew there would be no way to find the human agents at this point, if they were even still alive.

There was only one other option. Petrawnus hastily wiped his hands on his pants and started walking slowly but steadily towards the booth. In the distance, the sirens of incoming emergency and law enforcement personnel began to wail, adding to the chaos of panic and distress on the street. Hastily searching the shops and alleys as he walked, Petrawnus picked up his pace and concentrated on finding his targets as throngs of people scattering in all directions mingled with the traffic filling the streets and sidewalks.

He knew it was going to be next to impossible to find the two men among the gathering crowds of onlookers and emergency personnel who were just arriving at the scene. Still, Petrawnus continued to deliberately push his way through unabated towards the booth, scanning the sidewalks and alleys.

Out of the corner of his eye, he caught the back of a hooded figure moving up the far sidewalk of First Avenue leading out of the U.N.'s provincial location. Petrawnus strained to see through the crowded streets, when again he caught another quick glimpse of the hooded figure now joined by a second. Petrawnus abandoned the phone booth pursuit and hurriedly crossed the street to the far sidewalk.

Speeding up his pace, he worked through the crowds to close the gap between himself and the two suspicious figures who seemed very intent on heading out of the area. Petrawnus had to stop as two NYC heavy security cruisers made their way through the crowd. He waited for them to pass and continued his search looking to where he had last seen the two strangers.

They were gone. Clenching his teeth, Petrawnus pushed through the thinning crowds until he finally stopped at an alley way on his left. Without pausing, he made his way into the alley and then further on into its gloomy passageway. *There is no other place for them to go,* he decided as he continued to creep along stealthily. He caught sight of them about 50 yards further down into the alley, just as they shot towards the sky in their reptilian bird forms. *I knew it...*

Petrawnus took off running after them looking for a chance to go airborne after the two escaping Doon Esha. He found the side alley doorway his targets had ducked into to escape and used it to change into his winged form. He shot out of the alley and up into the air where he quickly spotted the two Doon Esha flying low over the rooftops.

He pounded the air for altitude to gain the high advantage and then used it to swoop down on his targets who had spotted him. Thinking quickly, they dove down into another maze of the city's seemingly endless alleys. Petrawnus closed the gap, diving close behind them.

Petrawnus pursued the two-winged reptiles relentlessly through the twisting and winding alleys. The first rank led the second rank Doon Esha in a race to evade the Tryistan at all costs. A homeless man sat against a brick wall next to a tipped over eroding dumpster trying to read an old newspaper with one hand and hold his wooden flask in the other. The first rank blew by him rattling the dumpster and tearing the paper from his hand. Grunting, the poor man leaned over and retrieved the old newspaper ignoring the incident. As he settled back down, the second rank Doon Esha shot past him with equal speed pulling the newspaper from his hand a second time.

The old man hesitated, looking up and down the alley first before retrieving his paper. Finally, he reached out and picked up the paper again settling back down to read. Petrawnus pitched past the man at breakneck speed tearing the paper from his hands for the third time. This time, the old man gruffly grabbed the tattered newspaper and pushed himself up the wall. Looking up and down the alley warily, he opened the cover to the dumpster, climbed inside, and slammed the lid shut.

Petrawnus continued to gain on the two Esha as the trio zipped through the winding, twisting alleys. Without warning, the two fleeing creatures came to a junction and split up, leaving Petrawnus with only a moment to decide which one to follow. *The second rank...*

The second rank Doon Esha had taken the left alley with Petrawnus now in hot pursuit. They flew up and down, twisting and turning down the long lifeless alleys knocking over stacks of crates and whatever else stood in the way. Petrawnus continued to close the distance to his target while the frightened Doon Esha frantically searched for any way to escape his pursuer. Then, as the Doon Esha turned to look back at the pursuing Tryistan, the hapless second rank misjudged its next turn and slammed headfirst into a concrete garage barrier breaking its neck with a sickening snap. The beast's body continued spinning on out of control until slamming into the pavement where it skidded to a halt.

Petrawnus landed a few feet from the stricken Esha and stepped into his human form. Looking up and down the back alley, Petrawnus approached the dead Esha and took a moment to study it over. It was definitely a second rank, and the Tryistan Elder had hoped to take it alive so it could be questioned. *Not going to happen now...*

Stooping down, Petrawnus reached down and put his right palm against the rib cage of the dead Doon Esha and closed his eyes. A soft ribbon of yellow-orange light slowly traced itself around the outline of his hand, which then turned into an expanding flow of tiny-banded orange-yellow flames. The small flames began to emanate outward from his hand, racing to engulf the entire body of the Esha. Opening his eyes, Petrawnus pulled back his hand and stood up to watch the body of the Esha quickly disintegrate into a small pile of gray smoldering ash.

Realizing the first rank was long gone, Petrawnus watched as a lazy breeze began to quietly scatter the ashes of the dead Doon Esha until there was no trace of the creature left to see. The sky was just beginning to announce the departure of the sun as it turned deeper and deeper shades of blue.

Petrawnus found a soft spot on the pavement and sat down with his back against an old wooden box. He was tempted to step into his flying form and take off, but decided to wait until it was dark. While he waited, Petrawnus thought over the events of the day and concluded how nearly unbelievable it was that not a single human had witnessed the bizarre alley chase except for the one in the dumpster. *Won't worry about that one...*

Two hours later as darkness settled on the city, the alley sat deserted as if nothing had ever happened there.

GLOBALCOMNEWS.NET
World Situation Report #4

"...and it has not yet been determined who is responsible for the bombing in front of the United Nations building costing the life of the Chairman of the Security Council and another six lives with no accurate count of the wounded, according to our most recent reports. We have not yet received the names of those who were killed or injured except for the Chairman himself.

"Again, no one has come forth to claim responsibility for the bombing but there are a number of circulating theories as to who may be responsible for this tragedy. At the moment, very little is known about the motive for this bombing, and we can only hope that there will be swift and judicial action to this heinous event.

"This is Gail Childers, GlobalComNews.Net live from our studio in New York."

CHAPTER EIGHTEEN

A KINDRED SPIRIT

Gharius sat quietly in the darkened chamber of the sacred archives. It had been a long day, and the night had swiftly set in. He decided he would take one last stroll into the main chamber lobbies to give everything a last check before turning in for the night. He could feel his eyelids getting heavy and did not resist the temptation to let out a voracious yawn. *In a few minutes...*

What... Opening his eyes, Gharius blinked several times before realizing he had drifted off to sleep. Sitting straight in his chair, he stiffened up as the notion that something wasn't quite right in the chamber came over him. He scanned the darkened chamber for a few moments until his eyes caught a faint hue emanating from a modestly decorated jewelry box. The box was sitting on a small table in a corner and now garnered his full attention. Gharius slowly rose from his seat.

Crossing the chamber, Gharius reached the small box and sighed heavily, staring down at the faint hue emanating from the inside of the box. He hesitated a few moments before finally reaching out to gently grasp the handles of the two small panes attached to the side of the box. Slowly he pulled the two panes apart and felt his eyes begin to moisten.

Gharius gingerly reached into the jewelry box and pulled out a small candle whose flame was delicately bobbing up and down the wick. He studied the candle for a moment, watching the soft flame and waiting for an answer to the only question on his mind. *Who is it?*

The dancing flame appeared to calm itself down enough allowing Gharius to ever so gently put out his hand and hold it over the flame, narrowing his eyes. *Ploruvus...*

Suddenly, the little flame seemed to be trying to leap higher as if it was struggling to reach Gharius' hand. Despite that, he continued to hold it over the candle. Slowly he lowered his hand until the tip of the dancing flame made contact with his flesh. There was no pain, and Gharius watched as the little flame softly caressed his fingers. *I know, my friend...*

Gharius gently picked up the candle with his free hand while keeping his other hand in close contact with the candle's flame that was dancing between his fingers. Turning to his left, Gharius quietly strode to the back of his archive chamber until reaching a pylon. He spoke softly in his ancient tongue and waited as a doorway slid open revealing another adjacent chamber. He moved into the next chamber and spoke again, waiting for the door to close.

The chamber was dimly lit with a single chandelier hanging just below the ceiling rafters. Gharius approached an enormous, enclosed curio, the only furnishing in the sparse chamber. As he stood in front of the two large panels, he spoke again in the ancient language and waited as the panels slowly and silently slid open. The room was immediately filled with the penetrating lights of a number of flickering candles coming from within the curio.

Holding the candle up, Gharius removed his hand from the flame which instantly calmed down to little more than a glow on the wick. With a heavy heart, Gharius gently placed the candle into the curio and set it down beside another candle burning with the same flame. Pulling his hand away, he paused to gaze upon all the many candles burning away with flames of their own. Finally, he turned his attention back to the candle he had just placed in the curio and noticed that he had set the candle down beside the candle of Nezfur.

"Do not worry, Ploruvus, my friend," whispered Gharius. "Our time will come."

With that, Gharius whispered the ancient words again and waited for the curio panels to come together. Hearing the locks snap shut, he turned and exited out of the adjacent tunnel back into the archive chamber. He was tired. So very tired. *I'm going to rest awhile...*

The leader of the Tryistan order blew out the candles in his archive chamber and retired to his personal quarters.

CHAPTER NINETEEN

THE VISITOR

It was early morning, and the fortress of the Order was coming to life. The young Tryistan panted heavily as he ran down the long, lit corridor towards the living quarters of the Council of Twelve. Stopping only long enough to apologize for bumping into an occasional occupant, he made his way quickly into the chambered living quarters area. Running up the narrow corridor lit by torches and past the council members' private quarters, he reached the end of the corridor, which housed the personal chamber of Gharius. Two Guardians blocked his entrance.

The young man was out of breath and could barely respond to the Guardian's request for his purpose. He bent over, placing his hands on his knees, fighting to speak and breathe at the same time. Sweat covered his brow, staining the collar of his shirt and continued to pour down his back. He tried several times to give the Guardians a coherent response, and as he was struggling to explain himself a third time, the door quietly slid open, and Gharius stepped out into the hall.

The young man dropped his head immediately, "Lord Gh...Lord Gharius! I-I was sent to re-request your...presence..."

Gharius motioned to the Guardians who immediately backed away and resumed their watch. Stepping forward, Gharius took the young man by the shoulders and helped him to stand upright.

"Now, take your time. Who sent for me?"

The young Tryistan was more than a little unnerved by the strength of his Lord's arm in picking him up. He closed his eyes for a moment and took a deep breath.

"Lord Gharius, Elder Johhanicus sent me to request your presence in the West wing. The Watch Commander from the wing reports that two Guardians have brought in a Doon Esha whom they intercepted at our borders. The Doon Esha submitted to them and is asking to see you personally, my Lord."

"Has he been contained?" Gharius questioned.

"Yes, my Lord, they have him in quarantine in the West wing bunker. Elder Johhanicus is assured there is no danger."

"Very well. Return to the West wing and report that I'll be there shortly."

"Yes, my Lord." Then he stepped back and bowed before turning around and running back down the passageway.

Gharius called out, "Young man?"

The lad stopped dead and wheeled about. "Yes, my Lord?"

"Did you get the name of the prisoner?"

"No sir, except that he is an Elder, my Lord."

Gharius rubbed his chin. *An Elder is it?*

"Very well, young man. Please continue with your duties."

Bowing again, he called out, "Yes, my Lord," and took off again down the passageway.

With a slight wave of his hand, the entrance to Gharius' chamber slid shut. With a nod to his Guardian detail, Gharius proceeded to leave for the West wing. He took his time as he went, pausing only to acknowledge those who greeted him along the way.

The fact that a Doon Esha Elder had yielded to the lower ranked Guardians raised several curious possibilities. Gharius pondered each one in turn as he passed through the central courtyard of the main chamber heading for the West wing tunnel formations. He was suddenly glad his Guardian, Neeash, was not on duty tonight. Chances were it very well could be this visiting Elder who had killed the Guardian's mate, which would certainly lead to a lethal confrontation.

Quickening his pace, Gharius continued to ponder the possibilities as he passed into the connecting corridor leading to the West wing. The corridor was oddly vacant, which Gharius realized was part of the precaution of keeping the Doon Esha Elder prisoner in the West wing. Should the Elder suddenly change his mind, there would be an absence of Tryistans in his way. Then, of course, if Johhanicus was in the West wing, it wouldn't matter. Johhanicus easily outranked whatever Doon Esha Elder they had in custody. Celetin would never promote any of his followers within his own tribes to such higher ranks of power that could be used to contest the ruler of the Doon Esha.

Finally, he arrived at the West wing main chamber. Rynsith, the West Wing Watch Commander met Gharius as her Lord entered. Bowing at the waist, the Watch Commander greeted him. "Lord Gharius, thank you for coming. My messenger reported you were on your way."

"Good to see you, Watch Commander," Gharius said and warmly shook the Tryistan's offered hand. "I understand we have a visitor?"

"Yes, my Lord," the Watch Commander began. "The Guardian's intercepted him some 50 miles out on the southern border. He immediately yielded and requested to speak to you, my Lord. They escorted him to our West wing facility. He is currently in isolation."

Gharius looked passed the Tryistan, then said, "This is interesting. We haven't had an Elder of the Doon Esha here in... well, I'm not sure I can remember when. Do you know his name?"

Gharius' Watch Commander lowered her voice, "Yes, my Lord. It is Elder Fiomass."

Gharius looked down at the floor. "I was afraid you'd say that name," he said softly.

"My Lord, it could be a trap, a distraction. Perhaps he is here to cause a diversion. I've doubled the Guardian stations throughout the fortress and requested six more dispatched to the perimeters. He has requested to see you. What shall I answer him?" the Watch Commander asked.

Pausing for a few moments as he looked around the great chamber, Gharius decided to grant the Elder's request. "Tell him I will see him now."

The Watch Commander's voice betrayed her surprise, "Now, my Lord?"

Gharius looked at his Watch Captain, "Yes, right now. Where are you holding him?"

The Watch Commander hesitated, and then stepped back, "This way, my Lord. He is this way."

Gharius silently followed after the Watch Captain who hurriedly escorted him to the holding chambers. The dimly lit passageway was oddly quiet and would have seemed uninhabited except for the two pulsing blue serpentine forms of the Guardians stationed at the last chamber. As Gharius approached, both forms began to pulse more erratically, static bluish lights dancing over their opaque bodies. Gharius reached the end of the corridor and stopped, the Watch Commander positioning herself behind him.

Looking over his shoulder Gharius said, "That will be all, Watch Commander. I will need you to keep these events quiet until you are told otherwise. Do you understand?"

"Yes, my Lord." With that, the Watch Captain excused herself and went off to return to her stations.

Both Guardians began weaving back and forth and emitting soft rumblings. Gharius raised a hand towards them.

"Miraz. Sylista, greetings. It is good to see both of you again. So, you've brought me a visitor?"

Both of the Guardians immediately displayed darting and dancing minute flashes of red intermingled with the blue. They appeared agitated.

Putting down his arm, Gharius smiled. "I see. You have both done well. I will see the prisoner now, and I will see him alone. Please remain at your posts here outside the chamber."

This time, the Guardians displayed fluctuating patterns of red and blue mixing with erratic emanations of purple-green. Gharius knew they were vehemently protesting the idea of leaving him alone in the cell with the Doon Esha and were vividly communicating their alarm. Gharius put his hands up to calm them down.

"I understand, but you need not be concerned. I will be in no danger, I promise." Gharius spoke in his most assuring voice.

The lead Guardian's purple-green display calmed somewhat as it continued to rumble firmly, but with a softer tone.

Gharius stepped closer, putting his hands down, "I know this Elder may be the one responsible for Nezfur's death, and maybe the deaths of the other Guardians. If this is so, I will not let this go unpunished. Rest assured, there will be justice. I am, however, ordering both of you to keep this visit absolutely quiet. I have my reasons."

Both Guardians calmed to only faint and occasional lesions of red under the dominant blue flashes signaling their compliance.

Miraz lowered his serpentine head, and Gharius reached up to put his hand on the Guardian's cheek. "Long have you served me faithful friend. I have never forgotten," Gharius whispered. "We will all make it through this together."

The Guardian rumbled softly and lifted its head up. Without another sound, both of the Guardians turned and took up a position on each side of the door. Gharius stepped up to the door and waved his hand over a small oval pylon. The door quietly slid open. Sitting against the back wall in human form sat Fiomass, First Elder of the Tribes of the Doon Esha.

Gharius stepped inside the solitary confinement cell barely acknowledging the door sliding shut behind him. Fiomass made no effort to stand, but offered what seemed to be a slight, if not involuntary bow. Gharius returned with the slightest nod and said nothing for several moments. The silence appeared to have no effect on the Doon Esha.

Finally, Gharius spoke, "You have taken a great risk in coming here, Elder. Whatever your reason, I assume it is of the utmost importance."

Staring at the floor, Fiomass replied, "That will depend on you, leader of the Tryistan."

Gharius walked over to a bench posted against the opposite side of the cell and gently sat down. He studied the Elder for several moments and then leaned forward.

"I was told that you would speak only to me. Well, Elder, I am here at your request. What is it that I can do for you?"

Keeping his eyes on the floor, Fiomass replied, "I have come to inform you that your servant Ploruvus is dead. He was exposed, and Celetin executed him. I suspect you have a traitor in your midst."

Gharius rubbed his chin, "I am well aware of the demise of one of my own ranks. Ploruvus was a great Tryistan and a good friend. We will mourn his loss, as we do all of our friends whom agents of the Doon Esha have managed to destroy. That would include the Guardian your forces killed recently. Her name was Nezfur. Tell me, why have you risked so much to come here and tell me this yourself?"

Fiomass sat in silence for several moments. Gharius said nothing, allowing the Elder to reflect on his question. The Elder seemed somewhat distracted but not necessarily nervous. The Tryistan sensed that the Doon Esha Elder had something else on his mind and was struggling with deciding to reveal it or not. Gharius waited several more moments and then decided to accelerate the Elder's decision making.

Gharius rose to his feet, "Thank you for the information, Elder. I will make arrangements to have you escorted safely beyond our borders." Gharius stood up and began to move towards the door.

"Wait..." a rasping voice called out.

Gharius stopped and stood in silent patience. Nothing. "Very well then. Goodbye, Elder," the Tryistan said moving toward the door. Gharius raised his hand to the pylon and hesitated. Finally, sighing, he lowered his hand. The door began to slide open.

"There are rumors within our ranks..." Fiomass rasped again.

The sliding door stopped. Gharius waited a moment. "Go ahead, Elder; I am listening."

"This I speak must not go beyond that door," Fiomass rasped yet again.

Nodding to the two curious Guardians peering in, Gharius waved his hand back over the pylon lock and the door closed. Gharius turned around and faced the Elder, "Then your words shall stay where you speak them."

The Doon Esha Elder was wrenching his hands with his eyes still locked on the floor. Gharius gave him enough time to continue. Fiomass finally leaned forward and relented.

"There have been rumors of dissension within our upper ranks," he stopped.

Softly Gharius said, "Please continue, Elder. I've given you my own word. Your words shall stay where they are spoken."

Hesitating a moment, the Elder continued. "A small number of our upper ranks are preparing an attempt to overthrow Celetin. A plan has been both conceived and well received. We... I mean, they, are preparing even now. The plan is a good one but one, I believe, which will ultimately fail. Celetin is simply too powerful for the plan to work. I fear all involved will be destroyed. You must understand this. Celetin has become as if mad. His power cannot be answered by any within our ranks. Your servant Ploruvus learned this through fire."

Gharius stepped back to the bench he'd occupied earlier. It creaked as he sat down hard this time and leaned forward clasping his hands. "So, you have come here with far more than a message to offer to me. You have another plan, and you want my help to carry it through."

Several moments passed. Fiomass spoke next, "You are the only one powerful enough to defeat him. Not even the members of your own council could prevail against him. He cannot be stopped. He is insane; I tell you the truth. Long have I served him, but time and power have made him into something of which I know not."

Gharius tugged at his chin pondering the Elder's charge. "You know, Elder, the only Esha to disappoint my father more than you was Celetin. Although Celetin was one of his most trusted pupils, my father often used to speak most highly of you. Tell me, what have you brought to me to offer as proof? Do you think me some kind of fool?"

Fiomass looked up and met Gharius' gaze. Slowly, Fiomass rose and turned around unbuttoning his tunic. Reaching around to his back, he slowly lifted the shirt up above his neck to reveal the crisscross scars and fresh lesions that now formed in layers on the flesh upon his back. He waited several moments until he was satisfied that Gharius had seen enough, and then lowered his shirt back down, pausing to button it back up again. Turning around without a word, he sat back down on the bench and waited, putting the burden of the conversation back upon Gharius.

Softly, Gharius spoke, "It was only a matter of time. His pride and arrogance have driven him to madness. It was so from the beginning."

Fiomass shifted, "Yes, except now he is planning the end."

"The prophecy then..."

"More than that. He intends to either enslave mankind to serve him or destroy it if they will not. It will be a holocaust not seen since the wars of the great beasts, nor of the ancient wars of men." Fiomass hesitated.

Gharius rubbed his chin thoughtfully, "Yes, I remember them. It was a terrible time. I wonder how the humans would feel if they knew all of the truths of the past. I do not think even we will ever know how many lives were burned and destroyed during those years. Had the world been more populated by men, they might have better recorded such events and given us all away. Like many things, however, mankind holds but a few records of that which is lost forever."

Fiomass answered, "It is better for all of us that they never come to that truth. However, if Celetin has his way, there will be yet one more extinction holocaust, only this time it won't be beasts or reptiles. He has the power to do so. It is not your Order that stands in his way; it is you. He intends to try to kill you, Tryistan."

Gharius looked down and studied the dull stone floor for a minute. Finally looking up at the Elder he said, "I understand. Tell me, how are you going to explain your absence in coming here?"

Fiomass slightly smiled, "He has sent me on a mission of redemption. You could say I was in the neighborhood."

"Alone?"

"Not exactly. But so go the casualties of war."

Remembering the scars on the Elder's back, Gharius asked, "No doubt, you did not fail this time in your task?"

The smile flatly disappeared, "No doubt."

"You could simply disappear. Start over somewhere else. It would be a most grueling task, but in time, with patience and proper action, anything is possible."

Fiomass looked towards the door, "Not possible, Tryistan. I cannot serve you, and I will no longer serve Celetin, at least, not in my heart. For now, I bear it, but I am committed to any plan that stands a chance to succeed with or without your help. We will overthrow Celetin, or we will die trying. It cannot be any other way."

Gharius stared hard into Fiomass' eyes, "There is always, another way." Standing up, Gharius brushed off his pants, "But, I will consider your request, Elder. If there is nothing else, you should be on your way."

Taking his cue, Fiomass rose. Gharius stepped over to the door and again waved his hand across the pylon. The door slid open, and Gharius stepped out motioning to the Guardians waiting outside. Fiomass stepped to the entrance but made no move to exit the cell. Gharius gave his instructions to the Guardians to escort the Doon Esha Elder out of the secret passage of the West wing chambers and to do it quietly. There was to be no word of this that might reach the ears of the Guardian, Neeash or anyone else. At least, not for now.

Satisfied that everything was secure, Gharius turned and nodded to Fiomass who took a step out of the cell. The Guardians took up their escort positions on both sides of the Elder as Gharius handed a dark hood to the Doon Esha. Fiomass hesitated and leaned forward.

"There is one more thing, Tryistan, which I might mention." he whispered.

Gharius moved closer to cover the conversation. He was not afraid of the Doon Esha Elder, and the Elder knew it.

Fiomass continued, "Celetin has made locating your daughter youngling a top priority. My information is that they are very close to finding her." He leaned back.

Through clenched teeth, Gharius asked, "Why is it he seeks my daughter?"

Fiomass glanced at the ground, "Celetin believes that her punishment has been delayed long enough. He will most certainly claim that the time has come to enact the law which requires her death. He is most adamant that the law be fulfilled, and her sentence carried out without any further delay."

Gharius huffed, "The sentence is mine to carry out when and where I so desire. It is not up to Celetin to make those determinations."

Without looking up, Fiomass continued in an audible whisper, "He has the right..."

Gharius growled, "He has nothing! He himself has broken the laws and yet lives, and it would do him well to remember that."

Looking up, Fiomass kept a subordinate tone, "It is as you say, but he still intends to hunt the child down and carry out the sentence."

This time, Gharius stepped up within mere inches of the Elder's face. With a husky whisper forced through gritted teeth tipped with the smell of burning sulfur, the Tryistan replied, "Should your information be true, and any harm comes to her, the power *I* will show your kind in my wrath will make Celetin's power look like a fairy tale."

The Elder's face suddenly paled considerably as the Doon Esha trembled, unable to hide a shudder. Regaining his composure, the Elder whispered again, "There is one more matter of some importance."

The Elder whispered something inaudible to anyone else besides Gharius. Gharius responded with a nod and stepped back as Fiomass shakily placed the hood over his head. Then, the Guardians began to escort the Doon Esha down the corridor to the private passage out of the fortress. Gharius watched after them for a minute until they disappeared around a corner. The Watch Commander stepped up to his side.

"My Lord, forgive me, but are we going to let him walk away? He may be responsible for the death of Neeash's mate. I don't understand."

Turning to his Watch Captain, Gharius calmly answered, "I know that eventually Neeash will hear of this visit. It's alright."

"So, he is free to leave? I don't understand, my Lord," the Watch Captain asked again.

Gharius looked over at the open cell, "What I have done is set a worm to the apple."

"My Lord, I still don't understand."

Gharius suddenly stepped out and began to stroll down the corridor towards the main chamber lobbies calling back over his shoulder, "You will, Watch Captain, you will."

The Watch Captain hurried to catch up and escort the Tryistan leader down the corridor.

Sometime later, the Elder of the Doon Esha soared off alone into the night.

CHAPTER TWENTY

SHADOWS OF DOUBT

Jade sat alone on the cold steps of her apartment building half-heartedly listening to the early morning sounds of vehicles racing up and down the street steering to dodge the occasional potholes. She had spent weeks essentially confined to her apartment and unable to leave without at least two of her brothers in tow. The weeks were starting to feel like months, and Jade was getting tired of all the security precautions she was taking. *More like bored to death...*

There had been little word over the past couple of weeks from anyone connected to the Order, although the world news outlets lately had much to report on events occurring around the globe. Jade and her brother were trying to keep up with it all as best they could, but even Jesse had admitted to the tediousness of trying to keep track of all the world events and the many possible ways they could be interpreted.

She realized that the lack of interesting events happening around her could easily lead to dangerous complacency. She felt like they were sitting in a remote outpost somewhere, "out there," waiting to receive further instructions that might never come. It was becoming maddening as if there was the distinctive feeling of being deliberately left out of something important. This resentment annoyed Jade, putting her in a persistent state of restlessness.

"Hey, sis," Jesse interrupted as he burst through the apartment doors and hurriedly made his way down the steps.

"Here," Jesse handed his sister a fresh cup of brewed black coffee, which she quickly took into her cold hands and began to sip.

Jesse took a seat on the cold concrete beside his sister sipping away at his own cup of hot coffee. The two sat in silence for a few minutes working on their steamy mugs and watching the morning commuters pass back and forth. The rising distant sun to the east began to cut through the light fog that had settled in sometime during the night.

"I have some news," Jesse suddenly whispered staring straight out across the street.

Jade shot her brother a quick glance before taking another sip of coffee. She waited for him to continue.

"I spoke to father late last night while you were all sleeping. I'm afraid it's not all good news, sis."

Jade took a deep breath and braced herself for the worst. "Well? You might as well give it to me straight, Jesse. It's not like we haven't waited long enough."

Jesse pursed his lips for a second before continuing, "Do you remember Ploruvus?"

"Of course, I do. I often sat with him in the libraries. He was very studious, I mean, you know, very intelligent. Why do you ask? What's wrong?"

Jesse put his cup down on the step beside him and clasped his hands. Looking down he took a deep breath.

"Ploruvus is dead."

She turned to her brother, eyes narrowing, "What do you mean he's dead? How can he be dead? Jesse, what the..."

"I don't know," Jesse answered barely avoiding sounding snappy. "I wasn't given any details. All I know was that he was on an assignment and vanished. Father said he has confirmation Ploruvus is dead. That's all I know."

Jade looked away from her brother and ran a hand through her hair trying to wrap her mind around this new development. *How can Ploruvus be dead? Who would do that?*

Jade put her cup down on the step and began to rub her legs in an effort to warm them while Jesse continued to stare straight ahead without any further conversation.

"Is there anything else, I mean, was that it?" Jade demanded.

"No," Jesse answered in barely a whisper.

Jade stopped rubbing her legs and picked up her cup of coffee. The black liquid was beginning to turn cold, but she took a sip anyway, waiting for her brother to say something.

"We lost another Guardian," Jesse continued quietly.

Jade was beginning to get impatient with Jesse's trickle of information as though he was trying to decide what to tell her and what he should quarantine.

"Okay, Jesse. Which one?" Jade's irritation was starting to show.

"It was Nezfur, Neeash's mate," Jesse answered staring down at the steps.

Jade's coffee cup shattered as it hit the concrete step, spraying what little was left of the black brew on her boots and down the steps. *No! Not Nezfur, no...*

Brother and sister sat in silence for a few moments ignoring the broken mug and the sounds of the awakening city. Jesse slid over closer to his sister and wrapped his arm around her as Jade fought and failed to hold back the tears. He knew full well the strong relationship that had existed for a very long time between Jade and the fallen Guardian.

The Guardian Nezfur had been one of two Guardians assigned as Jade's nurse mates shortly after her birth. In the years that followed, as Jade grew, she became strongly attached to Nezfur particularly after Jade had grown old enough to begin to form to the basic images every Tryistan was required to master. The child and the Guardian had formed a strong bond lasting for years and years. Nezfur had been nearly inconsolable when Jade had been forced to leave the Order.

Jade tried to hide her face from the street as she pawed away at the tears staining her face. Jesse felt his own eyes begin to moisture more over the pain he knew Jade was feeling. He had never had a close relationship to any of the Guardians during his formative years. Rather, his relationships to his sister and his brothers had become the bonds he thrived on along with the unbreakable bond with his father. He was secretly thankful he had not yet suffered the loss of someone close to him.

"I'm sorry. I know how close you were to Nezfur," Jesse whispered in Jade's ear.

Jade tried to say something, but nothing came out. She pushed away from Jesse and stood up glancing up and down the street wiping away the cold streaks from her face. Then, turning toward the apartment doors, she faced her brother.

"I'm going to get a bag and pick up my cup," Jade said flatly.

" I don't mind doing it, I mean, I'll take care of it," Jesse answered.

She shook her head and started up the steps.

"Wait," Jesse stood up and started to follow his sister up the steps.

"No, I can get it," Jade answered and took the next step up.

Jesse stepped up again to follow her. Suddenly, Jade turned back to lock eyes with her brother.

"Jesse, what is going on? Why are we stuck here? I'm sick of this, and I don't want to do this anymore. I just..."

Jesse reached out and touched his sister's arm, "Hey, I know you're hurting. I know. Look, if you just want to go inside and need some alone time I understand. I can get the stupid cup."

"It's not about the stupid cup!"

"I know it's not about the cup, sis. We just need to..."

"Need to what? We really don't know what's happening here. Maybe we're just really overreacting, and this is all just a big mistake." Jesse let his sister talk and just listened.

"We don't really know what the prophecy says," Jade continued. "We don't even have most of the pages to it anymore. I mean, c'mon, what do we really know?" She took a deep breath.

"I just feel like we're helpless here, or maybe useless is the better word. Sometimes I wish this was just over and everything could go back to the way it was. I'm tired of looking over my shoulder all the time and wondering who or what might be there. I'm tired of jumping at my own shadow, and I'm sick and tired of feeling like I'm being left in the dark. I'm tired of it, Jesse!"

Jesse nodded, "I know, sis. I admit, some days I have my doubts too. I think it's just natural given that we seem to be a little isolated here." *A little isolated? Yeah, Okay...* she thought.

Jesse shivered in the cold and cupped his hands to blow his warm breath into them. "Listen, why don't we go inside, it's starting to freeze out here. We can get the cup later. Okay? Besides, I didn't get a chance to tell you the rest of the news father gave me. Believe it or not, there is some good news as well."

Looking up the street one last time, Jade regained some of her composure and tried to wrestle something of a smile, "Okay, I could use some good news for a change. But don't misunderstand me, Jesse, whatever happens or is going to happen, I intend to go to father, face-to-face if I have to, and even if I don't have any rights anymore. I want to know what happened to Nezfur. I want to know who is responsible, and I want to know what he's going to do about it."

Jesse put his hands up, "Okay, Jade, I understand perfectly. I'm just not sure how or when you are going to get the chance to do that. If there's any way I can help, you know..."

"I know, I know. Let's go."

"After you, sis," Jesse gestured toward the doors.

Jade slowly nodded and headed up the steps to the apartment doors with Jesse right behind her. A few flurries of snow began to drift lazily across the street as the sun slipped behind a gray curtain of gathering clouds announcing every sign of a coming storm.

Once inside, Jade excused herself and made her way to the bathroom. Closing the door behind her, she reached down, twisting the faucet knob, and waited for the water to turn warm. Once at the right temperature, she ran her cold hands under the faucet in an effort to warm them up.

Jade dried her hands on the hand towel next to the sink and took a moment to look at the face staring back at her from the mirror over the sink. Her eyes traced over her slight Asian features until finally coming to rest on the green eyes staring back at her. It was then that she suddenly realized those same green eyes were holding back the tears she had not allowed herself to shed.

As the first tear streaked warmly down her cheek, she closed her eyes.

Father... Father, I am so sorry. This is all my fault, and there is nothing I can do to help you. What have I done father? Who am I kidding? Of course, I want to come home, I've always wanted to come home. Please father... Whatever it takes, I want to come home...

CHAPTER TWENTY-ONE

THE MEETING

Zelotus, a member of the Tryistan Council of the Twelve sat quietly watching a local D.C. news channel on the small monitor attached to the bright beige wall as he reclined on the soft sheets of the hotel bed. It was now just after 9 p.m., and the Tryistan was beginning to become restless as the evening wore on. Darkness had long since enveloped the capital city, and the normally busy streets had all but emptied themselves of their daily commuters.

Having booked the room several days prior, Zelotus had dutifully checked into the front desk of the hotel by the 6 p.m. deadline. He had taken his digital room key and had quickly found his room. He carried nothing but the small black backpack he usually carried just about everywhere he went. There hadn't been any reason to pack anything more; Zelotus was fully aware he wouldn't be staying the night.

He picked up the TV remote and began flicking through the list of cable channels as the news channel had failed to hold his interest any longer. He mused over how entertainment had changed so much over the years and how it was becoming more and more difficult to find anything worth watching. He continued to lazily flip through the channels looking for anything he thought could capture his interest. Nothing.

Zelotus slowly made his way through the rest of the channels on the cable listings until he found himself staring back at the news station again. Sighing out loud, he settled himself back into the lush pillows and tried to force himself to find something interesting about the story being covered at the moment.

The newscaster was describing a murder scene which had happened earlier in the day involving what appeared to be a case of road rage. Two people had been shot in their SUV by a suspect who later, having been apprehended, claimed the driver of the SUV had cut him off. Both of the victims were pronounced dead at the scene, and the suspect was being held in the local precinct. The names of both victims and the suspect were being withheld pending notifications of next of kin.

In other news it appeared the United Nations was meeting... tomorrow. The TV remote slipped from Zelotus' fingers and landed on the soft rug, bouncing under the bed.

What? Zelotus opened his eyes and suddenly sat up on the bed waiting and listening. *There it is again.* There came a soft knock on the door of his room. Slipping over the side of the bed Zelotus reached down and grabbed the remote to shut off the television. He then quickly adjusted his shirt and hair trying to look like he had not fallen asleep. Satisfied, Zelotus stepped across the room and grabbing the door handle, slowly opened the door.

His visitor did not wait for an invitation as an Elder of the Doon Esha pushed his way past the startled Tryistan. Turning around without so much as a word, the Elder impatiently motioned for Zelotus to close the door. The Tryistan quietly pushed the door until the clicking of the lock engaged the security panel. They were alone.

Haxiss, Elder of the Doon Esha strode over to the single French-style chair and took a seat, not even bothering to take off the oversized trench coat he wore. He set his gaze squarely on Zelotus who took a seat on the edge of the bed.

"Tryistan, I am not accustomed to being made to wait at a door."

"I apologize, Elder Haxiss. I was washing my hands in the bathroom when you knocked."

"Yes, of course," Haxiss quipped. "I am not here for a long happy chat, Tryistan. Do you have the information I'm looking for?"

Zelotus shifted nervously on the bed, "I have it. And you, Elder, do you have what I have asked for in return?"

"I have what you have asked for, Tryistan," the Elder answered abruptly.

Zelotus reached into his pants pocket and produced a small, folded piece of paper. He laid it down on top of a coffee table situated between the bed and the chair occupied by the Elder.

"This is the information you asked for. It contains the current address of Gharius' daughter in Atlanta, Georgia. The information is good. I have personally verified it myself."

"It had better be correct, Tryistan," The Elder growled. "The price you have asked for is, in my own opinion, far too high."

"Is it?" Zelotus raised his eyebrows. "Perhaps the final outcome from the information I am giving you could be worth twice as much."

The Elder let out a snort sounding like something between a growl and a chuckle. "That will all depend, Tryistan. As agreed, this is the down payment you requested. You will receive the rest when we have what we want."

Haxiss reached down into his overcoat and produced an envelope. Reaching out from his chair, the Elder placed the envelope on his side of the coffee table directly across from the small piece of folded paper Zelotus had placed there.

The Elder watched as the Tryistan sat staring at the envelope. Haxiss could feel the Tryistan's greed flowing through the room like the currents of an air conditioner. He waited to see what Zelotus would do, but both of them remained seated.

"Tell me, Elder," Zelotus said suddenly. "Your human form - did you assume it, or did you assimilate it?"

"What is that to you, Tryistan?" The Elder retorted.

"I have always been curious about the assimilations you and your kind have engaged in over time. I would have liked to..."

"Forget it, Tryistan!" The Elder jumped to his feet. "It is not for you to know."

Zelotus fidgeted on the bed, "The Tryistan you wanted captured..."

"Has been taken care of, Tryistan. You have completed your end of the bargain. When the daughter of your Order's leader is in our custody, you will receive your final due."

Zelotus nodded and slowly got to his feet. Looking down at the table Zelotus said, "So, how do you want to do this, Elder?"

Without warning, the Elder stood up and stepped forward. Reaching down, he abruptly snatched up the piece of folded paper and jammed it into the pocket of his overcoat.

"Like that, Tryistan." The Elder forced a smile. "Our business is concluded here."

Zelotus said nothing as the Elder strode back across the room, grabbed the door handle and quietly slipped out of the room. The door came to rest and shut itself with an audible click, resetting the security panel.

The Tryistan slowly reached down and retrieved the envelope from the table. Sitting back down on the bed, he carefully tore off a side of the envelope and retrieved the document inside. His hands trembled as he opened the documents to review the contents. After several moments and barely able to keep a deeply satisfied grin from taking over his face, Zelotus folded the document and pushed it back inside the envelope.

He reached down under the bed and retrieved his backpack, taking the time to stuff the envelope into a side pocket until he changed his mind and pushed it into his pants pocket. Zelotus walked over to the small desk in the corner and opened the center drawer to retrieve the room's security entrance key. The numbers on the desk's digital clock announced it was 10:05 p.m.

Looking around the room one last time, he tossed the security key on the bed and moved to the doorway. Slowly, he opened the door and quickly scanned the hallway and after finding no one present, he stepped out of the room and quietly let the door close behind him. *Time to go...*

<hr>

GLOBALCOMNEWS.NET
World Situation Report #5

"In what appears to be the single largest military joint training exercise in recent memory, Russian and Chinese forces continue to conduct extensive training operations in and around the South China Sea. Just yesterday, these forces were joined by several units deployed from nations of the EU who have recently voted to join the ranks of the evolving UNWC. We understand the vessels from the EU, however, are operating only as observers as the EU members are all still considered interim members of the UNWC.

"The United States, along with representatives from Vietnam and Japan, have voiced grave opposition to the training operations of the UNWC forces, stating the operations will lead to a more unstable environment, which could affect the role of the South China Sea in terms of the billions if not trillions of dollars of commerce traveling through the region.

"American Navy and ballistic forces in the Pacific theater have been put on heightened alert to DEFCON Four as have local forces operating in Japanese territorial waters. It has come to our attention the possibility that the United States is preparing to deploy a carrier battle group just outside of the region, possibly in a show of force aimed at projecting a strong American presence in the Pacific and assuring continuing American commitment to its allies and interests in the region.

"Elsewhere, efforts to investigate the recently sunken Chinese merchant ship and the loss of all hands, including the Chinese Ambassador, Li Sun Chen, have come to a near standstill due to deteriorating local weather conditions.

"We will continue to keep you up to date with the latest information as we receive it. For now, this is Connie Matthews, GlobalComNews. Net, live from our studio in Miami, Florida."

CHAPTER TWENTY-TWO

THE STIRRING

It was late as Gharius strolled through the near empty corridors of the Order's fortress, only occasionally pausing to give a greeting or answer questions from the more curious members of his Order. The Tryistan leader was headed towards the chambers of the north section of the immense compound and was not attempting to draw any special attention to himself as he made his way through the central chamber courtyards.

It had been a long day as reports continued to flow into the Order's command and communications center relaying the events occurring across the globe. As he continued towards the north chambers, Gharius wondered if he had revealed too much information to his son, Jesse. *It doesn't really matter now...*

Gharius knew quite well how badly Jade must have taken the news about the fallen Guardian, Nezfur, and he felt her pain. He realized had he arrived a little sooner that fateful night on the border, he might have been able to halt the conflict before it ever began. An Elder of the Doon Esha and a couple of first ranks would have presented no threat to him whatsoever had he been there when it had started.

Even though Gharius felt some degree of responsibility, he realized where the full responsibility ultimately lay: A Doon Esha had killed a Guardian, and Gharius had been dead serious when he had told the Elder dragon this could not pass away.

He turned his mind back to the events of the day by pondering over the situation evolving in the Pacific between the West and the East. He was well aware that the American military forces were on heightened alert including their ballistic forces, which gave him sufficient cause to be concerned. In Gharius' estimation, there was no need at this point to bring ballistic forces into the picture, and he wondered as to the reasoning behind such actions. If the Americans were bringing their ballistic forces online, then the Russians and most likely the Chinese would almost certainly follow suit. *But the Americans would know that. Why the provocation if only to make a show of force?*

Gharius arrived at the entrance to the north section of the fortress and glanced over his shoulder. Nothing appeared out of order, and the Tryistan leader proceeded into the north section corridors leading to the chamber areas.

What bothered him the most as he mulled the day's events was a strange sense of déjà vu. The Tryistan lead had been watching for a long time as populist leaders emerged on the world scene and many nations were encamped in a fierce spirit of nationalism. Additionally, a number of countries had initiated arms campaigns in the effort to bolster their military defenses while others were hastily building up their military might. This seemed somewhat disproportionate to what was actually happening around the world.

As he continued through the main north corridor it suddenly dawned on him. *I have been here before. I have seen all of this before... War...*

The reality hit Gharius like a ton of bricks, and he stopped in his tracks. Taking a deep breath, he continued down the corridor. He felt calming satisfaction about the decision he had made just 24 hours prior. He believed he was right to order the other 11 members of The Council of Twelve back to their respective continents.

Gharius knew they would all be watching and listening to the events unfolding around the globe as he was. He made a mental note to get an update on where the Australians stood on their invitation to join the UNWC although he was almost sure they would refuse. He also wanted an update on the recent uprisings in the Middle East as well as situational updates concerning a number of nations on the African continent.

Finally arriving at the entrance to the north section main entrance to the chambers, he checked to make sure the small pack he was carrying was still tightly bound. He stepped into the main chamber and was immediately greeted by the formal opaque flashes of a Guardian on watch as it effortlessly dropped to the ground.

"Talzon, old friend, how are you?" Gharius asked.

The Guardian rumbled a cordial reply as the blue flashes throughout her body deepened in intensity.

"I am happy to see you as well, Guardian. Tell me, is all well?"

She rumbled another deep reply.

"Excellent! Is the section Watch Captain available?" Gharius inquired.

The Guardian turned and motioned through the chamber towards the command station set squarely in the middle of the chamber. She let out a soft deep rumble dipping her head slightly.

"No, Talzon, thank you, but that won't be necessary. I can find my own way. Please, resume your duties."

The Guardian lifted slowly off the ground and returned to her post on a ledge just on the inside of the chamber entrance. Gharius gave a quick wave and headed to the command station to let the Watch Captain know he was there.

When Gharius reached the command station, he tapped on a window to get the Watch Captain's attention. The Watch Captain appeared to be startled but Gharius held out his hand and shook his head to let the Captain know everything was alright. Then the Tryistan leader pointed towards the back of the chamber, indicating where he wanted to go. The Watch Captain nodded though looking somewhat puzzled. Gharius gave the Captain a hasty thumbs up and headed towards the far end in back of the main chamber without any further word.

Upon reaching the back of the main chamber, Gharius began to follow the rocky walls north until coming to a small pylon nearly hidden behind the shadow of a small ledge just above him. Gharius turned to look in both directions before waving his hand over the pylon and taking a step backward.

Without a sound, a large opening appeared as the rock slid sideways revealing a dimly lit tunnel on the other side. Taking a firm grip of the small tightly bound pack he carried, Gharius stepped through the doorway to the tunnel making sure to touch the pylon on the inside of the tunnel and sealing the opening behind him.

He made his way through the damp tunnel barely pausing to notice the small dim lamps, which lit his way down the tunnel until he reached the steps. Gharius paused before taking the first step down as he headed deeper and deeper towards the rocky cavern. After several minutes, he finally arrived at the entrance to a large cavern. *The crypts...*

Stepping into the cavern, Gharius made his way through the maze of monuments and tombs until finally catching a glimpse of what he was looking for. *There...*

He turned and strode towards the tomb he was looking for, noticing it had not yet been sealed as per his orders. As he reached the open casket of carefully and elaborately carved stone, he put his hand out and carefully traced the name inscribed on the side of the tomb. This was it.

Gharius placed the small package he had been carrying on the side of the tomb and began to unfasten the buckles used to keep the package tightly wrapped. After several moments, he pulled the leather cover back and reached into the pack to retrieve a small jewelry box. Placing the box down beside the pack, he took a deep breath before reaching down to open the two small panels on the front of the box.

As he gently opened the panels, a soft glow began to immediately emanate from within the box casting both light and shadows all around him. Reaching a hand into the small box, the leader of the Tryistan Order slowly retrieved a candle bearing a small flame bobbing up and down the wick. Gharius looked over the small flame, which looked more like soft luminous light in the shape of a flame than actual fire.

As he held the candle in his left hand, he gently moved his right hand over the flame, which seemed to suddenly reach up as though straining to touch him. Lowering his right hand down to the wick, he pinched two fingers together and pulled his hand away from the candle. The dancing flame continued to bob and dance between his fingers as he gently put the candle down on the side of the tomb.

Putting his left hand over his right, Gharius very gently turned both his palms upward towards himself allowing the flame to slip through his fingers and settle itself in the midst of his cupped hands. He stared at the dancing little flame, which seemed like it wanted to stay right where it was. He suppressed a smile. He could feel his eyes begin to moisten. *Now...*

Gharius bent over the tomb and reached down, gently placing his hands on the body within. Pulling his hands apart and away from each other, the little flame landed on top of the body and continued to bob up and down. He watched and waited a moment before reaching down into the tomb, placing his right hand just above the dancing flame, which began to leap up and down from the body to his hand.

Waiting for the right moment, Gharius suddenly pushed his hand down hard on the body in the tomb while he whispered in his ancient language. He held his hand tightly against the body and continued whispering for several moments until finally pulling back his hand out of the tomb. The little flame had disappeared from on top of the body. He watched and waited for what seemed longer than he had expected.

His waiting was rewarded when he noticed the faint glow of soft light beginning to spread over the body until finally engulfing the entire corpse.

Satisfied, Gharius placed the candle back inside the jewelry box and shut the panel doors. He quickly wrapped the box back in its leather sheath and buckled the leather straps. It was getting very late, but it mattered little to him. He would wait.

He grunted as he took a seat with his back resting against the open tomb. Rubbing his eyes, he tried to guess the time realizing he was too tired to reach in his back pocket to retrieve the timepiece. He closed his eyes and lost himself in the moment when he had last seen Jade at her apartment. How her green eyes had flashed such surprise at the pendant. *If she would just move closer... Closer to the Order... Closer...*

A light. Moving and moving as if all around. Gharius jerked awake, opening his eyes to a light that caused him to squint repeatedly. He rubbed his eyes, struggling to see while turning his head away from the source of light shining down on him.

Grasping the side of the tomb, Gharius pushed himself to his feet and looked down into the stone casket. It was empty. He turned and looked up to see the Guardian radiating brilliant blue and red colors in all her glory. She slowly drifted to the ground directly in front of the Tryistan leader, and without waiting for permission, leaned in and wrapped her head and neck around the neck and shoulders of her master.

He reached around the Guardian as best he could to embrace her, burying his head into her opaque body as it flashed brilliant hues of blue and green. After several moments, Gharius slowly let go of his Guardian and stepped back looking her over head to foot.

"Nezfur, I am so glad to see you! Welcome back my old friend!"

The Guardian rumbled with excitement while her flashing colors intensified.

"Yes, Nezfur, yes. Now, if you will follow me, I believe there are a few of your comrades in arms who would very much like to see you."

He reached out, picked up his leather backpack and turned towards the tunnel entrance. "Are you ready to return, Guardian?" he asked playfully.

The Guardian emitted a series of excited rumbles to which Gharius replied, "Good, I have need of you. Let's go."

Gharius led the way out of the cavern and up the steps with his Guardian following close behind him emitting intermittent rumblings along the way as they headed back up the tunnel. This time, Gharius, leader of the Order of Tryistan, let his tears flow.

CHAPTER TWENTY-THREE

DEFCON 3

DEFCON 3: Increase in military forces readiness above that required for normal readiness. Forces ready to mobilize in 15 minutes.

The enormous and sleek, cigar-shaped, submarine calmly broke through the surface waters only a mere 350 miles due west of the North American continent. Heading North by Northeast, the silent behemoth sailed on its way at roughly 15 knots for its cruising speed. The deep, dark night sky provided extremely limited visibility to the naked eye, which mattered little because there were no naked eyes to perceive the cold darkness outside of the ship.

Invisible pulses of encrypted information emanated from the submarine's small mast bearing the ship's electronic transmission systems. Messages were being sent and received as the massive vessel maintained its course towards its selected coordinates. The round lids lining the dorsal cavity were tightly sealed so as not to allow any moisture to seep into the large missile silos, each containing a single medium-range missile and tipped with multiple nuclear warheads.

In American Navy slang, the enormous ship would be designated a "boomer." However, this particular ship was not registered to the U.S. Navy. A fading single red star graced the conning tower just below the large sail planes that helped steer the vessel underwater.

The submarine would travel another two miles before slipping back into the deep ocean depths, continuing onto eventually reach its final destination.

"Sir?" There was a knock at the door.

It was early morning, and President John D. Wesley had barely touched his coffee having just arrived at the Oval Office 15 minutes earlier. He had gotten little sleep over the night and had hoped for some time alone in his office before attending his morning scheduled intelligence briefing, which wasn't for another hour.

The knock came again, "Sir?"

"Yes, come in," the President barked.

The door opened slowly revealing the face of the President' secretary.

"I'm sorry, sir, I hate to bother you this early, but you have Admiral Westgate waiting to speak to you on line 2. He says it's urgent."

President Wesley glanced over at his encrypted phone and realized he hadn't even noticed the console was blinking. *It takes coffee to see that...*

"Alright, I'll take it, um, in here," President Wesley trailed off. He waited for his secretary to shut the door. At the sound of the door lock, President Wesley picked up the handset and touched the number 2 button.

"Admiral Westgate, how are you?"

"Good, Mr. President. Listen, I hate to bother you so early, but I believe we may have a problem, sir."

"Well, admiral, if one of the members of my Joint Chiefs of Staff thinks we have a problem, then we may well have a problem. What's up, Jack?"

"We've had another contact at 03 35 hours bearing due west of the California coast at about 350 miles. She looks like she may be headed northeast putting her closer to our shores than the other two previous contacts."

"Are you sure it's not the same contact, Jack?"

"No, sir. The other contacts and their positions plus their projected course estimates don't line up with this new contact. I make out at least three distinct contacts nearing our Pacific international waters over the last 24 hours."

"I understand. Have you heard any further word from NORAD?"

"No, sir, not for the last eight hours."

"Alright, Jack. I want you to get them on the line and see if they have anything else to add to this incident and any analysis they may have. And don't worry about submitting a report through the usual channels, it takes too long."

"Yes, Mr. President, I'll get in contact with NORAD immediately."

"Alright, thanks, Jack. I'll be talking to you later."

"Yes, Mr. President. Goodbye, sir."

President Wesley listened as the audio click informed him the conversation was over. Slowly setting the handset back into its cradle, he leaned over and took the still warm cup of coffee into his hands. Taking small sips, he sat back in his chair and mused over the events of the last 24 hours. There were a few things which didn't make any sense, including the new contacts in the Pacific.

Taking a deep breath, Wesley set his coffee down and grabbed the small stack of newspapers, which had been deposited on the corner of his desk earlier that morning. Taking the top paper, he looked over the front-page headlines and scanned the side index for any articles of interest. He found none and tossed the paper to the side while reaching for the next paper.

A knock sounded at the door. "Sir?"

President Wesley dropped the newspaper on the desk, "Yes, what is it?"

His secretary opened the door and slid into the office closing the door behind her.

"Mr. President, Mr. Richardson is here to see you."

"Daniel?" The President's brow rose slightly. "I don't see his appointment on my calendar."

"He's not on your calendar, Sir," his secretary whispered. "But he sure seems to think he needs to speak with you immediately. I don't think he's in any mood to be turned away."

The President sat back in his chair and took up his coffee cup, "Okay. Send him in."

"Yes, Mr. President." The secretary slid back out of the door. He could hear her speaking to Senior Advisor Daniel Richardson who apparently believed he could barge into the office of the President of the United States without an appointment.

Richardson thanked the secretary and made his way past her as she closed the door behind her. The senior advisor stepped into the Oval Office looking a little disheveled and gave the impression he hadn't slept much lately either.

"Mr. President, thank you so much for seeing me. I know I don't have an appointment, sir, but if you would just give me..."

"Daniel! Sit down. Can my secretary get you some coffee?"

"Oh, uh, no thank you, sir," Daniel replied, sounding out of breath.

The President sat back in his chair audibly sipping his coffee. "What can I do for you?"

Richardson clawed at his small leather briefcase until he retrieved a folder which he opened on his lap, nearly spilling the contents onto the floor. He pulled two black and white photographs out of the folder and handed them to the President.

"What's this?" he asked. He grabbed the photographs and began to look them over.

"It's a Chinese aircraft carrier, Mr. President."

"I can see it's a carrier, Daniel. Why am I looking at it?"

Richardson took a deep breath. "Mr. President, that photograph was taken just over 24 hours ago."

"We know the Chinese and the Russians are conducting large-scale training exercises in the South China Sea, and we have lodged out complaints at the U.N. So, what's the big deal?"

"Mr. President, that carrier is no longer in the South China Sea."

"Okay, Daniel, I give up, where is it?" The President was already tired of playing the guessing game.

"Mr. President, if you will look at the second photograph…"

Wesley dropped the first photograph down on his desk and began to study the second photograph. *I'm not in intelligence, Daniel…*

"Okay. I see a carrier and several ships cruising alongside it. What am I looking at?"

"Mr. President, you are looking at what our intelligence is claiming to be the possibility of a newly formed, UNWC backed, joint carrier battle group in the Pacific with a projected course estimated to reach within 500 miles of our western shores in two days."

The President continued to study the second photograph and realized he was looking at warships from both Chinese and Russian navies. The ships certainly did appear to be arranged in an engaged military deployment formation. Then he noticed something else.

"Have you had these photographs analyzed? Do we know what ship types we're dealing with here?"

"Yes, Mr. President. The two large ships flanking the Chinese carrier are Russian cruisers, the big ones, the ones capable of launching nuclear missiles. Two of the smaller vessels are Chinese destroyers, the newer class destroyers, and you can probably make out the two supply ships at the rear of the formation."

"I have my intelligence brief in about 30 minutes. This could have waited." The President dropped the second photograph on his desk.

Richardson shifted in his chair as he hastily collected the photographs and stuffed the papers back into the folder. He hurriedly placed the folder back into the briefcase.

"I'm sorry, Mr. President, I didn't think this could wait. What I really wanted to do, sir, is to see that you had this information before your morning meeting with your intelligence staff."

The President continued to sip his coffee. "Oh? Is there any particular reason you don't trust my intelligence meetings, Daniel?"

"Vice President Monaham will be present this morning as well."

A hint of surprise crossed the President's face. "And how is it you know the VP will be there this morning? I didn't even know he would be there."

Richardson allowed himself the faintest grin, "I know, sir, because that's what you pay me for. The Vice President will be at the meeting this morning."

"And you have a problem with that, Daniel?" The President sounded irritated.

Richardson cleared his throat before continuing, sensing he was walking on thinner ice than he was comfortable with.

"Mr. President, the Vice President still believes diplomacy is the only real option we have in settling our differences with the UNWC. I have shown you some of this new intelligence, and your intelligence staff meeting will show you the same thing, at least I would hope so. I also know that we have had two submarine contacts in the Pacific not too far from our west coast and..."

"Make that three contacts, Daniel," President Wesley added.

"Three contacts, yes, sir..." Richardson stopped.

"I have my own intelligence sources too. What are you getting at?"

Richardson inhaled and continued as he shifted again in his chair. "Mr. President, as your senior advisor I am advising a higher level of alert for our forces. I mean, just as a precaution, sir. We have, three you said, submarine contacts in the Pacific, which are most likely armed with nuclear missiles. We have what looks to be a carrier strike group headed our way with two Russian heavy cruisers most certainly carrying nuclear weapons as well."

The President put down his coffee cup. His intelligence meeting would commence in about 14 minutes.

"We know all of this. What's your point?"

Richardson continued. "Mr. President, you have all of these events occurring while the bulk of the Chinese and Russian forces have assembled for large scale training exercises in, and now around, the South China Sea."

"Yes, I understand that. I still don't see your point."

Daniel Richardson rubbed his eyes for a moment before delivering the last of his analysis.

"Mr. President, do you realize that right now, at this moment, over 50 percent of Chinese naval forces and assets, and over 60 percent of Russian naval forces are deployed in the Pacific Ocean? Sir, that is a very high number of potentially hostile resources at large. sir, I remind you we have no sizable assets deployed at this time, and we are sitting at DEFCON Two.

I believe, sir, it is time to move beyond intelligence gathering and throwing up a mere posture of alertness. The UNWC knows we've gone to a heightened state of alert including our ballistic forces, but it's only for show. It has no teeth, and we've got adversaries who are currently deployed with assets easily over 50 percent of their available resources."

There. There it was... everything on the table. Richardson sat back in his chair and waited for the President's response.

"And you think there is a clear and present danger, Daniel?" the President shifted.

"Mr. President, if the forces of the UNWC under the guise of training exercises suddenly decided to hit us today, it would make Pearl Harbor look like a trip to Disneyland. May I add, Mr. President, that three of our four operational carriers on the West Coast are docked in port, and the other carrier is deployed too far east of the South China Sea to effectively intervene if the UNWC were to hit us."

The President sat up, "How do we know the Chinese carrier force we're talking about isn't just part of the training exercises?"

"Mr. President, the UNWC informed us in advance of the variables, timetables, and latitudes of their training exercises. It's standard procedure. However, this new Chinese carrier battle group is not part of the scenario they gave us."

President Wesley looked over at the wall clock and realized he had five minutes to make it to the intelligence meeting. Rubbing his chin, the President gently placed his coffee cup back down on his desk. It was time to go.

Rising from his chair, he extended his right hand, "Thank you, Daniel, you have given me something to consider. I don't want to be late for my meeting."

Daniel Richardson hurriedly stood up and shook the President's hand, "I understand, Mr. President. I can show myself out."

Richardson reached down and retrieved his briefcase and quickly crossed the room to the door. A moment later, he was gone.

President Wesley grabbed his suit coat from the back of his chair and slipped it on as he crossed the room to the door of the Oval Office. It was time for his meeting. *I'm going to have some questions...*

The meeting lasted over an hour longer than it had been scheduled for. Vice President Monaham had been present as well, and in total, the meeting had lasted just over two hours. When the meeting came to a close, the President and the Vice President retired quietly to the Oval Office. An hour later, an obviously disturbed Vice President departed the White House, leaving the President alone in the Oval Office.

Two hours later, the American armed forces received the order to set DEFCON Three.

Daniel Richardson hurriedly made his way down the street towards the bus station, annoyed at the drizzle that had begun to fall over the city. It was cold here, not like the tropical warm base of the Doon Eshas' fortress nestled in the Galapagos region. He missed it a great deal and wondered how much longer before his assignment would be over. Mezlash, an Elder of the Doon Esha was ready to go home.

Maybe it was really because the Elder could hardly tolerate the smell of the human he was assimilating for much longer. It was no wonder anymore why Celetin detested the humans so much. The stench of them was truly loathsome.

<hr>

GLOBALCOMNEWS.NET
World Situation Report #6

"... and we have just learned American military forces have gone to DEFCON Three alert. It is currently unclear as to what exactly is transpiring just beyond the South China Sea, but we do know that a number of naval vessels, which had been taking part in the UNWC backed training exercises in the South China Sea, have broken away and have formed what appears to be a deployed formation. The formation is believed to be heading due east by southeast.

"We have also learned from anonymous sources that the UNWC ships may be continuing their training exercises in convoy deployment training, although at this time, we are unable to confirm this information.

"U.S. forces have visibly stepped up their readiness presence as we speak, and we are beginning to receive some word concerning the redeployment of Pacific naval forces both here and overseas, possibly as a response to these new developments occurring as of yet in international waters. We have reached out to our sources within the Pentagon but are unable to confirm the rumors concerning the activation of ballistic missile sites located throughout the northwestern United States.

"We have further information. Negotiations between the West and the UNWC have all but broken down at the U.N. level. In addition, the Chinese and Russian governments have recalled their consulate staffs in Washington, D.C. We have also just learned the U.S. has just issued an order to recall U.S. ambassadors and staff personnel as well. It is unconfirmed at this point whether these new developments have any bearing on the events unfolding in the Pacific.

"This is Mya Truddlow, GlobalComNews.Net, live from our studio in Washington, D.C."

CHAPTER TWENTY-FOUR

SCENT OF WAR

"Things are going according to plan," Celetin softly hissed, small curls of dark smoke rising from his nostrils.

"Yes, my Lord," Fiomass answered.

Both of the Doon Esha, in their smaller dragon forms, looked over the large global map laid across the large center round table set in the middle of the information chamber. Celetin had taken the pains to create a sort of command center nestled deep in the Tribe's Galapagos fortress. Small desks equipped with computer monitors were placed throughout the chamber, the center table containing the maps used for tracking important information the fortress received.

An unusual mix of smaller creatures sat manning the small desks, eyes glued to their monitors, waiting to relay any information to Celetin they believed would be relevant to the ongoing operations. The chamber was sparsely lit with the overhanging chandelier placed just above the center round table acting as the strongest source of light in the room.

"The UNWC convoy has pulled into formation and is continuing to travel on course towards the North American coast," Fiomass added.

"Excellent, Elder Fiomass. Remember, it is crucial when the convoy reaches 500 miles from the American course to contact our agents and have them move to get those ships to engage in missile training exercises."

"Yes, my Lord," Fiomass flatly replied.

"And, Elder, continue to move the UNWC submarines to position themselves closer to the American international water boundaries. Also continue to ensure they are only to surface for no longer than 10 minutes at a time and only in the dark. When was the last time we were able to move the Russians into sending aircraft into American airspace over the Alaska regions?"

Fiomass thumbed through a log sitting on the edge of the table. "It's been over two weeks since their last incursion over the region, my Lord."

Celetin looked hard at the map. Timing was going to be absolutely critical if the plan was going to work. It had taken years of planning and placing the right resources in precisely the right places to come to this point. Everything was, in fact, working as planned. *Now, if we can just get them to start shooting at each other...*

Suddenly, one of the small creatures from a small desk just across the room called out, relaying its information to Celetin and Fiomass. Fiomass took a marker from his pocket and marked the new location of the UNWC convoy headed towards North America. *850 miles...*

Fiomass continued to stare down at the map in silence. Slowly but steadily, the marks on the map were beginning to match the marks on the planning map Celetin had been working on for so long. It was almost unnerving to Fiomass how accurate the maps were beginning to align with each other in how they were marked out by the numerous military units of various nations, where they were and where they would be going based on Celetin's projections.

In fact, the maps were so well articulated Fiomass' questions were answered before he could ask them. *Pity the prophecies are not so clear...*

"Elder Fiomass," Celetin chimed. "Have our agents move to initiate a Russian air force training excursion near the American air space towards the Alaska region tonight. Be sure they do not actually cross into the American air space; I just want them as close as possible. Send a bomber, one of the ones capable of carrying nuclear weapons and two fighters. See to it, Elder."

"Yes, my Lord," Fiomass dutifully answered.

"And one more thing." Celetin pulled a sealed envelope from under the map and pushed it towards Fiomass who reached out and retrieved the envelope from the table.

"Your next set of orders, Elder Fiomass. I trust, for your sake, you do not fail," Celetin's tone was both dangerous and direct.

"I will not fail you, my Lord," Fiomass answered carefully.

Without another word, the Elder pulled away from the center table, turned, and headed out of the chamber towards the communications towers. Fiomass could taste the temptation to order his highly placed Esha agents in the Russian military to move to have the aircraft flagrantly violate the American air space. He realized, however, that Celetin would have certainly planned for such a blunder and swallowed the temptation.

As much as the Elder had grown to resent the leader of the Tribes, there was no arguing that Celetin was a brilliant planner if nothing else. The fact that Celetin would have backup plans for the many, many possible blunders was certain. Besides, after taking so many years to formulate the plan, it made sense to have contingency plans and resources in place to ensure the operation's success. Fiomass may not have been all that certain about the contingency plans, but he was quite certain about the trove of resources they had in put in place.

It had taken years of painful planning and patience to get the Esha's agents into the right places of influence. The Americas and its allies had proven rather easy as far as the precise placement of the Esha's agents. The only real problem had been that American leadership changed every few years, requiring agents to be reshuffled, new agents put in or pulled out altogether to try again. Assimilation had solved the problem rather well when it had become necessary according to Celetin.

The Russians had been somewhat less cooperative, but the Chinese had proven to be very difficult to infiltrate. As a result, Celetin's time-tables had suffered one setback after another. Now, however, all of the planning and patience appeared to be paying off.

Elder Fiomass reached the fortress' main courtyard chamber, ignoring the somewhat less than chaotic activities all around him. He brushed aside several small Eshas creatures that collided with him as he made his way through the courtyard chamber towards the elevator shaft to the communications towers. *I hate beggars...*

Once inside the shaft, Fiomass activated the door pylon and punched a number on the console. In moments, he could feel the elevator speeding him to the upper tower centers where he would make his communications with his Russian Esha agents.

As the elevator proceeded, Elder Fiomass realized he was still clutching the envelope Celetin had earlier passed over to him. He leaned back against the elevator's wall and slowly opened the edge of the envelope, carefully retrieving the single folded piece of paper. Fiomass opened the paper and began to read the contents in their entirety.

After he finished reading, he folded the piece of paper and reinserted it back into the envelope, shoving it into the small case hanging from his belt. *So, this is it…*

As the elevator came to a full stop Fiomass tapped his foot impatiently waiting for the doors to open. Stepping into the corridor, the Elder looked over to the left passageway and seeing no one, he turned and strode into the right passageway towards the communications chamber.

It only took Fiomass a minute to reach the tower's communications center chamber. He quickly touched the door pylon and waited as the smooth rock panel slid to the side. Stepping into the well-lit chamber, the Elder was greeted by a busy collection of creatures and machines all working to keep the multiple lines of communications open and operating. Sophisticated transmission equipment and computer servers dotted the four lofts sitting high and nestled in all four corners of the chamber. Desks and computers, complete with monitors, dotted the chamber floor while two enormous monitors appeared to be floating, precisely centered against the back wall of the chamber.

Fiomass looked around the mass of living networks searching for the Elder in charge. It didn't take long to locate the communications Elder on duty as Fiomass heard a growling from his right near the south walls. It was definitely Deforax in his rustic dragon form. Fiomass smiled slyly; he knew how much Elder Deforax hated communications duty. The rustic dragon's specialties leaned far more towards operations planning and initiation, which put him in the perfect place to help Fiomass plan and initiate the orders Celetin had given him.

Fiomass began making his way through the busy aisles until he came up behind the communications Elder, who suddenly turned to greet his visitor.

"Elder Fiomass, welcome. Tell me, what brings *you* to this hall of chaos?"

Fiomass noted the tension in Deforax's voice. *He really hates this...*

"Your Lord, Celetin, has sent me to bring a message that must be sent," Fiomass fought the urge to smile.

"Ah now, did he indeed? Well, come this way and let's get this message sent by all means," Deforax replied gruffly as he began to lead Fiomass to the chamber center's central office. As Fiomass followed, he shrugged as he glanced around the bustling chamber. He had never really minded communications duty. It kept him busy, and it was to his advantage to be the first to get the most important communications before anyone else could see them. It also kept him far away from Celetin. The White Dragon never came up to the towers.

Upon reaching the central office, Deforax reached out and touched a pylon, causing the door to open immediately. Both Elders stepped inside the office hardly noticing the door sliding shut behind them without a sound. Strolling over to his large desk, Deforax took a seat in the large but elaborate couch and set his eyes on Fiomass.

Fiomass stepped up to the desk, "I need to send a message to our assets in the Western Russian Air Force. There is to be a sortie tonight of one bomber, nuclear-weapon capable, and two escort fighter aircraft.

They are to come as close to the American air space as they can without actually crossing over into their air space."

Deforax leaned back on the couch, "So, the usual harassment I see. Do you have a specific timeframe?"

Fiomass thought for a moment. "Make it about 2 a.m. Western time."

"Very well. It will take a few minutes to identify our appropriate agents. There shouldn't be any problems."

Fiomass appeared to fidget a bit. He had one other message to send, and it was probably not going to go well for his request.

Deforax appeared to frown and leaned his head forward, "Is there something else I can do for you, Elder?"

Taking a labored breath, Fiomass lowered his voice, "I need to get a separate message out to both Haxiss and the Tryistan, Zelotus."

A well-manicured set of claws suddenly slapped the desk as Deforax rose to his legs looking more than a little irritated. Fiomass stood up straight, staring down the communications Elder who suddenly appeared very agitated.

"Zelotus! Why is he even still alive? That little traitor should have been roasted a long time ago. I've got a good mind to go to Celetin myself..."

Fiomass pulled the envelope from his belt case and handed it to the communications Elder. Deforax snatched the envelope out of Fiomass' hand, tore it open, and retrieved the slip of paper. Dropping the torn envelope to the floor, he opened the paper and began to read.

Deforax slammed the letter on the desk in frustration. If there was one thing Deforax hated, it was a Tryistan traitor.

Fiomass stood quietly waiting for the other Elder to finish fuming. "It will take me some time to set this operation up, Elder Fiomass."

"I'll need to leave within 48 hours, Elder Deforax. The timing of the meeting and the actions we are to take will be critical, as you can imagine."

Deforax looked down at the letter he had nearly crumpled on his desk, "I do not envy you, Elder Fiomass. I wouldn't want to do it, no thank you. And I can't think of anyone else who would care to do it either."

Fiomass forced a curt smile, "I guess I'm the lucky one."

Deforax smiled back through tightly clenched jaws, "You were always the favorite."

With that, Fiomass snatched the letter up from the desk, gave a slight bow and turned to the door. He would coordinate his mission with Deforax a little later when the communications Elder had received message confirmations of acknowledgment from both Haxiss and Zelotus. Forty-eight hours was not going to be a lot of time to get his mission off the ground, but it was crucial that he did.

Fiomass exited the central office and headed back to the elevator shaft. There was no turning back now. *You knew this was coming...*

GLOBALCOMNEWS.NET
World Situation Report #7

"... again, three aircraft of the Russian Air Force approached within five miles of American airspace over the Alaskan region late last night. Two American F-22 Raptors were scrambled to intercept however, it appears the Russian aircraft broke off the engagement just short of violating American airspace. This has been the third such occurrence over the Alaskan region in the last three weeks.

"In other news, the UNWC Pacific convoy has come to a full stop just 500 miles from the U.S. Western coastline and has engaged in what appears to be missile training drills. The U.S. has lodged a series of dire complaints to the U.N. Security Council in an attempt to pressure the UNWC to cease all activity in the Pacific theater. This comes days after it has been recently revealed by our sources that a number of as yet unidentified submarine sightings have occurred near U.S. international waters. The situation continues to furiously escalate as U.S. forces continue to significantly heighten their activities in and around the Pacific region.

"In addition to this current development, we are just learning that a number of other naval vessels which had participated in the UNWC backed drills in the South China Sea have left the immediate region and are reportedly sailing East further into the North Pacific. We do not as yet know the course of the vessels or their intended destinations.

"In other news ..."

CHAPTER TWENTY-FIVE

THE TRYISTAN ORDER

It was just after midnight as Gharius sat tensely atop the watch office central pedestal set in the east chambers of the Order's fortress. Large monitors evenly spaced up and across the east wall continuously displayed their images of the reported events unfolding around the world. On the north wall sat a series of smaller displays which were being constantly monitored by on-duty Tryistans waiting for and reporting any piece of news or information they had been directed to detect. The south and west walls had been reserved for digital mapping displays which showed bright images of both moving and stationary icons radiating in a myriad of corresponding colors across their screens.

Several rows of desks, carefully arranged in the middle of the large chamber, were situated in the middle of the chamber allowing for a complete 360-degree walk-around of the outer perimeter of the chamber from one wall to another. All in all, to an outsider, the command watch chamber would have appeared overly organized and clean.

A prominent LED icon in the upper corner of the south wall's single enormous mapping display monitor continued to pulse on and off with an orange glow signaling its alert level based on the Order's calculations of the sum total of world events. Orange was the last alert level before red. Red was the last step to almost immanent war. *World war. Not again...*

Gharius listened intently to the whispers and murmurings of his staff as they quickly and quietly crisscrossed the chamber, sometimes leaving their desks to confer with each other and then returning back to their stations. Occasionally a call would ring out for the Watch Captain who would hurriedly make her way to the source of the call and take a report.

The Watch Captain and her staff were instructed to act as if Gharius was absent. The Tryistan leader did not wish to impose or interrupt the operations of his staff. He merely wanted to be present in case any issues of significant importance appeared. It was not that Gharius did not fully trust his staff, rather, he enjoyed watching them work in unison and never tired of observing the cooperation they displayed as they worked.

The watch command chamber was well organized into regional zones, which were designed to cover the planet. Information obtained from each zone was transferred into data that was then fed into the multi-server mainframe updating the massive databases.

Once the databases were updated, the information shown on the corresponding monitors changed to display the most current information as well as the digital mapping displays. Satellite uplinks ensured most of the information on the main digital mapping displays relayed information in real time.

As Gharius studied the south wall's main mapping display monitor, he sensed the chamber door had opened and realized Petrawnus was making his way towards the center command pedestal where Gharius sat watching the operations.

Petrawnus stole up beside the Tryistan leader and sat down on the adjoining chair as quietly as he could.

"Any further news, my Lord?" Petrawnus whispered.

"No, old friend, nothing yet. Having trouble sleeping?" Gharius whispered back.

Petrawnus shifted in his chair, "Actually yes, my Lord. As long as the alert warning beacon continues to remain in the orange, I always have trouble sleeping."

Gharius could relate to Petrawnus' concern. The Tryistan leader would have to admit the orange beacon could cause certain disturbances to well established sleep patterns, which were usually better supported by the welcome and steady glow of a green beacon. Tonight, however, there would be no green icon to indicate general worldwide stability.

"May I ask, have you heard from Jade or her brothers?" Petrawnus asked.

"I received word from Jesse earlier today. Apparently, both Jesse and Jade were to attend their first evening class at a local academy."

"Academy..." Petrawnus trailed off. "Would you happen to know what class they have enrolled in, my Lord?"

"Foreign relations," Gharius chuckled. "They thought, and I approve, that perhaps if we are to join the humans one day, it might be a good idea to begin to get more of our Order educated in their diverse cultures."

Petrawnus nodded. "That would seem prudent, my Lord. Tell me, do you think it is wise for them to be getting out and around at this very time?"

Gharius continued to stare at the main monitor, "I don't believe there should be a problem. Jesse and his two brothers are very capable, and I trust them completely. I am confident that should a real problem arise, we will know about it and respond accordingly."

Both Tryistans sat in silence for several minutes studying the various displays and listening to the calls for the Watch Captain. The tension in the room was palpable as the display screens continued to feed information into the chamber for analysis and investigations. Gharius was particularly interested in the recent developments in the South China Sea with the departure of UNWC forces from the region, which had now begun to spread throughout the western Pacific.

Petrawnus was keeping his own eyes on the UNWC convoy, which was now sitting stationary approximately 500 miles west of the American coastline. Both Tryistans knew about the submarine sightings and that it had been some 36 hours since the last sighting had been reported. The Russian Air Force's incursion near Alaskan airspace the night before wasn't helping to diffuse the tensions Gharius knew were running deep between the forces of the West and the East. *It feels like a dry tinderbox just waiting for a...*

Nearly a half an hour had passed with no remarkable information received yet. The Watch Commander supplied both Gharius and Petrawnus with fresh coffee. Both Elders watched intently as the Tryistan's duty staff continued to perform their assignments. Another half an hour passed before Petrawnus made his way to where Gharius sat watching the map displays.

"I don't like it, my Lord. This is not a good picture at all," Petrawnus muttered.

"I agree," Gharius whispered back sitting up straight. "Something is definitely wrong here. What is the most troubling..."

Suddenly, somewhere from above in the ceiling, the disturbing cries of a warning claxon began to fill the chamber. Tryistan staff all hurriedly returned to their desks and began to dig into their keypads.

"Watch Captain, Watch Captain, quick please!" One of the duty staff cried out from over near the east wall.

The Watch Captain hurried over to the desk of her staff caller and began to take information before dropping her clipboard and shooting a glance over to where Gharius and Petrawnus were sitting.

Gharius didn't wait for a response and was on his feet taking long strides down the pedestal steps towards the Watch Captain with Petrawnus close behind.

The Watch Captain nodded sharply to her staff caller who immediately began to input information into a computer terminal. Reaching the desk, Gharius didn't have to wait for an update.

"My Lord," the Watch Captain stammered, "there has been a single missile launch from one of the ships with the UNWC convoy just 500 miles from the American West coast."

"Those forces were already engaged in missile training exercises earlier today," Petrawnus injected.

Gharius looked sharply at his Watch Captain. "Can we determine the course of the missile from here?"

The Watch Captain turned to her staffer at the terminal and nodded. "Do it."

The Tryistan staffer's fingers flew over the keyboard for a few moments. A screen display appeared on the terminal's monitor, which was transferred immediately to the chamber's main screen.

Both Gharius and Petrawnus turned and waited until finally a missile track indicated by a blinking red dot was followed by a red line that appeared on the main mapping display. *No...*

The room grew eerily silent and nearly absolutely still as the faces of everyone in the chamber turned to the south wall's main mapping monitor. Multiple blue circles abruptly appeared, each one surrounding a number of projected possible targets on the American West coast ranging from military bases to major cities.

Gharius and Petrawnus stood side by side mesmerized by the blinking red dot on the main screen. As Gharius watched, he also listened carefully, waiting for any of the communications stations to detect anything in connection with the in-flight bound missile. Nothing. Nothing but the small background buzzing of static. *C'mon...*

The missile was now less than 150 miles due west of the coastline with multiple targets still circled in blue displayed on the monitor. *There...*

As the incoming missile closed to less than 199 miles, a blinking green dot suddenly appeared on the main screen as the whole chamber watched, many holding their breath. Not a word was spoken while the entire watch duty staff watched the blinking green dot streak westward across the main display on what looked to be an intercept course with the ominous blinking red dot tracing the UNWC's incoming missile's trajectory.

It was over in seconds. Both blinking dots suddenly disappeared from the main screen completely.

"Get me updates!" Gharius shouted.

The room exploded into a fury of action as Tryistan staff hastily manned their stations, slipped on their earphones and began punching buttons on their keypads. The communications sections manned by the duty staff became the new center of attention.

Five, then 10, then 15 minutes passed as the Tryistan staff reached out to every channel and frequency they could access. Twenty minutes passed before the first reports of the missile incident began to circulate among the major news agencies and radio stations. There was a great deal of conflicting information passing back and forth throughout the media platforms, all vying to be the first to present the world with the most updated details of the incident.

As Petrawnus assisted the Watch Captain taking reports and coordinating information updates, Gharius set himself beside the nearest desk where one of his duty staff was monitoring a report coming from a West coast news stations. From what he could tell, there was far more information confusion than confirmation, which was to be expected given the circumstances. After all, it was also pretty late in the night.

"Watch Captain, could you assist, please?" a voice called from behind Gharius in the chamber's communications sections. Gharius continued to watch and listen to the station where he had set himself. He didn't notice the Watch Captain motion to Petrawnus who hurriedly made his way to the communications section.

Gharius continued to stare at the staffer's screen until he noticed what appeared to be a small commotion behind him. Turning, Gharius fixed his gaze on what appeared to be a tense discussion between his Watch Captain, Petrawnus and what appeared to be a very frustrated Tryistan staffer manning her station.

The Tryistan leader immediately kicked away from the desk and strode through the communications station to the source of the commotion.

"Is there a problem?" Gharius demanded. The conversation went silent.

"I don't believe so, my Lord," Petrawnus started. "We may be experiencing a technical difficulty with this station."

"Technical difficulty? What kind of a technical difficulty," Gharius stared down at his perplexed Tryistan staffer.

The Watch Captain stepped forward. "My Lord, we can get a technician to look at this station immediately."

Gharius raised his hand bringing silence again.

"Besina, you are my staff operator. I'd like to hear what you have to say."

The Tryistan slowly rose from her seat, her eyes searching the ground. "M-my Lord, I don't think it's a technical problem, if I may, I believe it's a reception problem."

Gharius ran a hand over his beard. "What do you mean a reception problem, Besina?"

Petrawnus interrupted, "My Lord, it would seem necessary that we need a proper technician to diagnose..."

"Petrawnus, please. Let my staffer speak. Besina?"

Besina looked over at her monitor. "My Lord, my station is tasked with monitoring all communication both to and from the UNWC convoy that just fired that missile. I just received an encrypted burst transmission two minutes ago, but I've lost the signal again."

"What do you mean you lost the signal again?" Gharius asked.

"My Lord, the signals went dead almost immediately after the missile was fired. I continued to monitor the frequencies but there was nothing. Then, two minutes ago, I received a burst transmission lasting only a couple of seconds, and then the signal went dead again."

Looking around the communications section, Gharius noticed every other staffer was monitoring their stations, all of which appeared to be active. It was indeed odd this particular communications station had gone silent.

"Besina, do you have any thoughts as to why your station has gone dead?"

She looked down at her earplugs, "My Lord, if you are asking me for a technical answer, I cannot give you that. But, if I had to take a guess, I'd say the convoy is being electronically jammed but I cannot tell from where. Whatever it is, it cannot be jamming all of us because our other monitoring stations are active."

"Jammed?!" Petrawnus exhaled loudly.

"I can't think of any other reason for what's happening here," Gharius responded.

"But who would want to jam the UNWC convoy's radio transmissions?" the Watch Captain demanded.

"Someone would have to have a good reason," Gharius answered.

Gharius looked at his Watch Captain, "This is strange. Wait a minute."

He turned to his staffer, "Besina, did you get a copy of the transmission?"

Reaching towards her computer tower, Besina tapped the screen and then removed the external light drive from the console. "Yes, my Lord."

Gharius commanded. "Please take the drive over to the cyber section behind the second door over there. Have them decrypt it immediately. I want a printout of whatever is on that drive. Go!"

The Tryistan staffer disappeared towards the cyber section, leaving Gharius to confer with his Watch Commander and Petrawnus.

"This is a problem, a real problem," Petrawnus whispered. The chamber had quieted down considerably as the staffers had all but settled back into their stations dutifully monitoring their assignments.

"Watch Captain," Gharius ordered, "Why don't you return to your station and continue your duties. We should begin to get more reports very soon. Petrawnus and I will remain in the communications section waiting for that decryption."

"Yes, my Lord." The Watch Captain gave a slight bow, turned and headed off to her station. The chamber returned to some semblance of normal operations. The threat icon on the main mapping screen continued to blink orange.

After several minutes, Besina emerged from the crypto section and found her way to the communications station with a folded note in her hand. She found Gharius and Petrawnus and handed the note over to the Tryistan leader. Gharius took a few moments to scan the contents before handing it over to Petrawnus who quickly read the report over.

"Well, my Lord, at least now we know…"

"My Lord, the U.S. forces have just gone to DEFCON Two," the Watch Captain loudly announced with waves of concern in her voice.

Gharius turned to Petrawnus, "You stay here and keep the fortress. Alert the others on the Council to continue to monitor their regions and keep us up to date on what exactly they believe is happening. Make sure they initiate all the resources they have in place and tell them to get ready to move if needed."

"Yes, my Lord. I expect you will be departing?" Petrawnus stepped back.

"Immediately. It's time I introduced myself to someone."

Gharius turned and quickly strode across the chamber, disappearing through the entrance door and was gone. The digital threat icon on the south wall's main mapping screen suddenly jumped to red.

Minutes later, the rock panel concealing the Order's east entrance slid apart, and the Tryistan leader slipped through into the dark night. Gharius realized he was going to have to make great speed if he was going to get to D.C. within the next few hours. He stepped out onto the main ledge leading from the fortress entrance. As he neared the edge of the ledge, he morphed into his griffin form, feeling the mountain wind blowing hard against his face.

The Tryistan leader leaped forward and jumped from the ledge, dropping into a freefall towards the jagged cliffs far below and out of sight before exploding straight up past the main ledge and into the night sky. A minute later, a sudden boom resonated across the mountain range as the eastbound flight of the leader of the Tryistan Order broke the sound barrier.

CHAPTER TWENTY-SIX

THE TAKING

Haxiss stood quietly while Fiomass shifted restlessly on his feet. They had been outside and across the street for over an hour waiting for Jade to return to her apartment with her brother Jesse. Haxiss took a moment to look over the four first ranks who accompanied them, satisfied with their numbers.

Getting inside the apartment had been almost too easy. Up the stairs, a knock on the door followed by a little slice of mayhem and confusion had left both of Jade's brothers unconscious from the bitter stings of night venom. The two Tryistans would remain in a coma-like status for at least two days. There had been no good reason to destroy them as they had quickly submitted to Haxiss' rank once the two Doon Esha Elders had entered the apartment.

It had become immediately clear that the female youngling and her sibling were not in the apartment. Haxiss had angrily realized he should have taken the opportunity to interrogate the two Tryistan brothers before stinging them into unconsciousness, to which Fiomass had agreed.

What was really important now was the information Zelotus had provided. The address had proven to be accurate itself, yet the absence of the Tryistan younglings complicated matters.

Now the six members of the Doon Esha stood outside hugging the chain fence posted along the far sidewalk, each well aware they could not be present there much longer without arousing the suspicion of some of the locals. They were also aware they could not return to Celetin without their intended cargo.

Seemingly out of nowhere, a pair of headlights came rolling down the street across from the apartment complex. The dull gray, late model SUV rolled past the Doon Esha slowing as it went. The dark SUV's brakes lit up as it came to an easy halt 15 yards further down the road and parked along the sidewalk. The headlights went dark, and four doors opened almost simultaneously. Four hooded figures emerged from the SUV and began to make their way back up to where the Doon Esha stood waiting.

Stepping away from the chain fence, the Doon Esha slowly spread out into a semi-circle. Haxiss softly rumbled to his companions, "You first ranks, you have all been instructed in the ways of assimilation, yes?"

The reassuring whispers of the four first ranks assured the Elder it was so. Fiomass cautiously stepped to one side as Haxiss stepped to the opposite side placing the four first ranks in the middle. The four approaching figures appeared to be unconcerned about the intentional deployment of the Esha. Slowly but steadily, the four figures approached until coming to a stop a mere few feet away and directly in front of the first ranks.

One of the figures reached up and pulled his hood back revealing a tattoo-scarred face featuring a prominent "H" tattooed on his forehead. Neither of his companions moved a muscle as each group sized up the other. With barely a sound, the tattooed figure flipped out a switchblade knife holding it out to his side so as to be plainly visible.

Haxiss managed to subdue his amusement, "Is there something we can do for you?"

The lead member of the Horde gave a quick glance to his companions and stepped forward toward Haxiss. "You're on our turf."

Fiomass leaned forward, "Look friend, we're just waiting for a ride."

"Then we need to see some money," the lead Horde member snapped.

"Money it is, is it?" Haxiss countered reaching down into his jacket pocket. Pulling out a wad of cash, Haxiss held it up and waved it around for the four members of the Horde to see.

"You mean that?" Fiomass asked sarcastically, pointing at Haxiss.

"Yes," the Horde leader snapped reaching out his hand. "Give it to me!"

"Well then, my young friend," Haxiss smiled. "By all means come and get it."

The leader of the Horde took a step forward, but it was too late. Both Elders of the Doon Esha, in blinding speed, lunged forward and grabbed each one of the gang members by the face in their hands, which had turned to dragon's claws. As they held the struggling gang members, each of the first ranks chose one of the gang members and 'walked' into them, assimilating each member nearly instantaneously. The switchblade dropped noisily to the concrete. It was over.

Haxiss looked the four gang members over for a few moments. Then the Elder spoke to the member who had pulled the knife.

"Whom do you serve?"

"I serve only you, Elder Haxiss, and Elder Fiomass," came the answer.

"And whom do we all serve?"

"We serve our master, Celetin," the member answered again, in unison with the other three members.

"Very well," Haxiss hissed. "We will take the human vehicle and drive a pattern around these streets until we find the younglings."

Fiomass quietly rumbled a command to which the six Doon Esha made their way to the SUV and climbed in. Haxiss appointed the former lead member of the Horde to drive. The SUV's engine was still running, and the Esha pulled away from the sidewalk with little trouble. The SUV began to drive an ever-widening pattern through the streets as the Doon Esha eagerly searched for the Tryistan younglings.

After nearly 45 minutes of nothing, the SUV made its way into the back alleys only a few miles from Jade's apartment. The usual lights of the busy city were absent as the Esha made their way deeper and deeper into the labyrinth of back alleys joined and conjoined at intersection after intersection.

It was late, it was dark, and it was cold, accenting the stifling dreariness penetrating the stagnant mists as the SUV continued to search for the Tryistan younglings. After another 30 minutes, the SUV came to a rolling stop at a major alley junction. Shutting off its headlights, the darkness surrounding the vehicle was broken only by the dim light emanating from a dirty garage window on the far side of the junction.

Haxiss was becoming more and more frustrated while the rest of the Esha sat quietly waiting for an Elder to issue another order. Fiomass shifted back and forth in his seat trying to find the switch to lower the door window he was seated against. He found it and lowered the window all the way, feeling the cold stagnant air waft into his face.

"How long do you wish to sit here, Elder?" Fiomass mused.

"We sit until we have a plan to return to Celetin with what we came for or we will need a plan to decide how we end our own fates..."

Haxiss' observation was not lost on the other Esha, especially Fiomass who could still feel the recent welts on his back. The Esha sat quietly for several more minutes, each one pondering on how they might proceed. It was Haxiss who began to speak.

"Elder Fiomass, it might be prudent if we..."

"Shhhh," Fiomass held up a hand. "I heard something."

Several moments passed. "I hear nothing," Haxiss grunted. "I think..."

"Wait," Fiomass whispered, "there it is again. Voices."

The unmistakable sound of an ongoing conversation now reached the ears of the Doon Esha who silently sat and waited. The voices, as distant as they had seemed, were clearly getting a little louder. Someone was coming. Fiomass strained to listen, trying to determine the direction the voices were coming from. In a fit of frustration, the Elder tried to open his door only to discover the SUV had parked right up alongside an abandoned old beamer, so close, Fiomass had no way to open the door.

"There," Haxiss pointed as two silhouettes passed across through the dim light coming from a garage window in the alley directly in front of the SUV. The Esha could now easily make out the pair of humans making their way towards the junction. The humans stopped for a moment and then continued, heading straight for the Doon Esha.

"Hit the lights," Haxiss ordered.

Jade and Jesse both froze, suddenly blinded by a pair of headlights staring directly at them. Jade's heavy backpack was beginning to wear hard on her shoulders, making her wish she had not refused to let Jesse carry it when he offered. The rotting smell of moldy crates and musty dumpsters drifted up with the light mists filling the alleys.

Suddenly, three doors of the SUV opened, and four hooded figures emerged from the vehicle, barely visible to either brother or sister who was still trying to focus through the bright headlights of the SUV. The four figures begin to slowly make their way towards the pair, stepping in front of the near blinding headlights as they came.

Jesse automatically jumped in front of his sister while at the same time putting out his right arm to push her behind him. Jade resisted the arm, but Jesse was able to move into a position in front of her anyway. He felt Jade's hand come to rest on his shoulder.

Jesse whispered, "Jade, just give me a minute. I'll work something out."

Jade stared at the four hooded figures, "I don't believe this. Not again, you have got to be kidding me."

"What?" Jesse whispered.

"I knew there was something familiar about this alley. I knew it," Jade murmured.

"No, it can't be," Jesse exclaimed. "It's impossible."

"Really? Can you make out that old beamer sitting beside their SUV? Look familiar, Jesse?"

"I don't believe it," Jesse stammered.

The hooded figures were getting closer until Jade could make out the lead member's face and the prominent tattoo of an "H" on the forehead.

"Okay, it looks like the same one as before."

"Just let me handle this, Jade. I've got an idea."

"I would very much like to hear your idea, youngling," a deep rasping voice called out from behind the two Tryistans.

Jesse and Jade both jumped and whirled around to find two Elders of the Doon Esha in their dragon forms settling to the ground with their wings spread wide. The four hooded figures suddenly collapsed as the four first ranks stepped out of the humans, leaving their human bodies to crumple to the ground. Each of the four first ranks formed into a dragon-wolf and stood stone still waiting for further instructions. The Tryistans were surrounded.

Folding back their wings, the Doon Esha Elders settled back on their hind legs taking a moment to look the frightened Tryistans over.

Turning to the four first ranks, Fiomass sounded a low deep series of rumbles. Two of the first ranks stepped back a pace and turned to face each other. Nearly simultaneously, both of the Esha looked straight up into the night sky and opened their jaws wide.

There came sounds not unlike that of a soft crackling fire. The forms of the two Esha turned rigid as if both were turning to stone. A few moments later, the transformations were complete, leaving the two first ranks looking very much like a couple of old stone-cold gargoyle statues. Jade and Jesse could only stare as the wide-open eyes of the stone statue gargoyles began to glow brighter and brighter. A short plume of pale fire emerged from each of the stone-cold Esha's open jaws.

The alley suddenly turned darker as one of the other first ranks had returned to the SUV and shut off the headlights. The only discernible light in the alley junction now present shone from the jaws of the silent gargoyle statues. Jade and Jesse barely noticed the first rank who had returned from the SUV and taken up a position close to the two Tryistans joined by the fourth first rank. The alley junction was clear and alarmingly quiet.

"You are impressed, no?" Haxiss hissed at the pair.

"What is it you want with us?" Jesse stammered.

Fiomass moved to confront Jesse face to face. "We have come to deliver to you a personal invitation, youngling. We are here to see that you accept the invitation."

"What invitation?" Jade quivered.

"Why, a personal invitation from none other than Celetin himself!" Haxiss cackled.

"And what choices do we have?" Jesse countered.

"Absolutely none, youngling," Fiomass hissed.

Jesse pushed Jade back away hard and took a step to form. A large, padded tail caught Jesse across the side of his head, throwing him through the air for several feet before the young Tryistan landed on the pavement still in human form, completely unconscious.

Jade screamed and darted to her brother's side, coming down to her knees to look Jesse over. Running her hand over the back of Jesse's neck, she could feel the warm blood between her fingers. *We have no choice...*

With her back now turned to the Doon Esha, Jade carefully ran her other hand up to her neck and snatched her gold pendant, easily breaking the delicate chain. She leaned over her stricken brother and acted as if she intended to pull up his shoulders using the cover of Jesse's body to toss the pendant away into the dark.

She turned to the Doon Esha in tears, "You didn't have to do that! He was only trying to protect..."

"Enough!" Haxiss hissed. "We will take them both."

"Is that it?" Jade demanded. "Is this the part where you kill the both of us and present us as trophies to your precious master?"

Fiomass strode over to where Jade kneeled beside her brother and raised his head, towering over the frightened girl.

"Child, we have no intentions of killing you. We need you alive. Do not deceive yourself, if we had wanted you dead, you would be dead already."

Haxiss made a barely audible rumble, signaling the two remaining first ranks to move in close to Jade and her unconscious brother. In a moment, Jade and Jesse were surrounded by the four Esha. Jade realized what was coming and reached over, putting her arms around her brother. She buried her face in his chest just before feeling the biting sting of night venom curse through her veins. *Jesse...*

Fiomass motioned to the two first ranks, dropping two sacks out from under his wing, "Cocoon them quickly, and be sure the strapping is tight. We need to return at once. Celetin will be waiting." *Now Gharius, you have no choice... You must face Celetin...*

Minutes later, four winged figures soared out of the dark alley and headed into the night sky. The two gargoyle statues left behind would remain motionless until their fires burned out as they began to blow away, turning to dust. They had followed their orders. There would be no trace of them in the morning.

GLOBALCOMNEWS.NET
World Situation Report #8

"It has just been confirmed through our sources in Washington D.C., that U.S. forces have just issued a DEFCON 2 status, again, U.S. forces have set DEFCON 2. Many of you may know the order to DEFCON 2 significantly increases the likeliness of at least the possibility of limited nuclear actions taken for either preemptive or preventive measures by U.S. forces. These actions would be directed at world actors who have signaled a clear and present threat to the U.S. mainland and possibly in response to threats against U.S. allies.

"What will likely happen at this point will be the order to open U.S.-based ICBM missile silos stationed across the Midwest. Other U.S. nuclear assets certainly including submarine-based nuclear missiles will also receive communications to standby for their orders to launch their missiles at their predetermined targets.

"We can safely assume these same actions will be taken by those world actors the U.S. has deemed hostile in preparatory retaliation against any nuclear aggression.

"I don't think I have to explain how grave the situation is becoming. If there are any of you in our listening audience who believe in the power of prayer, it would seem now would be the time to start praying. God help us..."

CHAPTER TWENTY-SEVEN

GOOD MORNING, MR. PRESIDENT

The president's secretary was a mature and experienced woman who had served under the last four administrations at one time or another. She smiled warmly as her eyes met the familiar eyes of the Tryistan leader when he entered the room.

"Gharius. I had been wondering when you were going to show up. How are you? It's been too long."

"Stephanie, always a pleasure to see you again." Gharius stepped forward.

The President's secretary and the Tryistan gave each other a quick but well-meaning hug.

"I have come to see your President," Gharius smiled.

"I'll bet you have. You have a real knack for..."

Gharius chuckled, "I know. I haven't had the opportunity for an introduction yet. I thought given the current circumstances, now might be a good time."

The President's secretary turned to the two Secret Service agents, "Thank you. You can go."

Without a word, the two agents slid noiselessly out of the office leaving the two alone.

"Stephanie, I want to thank you for getting me in to see the president..."

"Oh, it was nothing. I added you to his calendar and cancelled another war meeting the president didn't want to attend anyway. Things are getting pretty hairy."

Gharius chuckled. "I would understand something about those kinds of meetings."

Suddenly, looking through his pockets, "I haven't forgotten, Stephanie, let's see, it's here somewhere... Yes. Here it is."

He produced a tightly wrapped, small white handkerchief, which he gently handed to the president's secretary.

Taking up the handkerchief, Stephanie smiled shyly at the Tryistan leader as she carefully unwrapped the gift. "Oh, it's beautiful!"

The president's secretary held up the sizeable black pearl, dazzled by the flawless gleam the gem possessed. "It must be priceless, Gharius, you really shouldn't have."

"It is now, Stephanie, and a price well paid for your consideration."

Stephanie quickly wrapped the gem back up in the cloth and stuffed it down inside the pocket of her dress pants. Glancing over at the clock on the wall, "I believe it's time for your introduction, Gharius. You'll have to be brief. He has another meeting in 20 minutes, and he's not in a good mood with all the things he's having to deal with."

"Good, I'm ready."

She rapped twice on the door to the Oval Office before opening the door to announce the president's next appointment was ready to be seen. Turning from the door, Stephanie gave Gharius a tight-lipped smile and nodded her head, "The President will see you now."

He nodded and slipped past her into the Oval Office. Except for some superficial modifications, the carpets, some paintings, and the size of the president's desk, not much else had changed.

President Wesley rose up from behind his desk setting his reading glasses down and held out his right hand. "It's Gharius, I believe? I'm sorry, I don't have a last name for you."

Gharius reached the desk and took the president's hand firmly. "Mr. President, it is an honor to finally meet you."

Breaking his grip, the president sat back down in his chair and motioned for Gharius to have a seat in the chair in front of his desk.

Gharius smiled, "Oh, thank you Mr. President, but I hope to be brief, if I may."

President Wesley gave a slight shrug, "Well, that's fine with me, uh, Gharius. Tell me, what can I do for you? I'm afraid my secretary neglected to list a reason for your appointment, but you are listed with a high security clearance, and she said it was important."

"Mr. President, I understand you are very busy at the moment, so I will get to the point if I may. It is an urgent matter."

"Very well. Things are getting a little hot around here, so the briefer the better. I have another meeting soon."

"I understand, Mr. President," Gharius reached up into his coat pocket and produced a folded piece of paper. Opening the small scrap, he handed it across the desk to the American president. President Wesley took the piece of paper, put his reading glasses on, and began to read it over quickly.

"What is this?" President Wesley asked removing his glasses.

"It's an intercepted burst transmission I received from the UNWC convoy which fired that missile."

President Wesley dropped the paper to his desk, "and would you mind telling me where you got this piece of information?"

Gharius shifted, "Mr. President, I am going to ask you to do something, and you are not going to agree with me."

"Look, Mr. Gharius, I understand you hold a high clearance, but even my own people haven't provided me with this information. Who exactly do you work for?"

Gharius sighed. "Mr. President, I will be happy to answer your questions, but I have a request. I am asking you to stand down from your DEFCON 2 alert status."

The president laughed under his breath. "Listen, I don't know who you are or who you work for but in case you've missed it, we're standing on the brink of World War 3. And I have to figure out how to respond in the interests of national security and the American people. I'm sorry, I don't have time for…"

"Mr. President, please. You have read the information I have given you. You now know that convoy's communications are being jammed. You have read it yourself; the missile fired from that ship was a malfunction. It was not an intentional act of aggression. And if you will check with your people, you have not sighted another foreign submarine near your international borders in over 24 hours."

President Wesley stood up from his desk, "How would you know about the submarines? Who are you, exactly and who do you work for? I won't ask you again!"

Gharius realized his diplomatic approach was not going to work. It was time for the real introductions to begin.

"Alright, alright, Mr. President," He got up and looked around the room. "You want to know who I really am? It will be more helpful if you know what I am." Gharius took several steps back towards the center of the room.

"Our peoples have been in contact from time to time, Mr. President. The last time I was in this office was nearly 50 years ago. It was the same then too, you know."

President Wesley nodded with a smile while slowly moving his hand to the phone, feeling his way towards the button which would usher in his Secret Service team in seconds.

"Please don't do that, Mr. President. What I am about to reveal to you is for your eyes and your eyes only. I only need five minutes of your time."

Gharius calmly smiled at the president and stepped out of his human form.

Five minutes later, the sudden frantic buzzing of the phone startled the president's secretary out of her train of thought. Stephanie jumped up from her desk and hurried over to the door of the Oval Office rapping twice before opening the door and stepping inside.

A bewildered President Wesley sat at his desk and was pulling his tie loose. Stephanie glanced at Gharius who was standing just to the side of the president's desk in his human form with a look of finality written across the Tryistan leader's face.

"Stephanie, would you please get me the Chairman of the Joint Chiefs on the line?" the subdued voice of the president seemed to drift up from his desk. "Now, please."

"Yes, Mr. President," Stephanie answered glancing again at Gharius and swearing the Tryistan had just winked at her. Turning to go back to her desk, Stephanie approached the office door and was nearly tossed aside as a disheveled Daniel Richardson burst in through the same door clearly unannounced.

"Mr. President!" Richardson rasped, out of breath.

Gharius immediately rushed over to put himself between the senior advisor and the president's desk. Richardson tried to sidestep the Tryistan and stopped. The two men sized each other up for a moment as President Wesley rose unsteadily from his desk. *You two know each other?*

"You!" Richardson shrieked. The senior advisor to the President of the United States took a step forward just as the head of a wolf-dragon emerged out of Richardson's chest, deep red eyes set squarely on the large window behind the president's desk.

"No, you don't," Gharius growled, instantly reaching out, grabbing the emerging wolf-dragon by the neck and pulling it with great strength. The wolf-dragon garbled out another shriek and began to burn to ashes under Gharius' iron grip as the Tryistan leader pulled the Doon Esha Elder from Richardson's convulsing body.

In seconds, Mezlash, an Elder of the Doon Esha disintegrated into a swirling cloud of flittering gray ash as Richardson's unconscious body finally collapsed to the floor. For a few moments, no one in the office spoke, and no one moved a muscle. All eyes were set on Gharius who began brushing ash from his suit as if swatting away a cloud of gnats.

Looking over at Stephanie who was planted against the far wall, hands over her mouth and eyes wide open, Gharius calmly nodded, "Stephanie, Mr. Richardson is going to require immediate medical attention. And I believe the President needs to speak to the Chairman of the Joint Chiefs."

Stephanie quickly nodded and hurriedly made her way out of the office. A stunned president, Wesley had taken his seat again, running his hands through his hair, his eyes never leaving his newly revealed guest.

Giving a slight bow, Gharius realized it was time to depart. "Mr. President, it has been an honor and a true pleasure to make your acquaintance, sir. With your permission, Mr. President, I have other urgent matters I must attend to. I believe we have an understanding between us, sir?"

President Wesley nodded, "Yes, Gharius. I believe we have a very good understanding. Will we have the pleasure of seeing you again?"

Gharius noted the president's sarcasm, it was understandable. "Perhaps, Mr. President, but let us hope not. I have every confidence in you and your office."

"Then good day, sir," President Wesley grimaced.

"And to you, sir," Gharius returned.

The leader of the Tryistan Order turned and made his way out of the Oval Office. Gliding past the desk of the president's secretary, Gharius nodded to Stephanie who winked back at the departing Tryistan. Gharius made his way to the lobby exit door and disappeared without any further word. With a good wind at his back, he would make it to Atlanta, Georgia before nightfall to check in on Jade and her brothers.

Back in the president's office, President Wesley sat quietly waiting and listening to his secretary who was speaking on the phone at her desk. He heard the click of her handset placed back into its cradle and picked up his own handset punching the flashing button, which demanded his attention.

"General, yes, no, listen, I need to see you right away. Yes, right now. I'm in my office. Okay, thank you." *I can't believe this is actually happening...*

CHAPTER TWENTY-EIGHT

FORTRESS OF THE DOON ESHA

Jade and Jesse were escorted through the Galapagos fortress by two security scorpulas of the Doon Esha. The large arachnid types made no conversation as the small entourage quietly made their way through the deserted tunnels. After several minutes of walking, they arrived at the entrance to the main central chamber of the Doon Esha fortress. Jade had to catch her breath as she and her brother took in the sight that lay before them. Nothing could have prepared them for the spectacle that presented itself.

Every rooftop, stairwell and every ascending outcrop or peak was occupied by a myriad of creatures of the Doon Esha. To Jade and her brother, it looked more like the long-gone scene of the glorious days of the Roman gladiator arena than the underground fortress city they were witnessing.

Calls, cries, and shrieks echoed throughout the entire hold, adding to the crescendo that was building within the enormous chamber. Although Jade had no choice, Jessie had agreed to retain his human form and their presence as they entered as it was already beginning to draw much unwanted attention.

Sensing the hostility, the scorpula on Jade's right went ahead and began to clear a path through the gathering crowds, sweeping its large threatening tail up and over its body while rapidly clicking its pincers. Jade and Jesse were hastily nudged to follow the lead scorpula as a path began to clear ahead of them. The group headed for the center of the chamber where their awaiting host was also causing a great deal of the commotion surrounding them.

As they approached the epicenter of the chamber, a gathering gauntlet of Doon Esha creatures hissed, barked and shrieked at the sight of the human forms. Many along the way bore their teeth and swiped claws and pincers at the prisoners. One particularly overzealous creature, a small, wicked hybrid of a velociraptor and a cheetah, leapt into the air, intent on sinking its bare canines into Jade's neck.

Just catching sight of the incoming blur of teeth, Jade shrank back and stared as the animal was instantly snatched up by one of her escort's pincers. With a powerful flick, the scorpula flung the creature some 30 yards into a Roman column support, breaking its back. The small, wicked creature slid to the floor with eyes wide open, blood running from its face.

Upon reaching the center of the chamber, the group was greeted by the sight of the white dragon who stood alone in the center. The jeering crowd gave Celetin a wide berth. The group stopped within 20 feet of the dragon as both scorpulas bowed.

"Master Celetin," one of the scorpula announced, "Your guests have arrived as per your orders."

With that, the scorpulas rose and took their positions on each side of Jade and Jesse awaiting further orders. Both of the Tryistans stared wide-eyed at the sights around them, taking a few moments to wrap their minds around what was happening. Jade's hand instinctively went to her neck finding only soft skin. *I hope you've found it...*

A hush began to fall upon the crowds as Celetin raised a winged claw calling for order in the enormous chamber. It took several long moments until the noise in the chamber subsided to mere whispers. Finally satisfied, Celetin lowered his claw and rose up to his full measure turning his gaze upon the two Tryistans standing before him.

"Welcome, my friends, to our most humble dwellings. As you can see, we do not often have the privilege of such royalty," Celetin's voice trailed off almost mockingly.

A host of jeers and some laughter broke out among the crowds for some time until the white dragon glanced hard around the chamber, calling for silence once again.

"What is it you want with us? Why have you brought us here?" Jesse demanded, stepping in front of Jade.

Jade sidestepped around her brother, coming back up beside him. "You have taken us against our will. I know who you are."

The white dragon smiled through curved lips, "Good, then we may dispense with the formalities. Both of you know full well why you have been brought here. The law has been broken, and the time of the sentencing has come."

The crowds broke out into chaos as creatures large and small raised their fists and chanted for death. Jade was again struck by how much the scene before she and her brother seemed to increasingly imitate the crowds in the ancient coliseum of Rome clamoring for the death of some poor condemned soul. *So, how does this work, thumbs up or thumbs down...*

Jade could feel the blood draining from her face. She had known for a long time her fate was to be determined but she never dreamed it would end up here like this. It was like a nightmare which could only end in a very bad way. The problem was that Jade could not figure out how Celetin could carry out a death sentence himself. No Esha was ever permitted to directly kill a human being, and indeed, a full human being Jade was.

Once again, the white dragon called for silence in the chamber and was met with almost immediate obedience. Celetin waited until the last of the echoes drifted up into the heights of the chamber.

Moving deliberately toward the Tryistans, Celetin motioned the two scorpulas away and came closer to where Jade and Jesse stood. The white dragon leaned down and studied the frightened pair looking them over like a pair of birds in a cage.

The dragon barely whispered, "It may have escaped your notice, but your father has once again foiled my plans to set the humans on fire. But this time, however, I have also planned for that possibility as well, and that is why you are here."

Jade and Jesse exchanged a quick glance. Jesse gave Jade an almost undetectable nod and moved closer to his sister. *So, father actually did it...*

"What does that have to do with me?" Jade asked, feigning her innocence.

The white dragon exhaled a blast from his nostrils while a drop of burning sulfur fell from his jaws, landing inches away from Jade's feet as it began to burn into the floor.

"It has everything to do with you, youngling. If I cannot have my way with the humans this time, I will have my way with you. One way or the other, I will have a victory!"

Jade flinched, then said, "You know full well our father will eventually come for us, and he will bring a thousand Tryistan warriors with him."

The white dragon pursed his lips, "I am counting on it, youngling, and I welcome the presence of your father to come forth and offer a defense for your life."

Taken aback, Jesse leaned forward, "You cannot hope to win against him, and you know that. Even if you attempt to carry out the sentence on Jade, in doing so, you yourself will be destroyed."

Stepping back, Celetin pointed at Jade.

"It is true that I cannot directly destroy you, youngling, however, it is permitted to render an accepted sacrifice in your stead under the law. No, I cannot directly destroy you, but I *can* destroy him," Celetin pointed squarely at Jesse.

"You can't do that!" Jade shrieked. "That is not up to you to decide…"

"No, youngling," Celetin smiled through clenched jaws, "I will not make that decision. I will leave that decision up to the wisdom of your father."

Jade turned and whispered to Jesse. Then, "How exactly does he intend to force our father into such a decision?"

Celetin rose up and stroked his lower jaw, "Your father is on his way here even as we speak. And it is true as you have just asked your brother. Your father will certainly be leading a force of his finest warriors. I, too, expect his arrival very soon."

"And what is to be done with us in the meantime?" Jesse blurted.

"Well, then," Celetin smiled through curled lips, "You will be my welcome guests until your great leader arrives."

Jade took a defiant step forward, "And how do you know my father will not destroy you and this fortress when he arrives?"

The white dragon again leaned down until his jaws rested inches from Jade's face.

"Your father is no fool. I know he will not attack me because I have you and your brother well within my keep."

Jade shrunk back from the force of the smell of Celetin's fetid hot breath. There was something in his

words that seemed to make the white dragon so sure of himself.

"I don't understand how you can be so confident your plan will work this time," Jade challenged.

Celetin rose up and began to cackle heartily. "Youngling, are you so ignorant as to not have read the prophecies? Know you nothing of how the end of your Order comes and thus the order of humanity? Or are you so naive as to believe all of this is really just about you?"

A symphony of laughter now filled the chamber as Celetin slowly circled his two Tryistan guests. The white dragon allowed his crowd of spectators to jeer and mock the brother and sister who could only stand in silence before the great mob. After a time, once again Celetin called for order, which took several minutes before his audience calmed down enough to allow any further words to be spoken.

Finally, "You see, younglings," Celetin raised his wings and waved them around as the white dragon now addressed the crowds, "There are those things which have been set in motion of which neither you nor I have any real control. It has all been foretold, and that which has been foretold is that which we all must now call our final destinies."

Once again, the crowds erupted into cheers, and chanting filled the chamber with the sounds of their voices granting their master the full unison of their approval. The noise rose louder and louder as Celetin raised his wings higher into the air.

Staring out across the crowds, Celetin bellowed, "And our final destiny is to rule!"

Jade and her brother covered their ears as the deafening noise of the cheering crowds reached a level causing slight tremors to race across the chamber floors. Rocks began to tumble from the higher ledges throughout the massive chamber as dust fell from the heights. As the ecstatic praise continued, a number of large boulders rolled down from their pedestals into the crowds crushing a number of the Doon Esha under the weight of untold hundreds of pounds.

Jesse and Jade threw their arms around each other while continuing to stare around at the jubilant crowds who were demanding their deaths and praising their leader. Time seemed to stand still as the relentless noise seemed to carry on without end. The white dragon continued to circle the two Tryistans now almost seemingly unaware of their presence altogether as the leader of the tribes of the Doon Esha appeared to bathe himself in all of the crowd's fervent adulation.

Jade looked at her brother who shook his head with sadness in his eyes. Both of the Tryistans knew there was nothing left to say in their defense. There was really no point in arguing any further with the dragon. The only thing left to do was to wait until the leader of the Tryistan Order arrived to make a decision which would decide their fates.

Finally, amid the decreasing volume of the cheering crowds, Celetin motioned to the scorpulas who stood at a distance.

"Escort them to our hold, I mean our guest chambers and keep them secured until I call for them again. Make sure they remain unharmed."

The security scorpulas moved quickly to each side of the Tryistans and began nudging them back towards the main chamber's entrance tunnel. The crowds began to chant again calling for death as the volume rose again to a feverish pitch, which filled the massive chamber up to its heights.

As they reached the entrance tunnel, Jade stole a look back over her shoulder just in time to see the white dragon disappear off into a side corridor. *Father... I know you're coming...*

CHAPTER TWENTY-NINE

THE DECISION

It had taken Gharius nearly three hours to make the flight to the Galapagos Island region. As he neared the central island which served as the base for the Doon Esha fortress, He glanced down at the small pack tied around his waist containing a scroll and a small golden pendant. *I will need them both...*

Landing on the outcropping of ledges, which served as the entrance to the fortress, Gharius stepped into his human form. Gathering up the small package, he tucked it under his arm and approached the rocky entrance waiting for the two sentries he knew were present to respond.

Two serpentine forms finally emerged from the rocks but did not approach the Tryistan leader. Instead, they both merely pointed to the opening, which had appeared in the side of cliff, bidding Gharius to enter. The Tryistan leader knew there would be no escort. He knew the way already, and it was doubtful any of the Doon Esha lower ranks would have dared to serve as his escort, given he was in his human form.

Stepping through the entrance, Gharius could hear the dim sounds of a gathering crowd up ahead in what he knew would be the main courtyard chamber. Holding the scroll tightly, he made his way towards the main chamber, noting the absence of any of the fortress Esha along the way. It was obvious the Doon Esha had purposely cleared the passages he would take to the main courtyard.

After several long minutes, he came within eyesight of the entrance to the courtyard chamber and stopped. Holding up the scroll, the Tryistan leader carefully broke the scroll's seal and waited. A moment later, he felt the bare wisp of a draft, which seemed to have blown into the tunnel from some unseen source. He carefully took the chain of the golden pendant and wrapped it around the scroll tightly. *It is time...*

Deafening silence suddenly filled the great cavern as Gharius stepped out of the entrance tunnel and into the main courtyard chamber. Holding the ancient scroll under his arm, he walked slowly and deliberately towards the center of the cavern where Celetin stood waiting, surrounded by his personal guard. Gharius's footsteps echoed with each step fueling the tension vibrating through the air.

Not one form moved as Gharius made his way quietly through their ranks. It was as if somehow, he was commanding a gauntlet, which had strangely formed before he'd even arrived. When he finally reached the center of the enormous central courtyard chamber still in human form, he stopped.

A dark-hooded figure stepped out from behind Celetin and approached Gharius. When the figure reached him, a hand reached up and pulled the hood back from his face. Zelotus stepped closer to Gharius and threw his arms around the Tryistan leader in an embrace that two brothers in arms might give each other after a long battle.

Gharius made no effort to return the embrace and after several awkward moments, Zelotus finally released his clasp and stepped back.

Casting his eyes to the floor, Zelotus softly sighed and pulled the hood back over his head. Slowly, he turned and walked away from Gharius, heading for an exit tunnel.

The multitude watched, offering only quiet whispers and murmurings as the Tryistan's footsteps resounded through the great hall. Zelotus suddenly stopped as the smack of a small black velvet purse landed just behind him. Deliberately taking three steps backward without turning around, Zelotus reached down and retrieved the small purse.

"Your wages for your conscience, Tryistan," Quoros, a Doon Esha Elder, called out, his voice echoing throughout the chambers. Without any response, the hooded figure stood up and stepped forward as he wordlessly made his way out of the great cavern.

Gharius, holding the scroll, addressed Celetin, "I would like to see my two younglings before we proceed."

Celetin looked back over his shoulder and nodded. From a side tunnel Jade and Jesse emerged escorted by two scorpulas. The foursome strode in formation until within a few yards, both brother and sister broke away and ran to their father. Gharius put both arms around his younglings trying to reassure them as their tears began to fall.

"Father, what are you doing? Where are the rest?" Jade cried.

"Jade..."

"She's right, father, where are the rest...?" Jesse stammered.

Gharius hugged his two children harder, "You both must leave at once."

Jade broke the embrace, "What? What do you mean leave? Father..."

"Jade, you both must leave now."

This time, Jesse broke the embrace, "Father, we're not leaving you..."

"Jesse, you must..."

"Ah, so touching," Celetin interrupted. "I am afraid; however, the younglings are quite right, Gharius."

"That was not the deal Celetin..."

"But Gharius, the deal is not yet complete. You have a decision to make."

Gharius stepped away from his children, putting himself between them and the white dragon. "The decision has been made."

Celetin drew himself back with a puzzled look crossing his face, "What is this? Have you come so soon to decide which one is to suffer the penalty?"

Gharius took a step forward, "The decision was made long before it was required, dragon. It will be neither these of my own to suffer the penalty."

A wide wicked smile slowly crept across Celetin's face. "So, the decision is made?"

"The decision is made," Gharius answered resolutely.

Celetin clasped his claws in obvious pleasure. Turning to his personal guards, the dragon announced, "Make ready the holding post."

Four scorpulas scrambled away towards a series of hewn steps rising up to a large ledge on the far side of the main chamber. The crowds quickly gave way to the quartet of arachnids that hurriedly cleared the way towards the steps to make the holding post sitting in the center of the large ledge ready for the white dragon's commands.

"It is time to release my younglings, dragon," Gharius warned.

"Release the younglings!" Jade shouted. "What are you talking about? Father..."

Jesse stepped up to his father reaching out, "Father, what is happening here? What do you mean about releasing us?"

Gharius turned to face his two younglings, "The decision is made."

Jade was nearly inconsolable, "Father, I don't..."

"You will in time, child," Gharius answered firmly.

The two young Tryistans continued to protest until their faces were awash in fresh tears. Gharius put out his arms and embraced them as he turned to the white dragon.

"If there is some other way..."

"I'm afraid that is not possible, Gharius. They are required by the laws to remain here as witnesses of your Order to the just execution of the sentence. They will be released immediately when the sentence is carried out to completion."

Gharius grimaced. He knew the law required witnesses to the sentence, and it hurt him deeply that Jade and Jesse would have to be those witnesses. The Tryistan leader consoled his younglings before finally breaking their hold and holding out the scroll to Jade. Jesse wiped his eyes while staring at his father.

"Child, you and your brother need to take this and hold it in your keep until the appointed time."

With tears clouding her eyes, Jade reached out and took the scroll, "Father, what is this?"

"It holds a key to your future, child, and to the rest of the Order. Take it and keep it safe."

"And what is this, Gharius?" Celetin snapped.

"Only my final wishes, dragon. They are of no concern to you. And you have made it clear you will release my younglings when this is over. It would be most unwise, dragon, to break the law otherwise."

"Your younglings will be released, Tryistan," Celetin snapped again. "Now, the time for the fulfillment of the sentence is ready. There must be no more further delays."

Celetin motioned again to the rest of his guards. The assembled crowds up to this point had remained in a near state of silence, appealingly hypnotized by the events unfolding before them. Four more scorpulas took up their position just behind where Jade and Jesse were standing.

"Father..." Jade whimpered.

"It is time," Celetin announced loud enough for the crowds to hear.

Gharius looked tenderly upon Jade and Jesse, "What I do, I must do alone. Remember to take the scroll and to keep it with you for it is my word. I love you both so much."

Two of the scorpula stepped forward and reached their pinchers forward, gently taking each arm of the two Tryistan siblings to firmly to hold them in place. As Jade and Jesse watched, they offered no resistance to their captors, choosing instead to stare through their tears after their father who walked away through the chamber towards the steps up to the ledge now prepared for the holding post.

The crowds parted silently as Gharius strode deliberately to the steps leading to the ledge. Just as he was about to take the first step, "Hold Tryistan," Elder Fiomass had appeared out of nowhere behind the Tryistan leader and handed Gharius a heavy wooden crossbeam. "You will have need of this."

Gharius took the heavy crossbeam from the Elder and hoisted it up on his own shoulders. Then, one by one, the Tryistan leader began to traverse the stairs, each step getting heavier and heavier as he went. Several times he nearly stumbled to the edge of the steps, threatening to throw him over the side but he continued to climb.

Finally, as the sweat ran from his face, Gharius reached the top of the stairs and stepped up onto the ledge bearing the holding post. It seemed to take forever as the crowds quietly murmured, anticipating and speculating as to how the sentencing would end.

Reaching the holding post, Gharius dropped the crossbeam and stood staring out over the ledge at the crowds of the Doon Esham and spotting Jade and Jesse. He managed a light smile and waited as two of the scorpula picked the crossbeam up and placed it over the holding post before dropping it in place, forming a T-shaped cross-member post.

Gharius offered no resistance as the scorpulas placed him against the holding post and tied his hands to the sides of the crossbeam. When they had finished, the scorpulas moved away from the holding post as Celetin, having taken flight, settled down on the ledge directly behind the Tryistan leader's post.

The white dragon raised its wings and called for silence, to which the crowds obeyed. As the noise subsided, Celetin looked out over his audience, "The time has come. You are all witnesses to the final sentence to the penalty which is due. I will now carry out the penalty which is demanded by the law!"

As the crowds cheered, Gharius watched and waited, securely tied to the holding post. Celetin turned and took a position close behind the Tryistan leader. The crowds were awash in anticipation as Celetin leaned in close enough for the leader of the Tryistan Order to hear.

"Foolish leader, your love for your own is your greatest weakness."

Without turning, "And your hatred for the humans is yours," Gharius replied.

"So be it," Celetin retorted, "I shall pierce you Tryistan and burn you with fire!"

It came without warning as the whip-like tail of the white dragon shot into Gharius' back, penetrating at an angle that brought the tip of the dragon's tail out through the side of Gharius' chest. The Tryistan leader cried out as the blood spurted from the wounds falling to the ground in large drops.

A scream cut through the air as Jade's legs fell out from under her, held up only by the pinchers of the scorpula behind her. Every eye in the chamber watched as the writhing body of the Tryistan leader fought to break the restraints holding him in place. Moments later, Gharius stopped fighting and slumped against the holding post, his breathing becoming irregular and ragged with each fleeting gasp. Then, the Tryistan stopped moving altogether as he looked out over the chamber through his dying eyes.

With his last breath, Gharius, leader of the Tryistan Order bowed his head as he gave up his final words, "It is over, and now... it begins."

For a few moments, there was nothing but absolute silence.

The rising orchestra of Celetin's sickening cackle began to fill the great cavern, growing stronger and stronger as its overtones rose filling the chamber. Raising himself to his full measure, Celetin spread his wings wide, looking down upon his cowering subjects. Turning his head towards Jade and her brother, "It is the final hour, and I am victorious! My name shall no longer be Celetin, leader of the Tribes of the Doon Esha."

Looking around the cavern, Celetin paused a moment, then declared, "From this moment on and forever, all shall know me by my new name. From this moment all of you shall call me what I am. You shall call me Chaos!" Again, the distorted symphony of dissonant cackling laughter, "Chaos, the victorious!"

The scorpulas released Jade and her brother who covered their ears as the deafening roar of the crowds of Doon Esha erupted again. They pumped their fists, claws, and pinchers, raising their voices to praise the victory of the white dragon. Something caught Jade's eye, and she looked down to catch a glint of light gleaming off the golden pendant while sealing the scroll she was holding tight in her hand. *This can't be...*

Jade touched her brother on the shoulder and held the scroll up as she tried to speak over the roar of the crowds. Jesse nodded as if he had heard her, but Jade knew her brother hadn't heard a word she had said.

Leaning into his shoulder, Jade cupped her brother's ear, "Jesse, this scroll is the same scroll I opened in father's sacred archive! It's the one that made me..."

"You're mistaken, Jade," Jesse frowned sharply, "That's not possible!"

Jade held the scroll up for Jesse to see shaking her head, "It's the same one, Jesse, the one that made me human."

A look of disbelief covered Jesse's face, "It can't be. That would mean father became..."

"Human!" Jade shouted.

The ground began to shake, barely noticeable at first. Then again and again, the ground began to shake. Suddenly, a sickening sound descended from the heights as if the ceilings were threatening to fall in on the chamber itself. Rocks began to fall from the sides of the great chamber sliding down the smooth walls until something much like an earthquake began to shake the entire chamber with force.

The crowds started to panic and run in every direction as the shaking continued opening small fissures throughout the chamber floors. The scorpulas on the holding post ledge scrambled away and across the wall in their panic to flee. Celetin quickly looked around the chamber as smoke began to rise up from the numerous fissures, which continued to open across the chamber floors. The fissures grew wider, swallowing numbers of the Doon Esha crowds scattering across the chamber in panicked masses.

Spreading his wings, the white dragon lifted off from the holding post ledge just in time before the entire ledge collapsed and crashed onto the floor below burying the holding post and the dead Tryistan leader in tons of rock. The massive chamber continued to rumble and quake, filling the air with dust and smoke until the moment the shaking came to an abrupt stop.

Coughing and blinking to clear their eyes, Jade and Jesse found themselves on their knees trying to make out what had just happened. Jesse touched Jade's shoulder and pointed across the chamber to where the holding post ledge once sat, now crumbled on the floor of the chamber. Cries and shrieks abounded from every corner of the central chamber as what was left of the crowds of the Doon Esha appeared to be stunned and disoriented.

After several minutes, the smoke and dust had cleared away enough for Jade and Jesse to make out clearly where the holding post ledge now lay in ruins. Rising to their feet, they both looked around trying to decide whether or not they were free to leave or if something else awaited them.

Celetin had landed near where the holding post ledge had collapsed and was conferring with a number of his personal guard of scorpulas. Small fires continued to burn from the many fissures that had opened during the quakes. The massive chamber now looked more like an earthquake-stricken city, rubble and ruins lie throughout its streets and passages.

Jesse noticed it at first and nudged his sister to get her attention. "What is that?"

Both brother and sister stared hard at the collapsed rubble of the holding post ledge and then noticed it again. A faint light emanated again from underneath some of the rocks. It was there and then it wasn't, as if the light itself was pulsing or was it shimmering?

Jade caught sight of the light again as Jesse looked to see if Celetin and his guards had noticed the strange light coming through the rubble from the shattered ledge. At the moment, no one in the chamber seemed to notice much less care about the light softly flashing on and off under and through the mass of rocks from the devastated ledge.

A nearly ear-splitting crack erupted as suddenly the entire floor where the holding post ledge had fallen gave way. In an instant, what was left of the collapsed rubble disappeared into an enormous new fissure forcing Celetin and his guards to hastily back away from the gaping hole now spitting smoke and flames into the air. What was left of the holding post ledge was gone.

"Jesse?" Jade spoke, uncertainty in her voice.

"I don't know, Jade. I think we need to find a way out of here, now."

Jesse looked over his shoulder, spotting the entrance tunnel out of the chamber. Grabbing his sister's arm, he began backing away towards the entrance tunnel looking around to see if anyone would notice their intentions to escape. With the chaos and panic still widespread in the chamber, it seemed unlikely any of the frightened Doon Esha would care enough to stop them.

The pair cautiously picked their way backward towards the entrance tunnel one step at a time until Jesse grabbed his sister with both hands and pulled her in tight. The center of the chamber's floor suddenly rose up and collapsed as if the ground itself had gone into a convulsion. Then, the floor rose up again and collapsed only faster this time as the convulsions were spreading further out away from the center of the chamber.

The ground continued to convulse almost as if with each rise and fall, the floor itself was keeping time to a heartbeat. The many Esha still left in the chamber flew into a frenzied mob trying to evacuate by any means possible. Then the convulsions stopped. Everything stopped.

Celetin and his guards who stood near the large fissure were staring around the chamber as did most of the Doon Esha who had not yet fled. An eerie quiet fell over the chamber as sulfuric-laced smoke drifted lazily towards the heights of the ceilings.

Jesse had managed to pull Jade to within a few feet of the entrance tunnel hoping to escape the chamber unnoticed through the pandemonium while trying to keep from drawing attention to themselves. Jade still held the scroll tightly against her side as the two stood barely daring to breathe.

With most of the attention in the chamber still focused on the center of the ground, a soft light emanating from the large fissure, which had swallowed the holding post ledge, went unnoticed at first. It was only after the pulsing light form began to rise from the fissure and reflect against the smooth rock walls that it began to draw attention.

Celetin and his guards turned just in time to see the pale glow of a silhouette rising from the fissure. Jesse and Jade both caught sight of the rising Phoenix pictured in exactly the way their ancient histories had described. The shimmering light pulsated and emanated from the rising form, which now hovered above the fissure in absolute silence.

"You!" Celetin snarled opening his jaws. An explosion of crimson flame shot from the white dragon's mouth threatening to envelope the Phoenix form. A blast of flame passed through the shining silhouette, hitting the glassy surface of the rocks behind.

"No! Nooooo!" The white dragon screamed as he drew himself up to fire another crimson blast. The second blast of crimson flame would never come. As fast as light moves, the Phoenix came forward towards the white dragon, a blade of pure light protruding from the edge of its wing. The blade sliced through the air, cutting straight through the white dragon's neck just under the head and severing the gaping jaws from the white dragon's body.

A look of total disbelief covered the white dragon's eyes as its head slowly began to roll forward away from his body. As the head fell, it began to burn as did the rest of the dragon's body. In nearly an instant, both body and head burned to mere bones scattering across the ground as they landed.

The ground of the chamber began to quake again as the Esha survivors shrieked and screamed, each one burning to bones, which fell to the ground in heaps and piles. The small earthquake lasted many moments,

forcing Jesse to throw Jade to the ground as he threw himself on top of her. The ground continued to shake for several more moments until finally the massive chamber grew still again. The silence was almost deafening as the ringing of echoes of the now vanquished Doon Esha drifted high up into the heights and faded away.

CHAPTER THIRTY

FAREWELL, FOR NOW

Tears hotly streaming down her face, Jade shakily pushed herself up from the ground as Jesse helped her to her feet. The smell of sulfur had abated as the last whiffs of the acrid smoke rose up, dissipating into the heights of the cathedral ceilings. The shattered and splintered bones of Celetin lie around the fallen cavern floor near the fissure while the masses of scattered bones of the fallen Doon Esha were littered about throughout the chamber.

Both of the Tryistans barely noticed the light of the silhouette now hovering behind them illuminating the entrance tunnel. As the pair stared at the carnage lying throughout the massive fortress chamber, it was Jade who suddenly noticed the strange pale light shining down on them. She reached out slowly and tugged Jesse's arm using her eyes to point to him behind where they stood.

Both brother and sister turned around and gasped. The Phoenix hovered, casting its pale light only feet from where they were standing. Jade looked down at the scroll in her hand. Wiping away at the tears on her cheeks, she glanced at her brother, nodding her head. Jesse nodded back as Jade took a step forward.

"Father? Father... is that really you."

"Yes, child, it is I. I am here."

"Father, what has happened here? I don't understand what's happening."

"All the laws and the prophecy are fulfilled now, child."

"What do you mean fulfilled? Father, I don't understand."

"You will in time. But now, I must go."

"Go? Wait father, no, wait! What do you mean go?" Jade choked.

"My time here is at an end. I cannot stay any longer. My task is finished."

"You can't leave me; please don't leave me. Take me with you father, please!" Fresh tears began to flow freely down Jade's cheeks.

"Jade, where I am going you cannot yet follow. You have your destiny. Follow it. Live among your brothers and sisters, and in time, you will see me again."

"Father, wait! Where are you going? I don't want you to leave. You can't just leave me here. You can't just leave us all now!" Jade began to shake as she sobbed. Jesse stepped up to his sister, putting an arm around her shoulders.

"Children, each of us has our own destiny. Each of us must travel our own path. My time here is done. Our enemy is defeated and all those who chose to follow him. I have fulfilled my destiny. Now I have another destiny to follow, and I must go to my Father."

"Another destiny? But what about me? What about us..." Jade pleaded.

"You must not worry, child. Remember what I have taught you. The time will come when we, you and I, will once again run together through golden fields and fly through the mountain passes. In that day, we will all find each other again. That day will come child, you must trust me. But not for a time."

Reaching out, Jade pleaded, "But you promised me! You promised you would never leave me father. I don't know where to go. What do we do now?"

"Listen to your heart. Listen and you will hear me. Look up and you will see me. I promised you I would never leave you, and I never will. My spirit is inside your heart and will always be as long as you will keep me there." The Phoenix's light form began to shimmer in and out, threatening to fade away.

Jade looked down at the tightly sealed scroll she held in her hand, "But father, what do we do with the sacred writings now?"

"You must keep them to remember from where you have come from and where you will go."

Looking up at her father, Jade asked, "So, the prophecy is truly fulfilled?"

"Yes, child, and that has now passed away. See that which you hold in your hand."

Jade held up the scroll. In her hand, she no longer clutched an old decaying parchment. Instead, she held a shimmering scroll of beautiful white parchment, the handles of which shined in the firelight-like fresh gold with new seals bound tight. Jade's eyes widened.

"Father, what shall I do with this?"

"Keep it and wait for the time when you will know to break its seal again."

Suddenly, Jade understood. "I understand father. We will keep your word."

"Yes, children, keep my words." The voice grew fainter.

Jade watched as the light began to disappear from around the edges of the Phoenix form. Realizing that her father was fading away, she stepped forward and reached out her hand. Jesse started to stop her, "Jade, stop! Wait, don't touch..."

Jade's hand moved through the light. It was warm and soft, like sweet gentle winds after a cleansing summer rain. She looked up into the translucent face of her father. She understood now. Strangely, she felt calm and assured. A warm shiver suddenly raced through her body that left her feeling like she'd just been born all over again.

As she stood looking up at her father, a small and nimble limb of light reached out and softly touched her cheek. She closed her eyes and let her mind caress the touch. It was so warm and safe. More real and true than anything she'd ever known.

Opening her eyes, she watched as the remaining light of the Phoenix lifted effortlessly from the ground and traversed upwards into the enormous cathedral chamber's heights. She continued to watch as the last of the shimmering light seemed to hesitate for several moments before disappearing altogether into the heights. "Goodbye, father," she whispered. "I'll see you soon... I love you..."

Jesse reached out to his sister and hugged her tightly. After several moments, Jade softly broke her brother's embrace.

"Jesse, we're not ready yet, are we?"

"No, Jade," gently shaking his head, "We're not ready and neither are the humans, at least not yet."

Jade took a moment to look over the scroll in her hand as if the ancient writ had just been created and handed to her. It began to dawn on her something felt different, something felt new, as if a shifting change like an epiphany had occurred. She glanced at Jesse who was staring at her with a puzzling expression across his face. *No... No way...*

Slowly, Jade laid the scroll on the ground and stepped away carefully from the precious container. She closed her eyes, concentrating hard and stepped forward.

"Jade!" Jesse exclaimed.

The form of a golden eagle stood where Jade had stepped. Majestic and regal, the eagle looked to the towering heights and spread its wings. The piercing cry of the great bird filled the chamber echoing off the walls and up into the heights. It was time to go home.

As brother and sister later made their way out of the deserted chamber and headed towards the fortress' main entrance, Jade reached out and locked her arm around her brother's arm.

Jesse smiled, "I don't think your boyfriend is going to like this."

"No?" Jade innocently asked. "Who says he has to know?"

"Jade, you can't..."

"Can't what? I don't know what you're talking about, big brother."

"You have to tell him."

"I don't have to tell him anything."

"If you don't tell him, I will."

Jade thought for a moment. *Boys!...*

Among the ruins of rock and smoldering debris, a single bone claw began to shiver. After several moments, the claw joined together with the rest of its bone parts and began to slowly drag the rest of the bony claws across the dirt, looking for the rest of its wrist. Once the bones of the clawed hand loosely reassembled itself, the bony hand began to slowly sink into the dirty sand, leaving behind a few scribbled characters from an ancient language long gone:

INSURRECTION

Greater love has no one, than he who lays down his life for his friends. I am very pleased and proud as I have witnessed these events unfold. It is most important for you to understand who I am, for it is I who declare that Gharius is my son, and I am his Father. May peace go with you into the far places and light go with you into the deep places. Farewell for the moment but know this; all is not yet concluded. Not yet ...

CHARACTER INDEX

Transformation ability on levels of 1 to 10. 1 equal to lowest level and 10 equal to the highest.

Name (Level), Position

Gharius *(Unknown)*, Lead figurehead of the Order of Tryistan

Petrawnus *(9)*, First Elder of the Order of Tryistan

Jasmetricus *(9)*, Second Elder of the Order of Tryistan

Johhanicus *(9)*, Third Elder of the Order of Tryistan

Philocus *(8)*, Fifth Elder of the Order of Tryistan

Zelotus *(7)*, Eleventh Elder of the Order of Tryistan

Jesse *(6)*, Son to Gharius

The Guardians *(5)*, Soldiers of the Order of Tryistan

Ploruvus *(4)*, Esha of the Order of Tryistan

Jade *(0)*, Daughter (Human) to Gharius

Celetin *(10)*, Leader of the Tribes of the Doon Esha

Fiomass *(7),* First Elder to the Tribes of the Doon Esha

Haxiss *(6),* Second Elder to the Tribes of the Doon Esha

Quoros *(6),* Third Elder of the Tribes of the Doon Esha

Mezlash *(6),* Fourth Elder of the Tribes of the Doon Esha

Deforax *(6),* Fifth Elder of the Tribes of the Doon Esha

First rank *(5),* Soldier of the Doon Esha

Second rank *(4),* Soldier of the Doon Esha

Third rank *(3),* Soldier of the Doon Esha

Fourth rank *(2),* Soldier of the Doon Esha

Fifth rank *(1),* Laborer of the Doon Esha

ACKNOWLEDGMENTS

I want to thank my publisher Lil and her team for taking an idea and making it a reality. I would also like to thank Jack and Ann, without whom, this book would most likely have never happened.

ABOUT THE AUTHOR

Ellis is a retired military veteran and has traveled worldwide. He graduated from a local university with honors majoring in philosophy and religious studies. He currently resides and works in a quaint small town in North Eastern Ohio. Ellis enjoys reading, writing, playing music instruments, hiking, and shopping on Amazon.